About the a

C000046527

The author was born in London in October 1944. She enjoyed school, adored Elvis and loved to dance. She ruined her feet in winklepicker shoes in her teens and swung in the swinging sixties. She worked as a personal assistant, married Dave, had three sons and then worked in their garden centre in Essex.

She moved to Cornwall in 1980. She worked as an administrative assistant for a government quango. She retired and brought and rented out villas in Tenerife. She lost Dave after nearly fifty-two years of marriage, and is currently surrounded by three sons with gorgeous wives and twelve grandchildren.

IMPACTUS

J A ELLERY

IMPACTUS

Vanguard Press

A CIP catalogue record for this title is
available from the British Library.

ISBN 978 1 80016 216 7

*Vanguard Press is an imprint of
Pegasus Elliot MacKenzie Publishers Ltd.*
www.pegasuspublishers.com

First Published in 2021

**Vanguard Press
Sheraton House Castle Park
Cambridge England**

Printed & Bound in Great Britain

Dedication

For Family Ellery with all my love

1

The second to last thought to go through her mind was the trailer behind the Land Rover was swaying violently and the last thought was she was about to die.

Sarah Cook was fifty-one years old, tall, her fair hair swept up in a perfect chignon, the elegant personal assistant to John Bartlett, head of the pharmaceutical chain John Bartlett Corporation with offices in the major cities of the world. Sarah worked out of the London office in Canary Wharf.

She was driving to Heathrow Airport in London to meet John to fly to Manchester where he was launching a new skincare product to a select group of businessmen. The groundwork had been done via teleconferencing, but this was the closing stage of the deal and he needed to be there in person.

Sarah had prepared the presentation and they had rehearsed the format many times. The venue was the Manchester Grand Hotel and Sarah had secured accommodation for the invited guests, gone through the catering personally with the head chef and secured the party gift bags with the all-important wrinkle reducing cream. Potential customers needed to know how the new product would bring value to their business and she had developed collateral containing useful information, as well as statistics to answer any questions the customers may have. John, who excelled at engaging his audience, would skilfully deliver the salient points she had prepared.

She smiled to herself, it was all perfectly organised. She loved her job. She enjoyed meeting people, knew everyone in the London office, from the cook who prepared John's lunch to the doorman, typists, secretaries and the directors.

She was wearing a duck egg blue suit by Karen Millen with a cream silk blouse, navy shoes and matching bag. She was the epitome of an elegant sophisticated woman with a little light make-up and her signature Red Door perfume.

The traffic was quite light for eight a.m. on a Monday morning. She was approaching junction four on the M4, the turn-off for the airport. Her car was behind a Land Rover towing an open trailer with some large drums moving around, an unstable load going far too fast. She pulled into the middle lane to overtake but suddenly the trailer swung to the right and caused the Land Rover to flip onto its roof that collapsed, almost flat. It slewed into the side of Sarah's car as she tried to get into the fast lane but a car was fast approaching, and as she pulled out, it ploughed into the back of her car pushing it into the central reservation crash barrier. She was pushed forward onto the wheel just as the airbag deployed and she felt tremendous pain in her chest and neck, and as she lost consciousness, she thought she would never see her children again.

The car that hit Sarah's spun and ended up facing the traffic that was desperately trying to stop but too many were too near the car in front, too late to brake.

Cars on the other side of the motorway were slowing and pulling over. People were running to see if they could help. A lorry driver got a crowbar from his cab and jumped the barrier to try to lever the crushed cab of the Land Rover but it was having little effect. He was saying, "It's all right mate, help is coming, you will be OK, hang on in there." Although, he could not see how anyone could have survived the impact.

The sound of screeching tyres, spinning, crashing cars was endless. Those who could get out of their cars were running to try to help those who were trapped and it seemed an eternity before the sound of sirens could be heard as emergency vehicles sped to the scene. Cars were still not slowing down, more and more were failing to stop in time, everything spinning out of control.

A fireman tried to open the door of Sarah's car but it was jammed against the barrier. They cut open the roof to get to her, a doctor squeezed in next to her. "She is unconscious with a weak pulse." They slid a board under her, put her neck in a brace, and gently, with the doctor lifting her and strapping her to the board, they pulled her free of the car. The ambulance drove at speed to the Hillingdon hospital, about three miles from the accident. She was alive, but what injuries she had sustained internally could not be determined.

2

The chauffeur carried John's bags to the check-in desk and he was soon through to departures and made his way to the executive lounge where he was meeting Sarah. He was a handsome man in his Savile Row navy blue suit, crisp white shirt and a light blue tie to complement Sarah's suit. He was fifty-five years old, his tanned face emphasised his amazingly blue eyes, his thick hair combed back with just a slight hint of grey gave an air of well-groomed distinction. He was his own man. Successful, determined, tough but fair. He made it his business to take a personal interest in his staff. He regarded them as family and treated everyone in the same courteous manner. He was married to Victoria and their children, Samantha, Mark and Paul had given them three adorable grandchildren. He knew he was lucky, but his father had always taught him, the harder you work, the luckier you get.

He looked at his watch; Sarah was not yet in the lounge. Not like her to be late he thought. He glanced at the television. There had been some sort of accident on the M4 near the Heathrow junction. His heart skipped a beat and his mouth went dry. The cameras were panning the scene and he saw a red Audi sports car crushed against the central barrier. Surely not, surely it could not be Sarah's car. He punched her mobile number into his phone and it went straight to answerphone. He tried the office, had Sarah called there first before going to the airport? She had not. He thought of her husband but realised Clive was in New York on business.

He asked his secretary to call the nearest hospital where the casualties would have been taken. She was told that a Sarah Cook had been admitted but no details could be given until the next of kin had been informed. He called the hospital and told them who he was and that Sarah should have met him at the airport and that her husband was in New York. He would find a way to contact him to let him know.

His secretary gave him Clive's contact number. The loud ringing of the telephone startled Clive Cook awake. He looked at the clock. It was four a.m. What on earth was going on? He looked at the slender form of Kiri, stirring and trying to focus. He reached for the telephone. "Hello, Mr Clive Cook?" a voice asked.

"Yes, it is, do you know what time it is? It is four a.m. and you had better have good reason to be calling me at this hour". There was a clicking sound and the voice of John Bartlett came on the line.

"Clive, its John Bartlett. I am so sorry to call you but Sarah has been in an accident. She is at the Hillingdon hospital. She was on her way to meet me at Heathrow when the accident happened. Clive, we don't know how she is, only that she has been admitted and they won't tell us anything until the next of kin has been informed. Do you have a pen handy and I can give you the number of the hospital." Clive dropped the phone.

"What is it?" Kiri asked.

Clive put a finger to his lips, "Shush".

"Hold on, John, is she OK, do we know how she is? Where is my pen? Oh my God where is my pen?" Kiri got it from the bureau and gave it to him. "OK John, give me the number. When I know anything, I will of course telephone you straight back."

"Thank you, Clive, if there is anything I can do this end?"

"No, I can sort it from here thank you. I will be in touch as soon as I can."

Clive put down the phone and Kiri came to him. "Baby, oh my poor baby, what has happened?"

"It's Sarah. She has been in an accident. I have to call the hospital. Oh my God, Kiri, please let her be OK. Please God." She held him while he made the call.

"Hello, my name is Clive Cook. I believe my wife, Sarah Cook, has been admitted to your hospital after an accident near Heathrow airport this morning."

"One moment Mr Cook."

There was a buzzing sound on the line and a voice said, "Intensive care unit, nurse Thompson speaking."

"My name is Clive Cook and my wife Sarah was admitted this morning."

"Mr Cook I will fetch the consultant."

There was a pause. "Mr Cook, my name is Richards and I am the consultant looking after your wife. Her condition is serious but stable. She suffered massive trauma of the neck and chest. Please come as soon as you can. She is unconscious on a ventilator."

"I am in New York! It is four a.m. and I will not be able to get a flight for another two hours and then it will be five to six hours before I can be at the hospital. I will contact my son, Adrian, and hopefully he will be able to get there within the hour."

"Thank you, Mr Cook, I will leave a message at reception that he is to come straight to ICU. Take care and we will see you as soon as you can make it. Goodbye."

Clive suddenly started to shake. Kiri held him tightly. "I must contact Adrian, his office is in Harrow and he could get there within an hour." He dialled Adrian's mobile number.

"Dad, everything OK. Dad, its four a.m. over there isn't it?"

"Adrian, thank God, where are you?"

"I am in the office. Dad, Dad, what's wrong?"

"Mum has been in an accident near Heathrow. She is in the Hillingdon hospital in ICU. Her condition is serious but stable. The consultant, Mr Richards said they will be looking out for you at reception. Oh Adrian, it's dreadful. I can't get there for at least eight hours, but I will keep you in the loop as to where I am. So sorry son, it's a terrible shock, but please can you get there?"

"Of course, I will go there right now. Oh Dad, try not to panic, take it easy, you can't do anything until you are here so just get here safely. I love you."

"Love you too son, take care." He put the phone down. He called John Bartlett. "Hello John, she is in a serious but stable condition. She is on a ventilator and unconscious. Adrian is going there now and I will get the earliest flight I can."

"OK. Can you let me have Adrian's number and I will see if he needs me to do anything at this end?" Clive gave him the number and they said their goodbyes.

He pulled Kiri to him. He was in shock. "Oh my God, how dreadful are her injuries, what if she doesn't make it, what if she is brain damaged, what if…" Kiri kissed his head, stroked his face, calming him. His head was in turmoil. He loved this beautiful young woman. He knew that now, more than ever before. She was everything that Sarah was not, and she had time for him, just him. No high-flying job that took her away, she was always there for him. She was petite, almost boyish with curly black hair tight to her head. Her luminous black eyes and smooth olive skin gave her an ethereal look. Her breasts were pert, erect nipples that he loved to suck, making her arch her back, and almost mould into him. She oozed sex, she dressed for sex, always so wanting, so giving and made him feel like no other woman had ever done before. She gently caressed him, he felt himself wanting her, moved to her and they held each other. He kissed her, she kissed him back and they made love. His need drove him with a desperate urgency, both of them trying to find release and when it came, they lay back, and silent tears rolled down Kiri's face.

She showered while he called the airport and booked himself on the six thirty flight. He knew it was tight and while he showered, she booked the cab and together they got to the airport forty minutes before take-off. They stood together as he checked in, and he had to go through departures almost as soon as he got there. Kiri looked at him. She loved him. She knew he had a wife but so far this had never been a problem. He had his life in England and they had theirs in New York. She was his personal assistant and they had instant chemistry as soon as they met. She found him an apartment in the Meat Packing District, a ten-minute cab ride from the office, and he took her to dinner and it seemed a natural progression for her to stay. They both loved the trendy bars and restaurants and Kiri was able to visit the designer shops there, Stella McCartney, Tiffany's and Alexander McQueen on her very generous salary. His time in the New York office was hectic, but each night they would be together and he never thought it could be a bad thing to do. He thought it was right and fine and he gave every bit of himself to her. She loved loving him. Her heart would soar with joy, knowing she could dance with his heart and she felt he owned her very soul. She shuddered at the thought of him leaving, not knowing when he could get back. It was a regular routine, ten days in Europe and three weeks back in New York, sometimes more, sometimes less. That would change now, of course it would, and she would be lost.

His flight was called and she clung to him. He tilted her head and held it in his hands. "I love you, baby, I will keep you in my heart and I will let you know what is happening. I miss you even now, be strong my darling. I love you."

She tried to speak but the tears choked her and she tried to smile and hugged him tight. "Be safe, be strong, I love you," she managed to say as he went through the barrier.

3

John Bartlett dialled Adrian's number. "Hello Adrian, I am so sorry about your mother. Dad has told me about her condition and that you can get there right away."

"Hello John, yes I am on my way now, we are in shock but my mum is a strong woman and she will fight to get back, I know that."

"Of course Adrian. Do you need me to do anything, inform anyone?"

"No, you're good John, don't worry I know, Mum told me there was an important meeting today and she would want you to go ahead and clinch it. Don't worry, we will be fine and I will keep you posted on Mum's condition."

"OK, Adrian, if you are sure, but please let me know as soon as there is any news."

"Will do John, hope all goes well in Manchester, Goodbye."

"Goodbye, Adrian."

John's mobile rang with Victoria's ID. "John, I have been trying to get through and obviously you know about the crash and I thought I saw Sarah's car."

"Yes darling, it's absolutely awful. She is in Hillingdon hospital and I was about to call you after contacting Clive and then his son, Adrian. Clive is on his way back from New York and Adrian should be at the hospital soon. He said I should go to Manchester, Sarah would not want anything different." His voice trailed off.

"I am so sorry sweetheart, poor dear Sarah. You can do nothing, John, her family will be with her and you both have worked so hard on this deal. Can you get Andrea to go with you?"

"It's all organised. She should be here any minute, and I have all the paperwork. Have to say I feel shattered before I even get there."

"Get a coffee and something sweet to eat, boost your sugar levels darling. Please keep me in touch with things. Let me know how things go and I will try and contact Clive when he is in London. Good luck John, go reel them in, I love you."

"Thanks Victoria, love you too sweetheart." As he put down the phone, Andrea his secretary came into the lounge, her face drawn into a frown.

"Oh, John, what dreadful news. Are you OK?"

"I am fine Andrea, and thank you for coming. Did the office arrange everything, tickets and paperwork?"

"Yes John, I double-checked that you had all the presentation and photocopied the list of attendees so that I could study them on the flight. I don't think we have forgotten anything." She was very efficient, and considering the circumstances remarkably calm. She always dressed immaculately, top to toe the essence of good grooming. John always surrounded himself with people who projected such an image. Appearances went a long way in his line of business.

"Thank you, Andrea. I knew I could count on you. Sarah is in a serious condition but stable. She is a fighter. I know she will do all she can within herself to come through this." His voice was flat, he felt torn and anxious, but he knew he must carry on. They got a coffee and he tried to eat a flapjack but his appetite was not there. They went over the presentation. Andrea had transferred it onto the computer so she knew it inside out and John was grateful for this. Their flight was called and they boarded the plane. They leafed through the paperwork in silence, both now concentrating on what was ahead. This deal would be the icing on the cake for the company in London. The product would revolutionise the beauty industry and Bartletts would be the pioneers. John was hopeful, he felt that they had it covered, and the one thing he knew he was good at was putting the deal across to even the most hard-nosed businessman. The plane touched down, the chauffeur met them and whisked them to the hotel. He silently prayed for his right-hand man to come through, walked to reception and booked in. The game was on.

4

Clive Cook was exhausted, his head in turmoil, his emotions drained, pulled this way and that and as he fastened his seat belt his mind was praying that Sarah would hold on, that she would pull through.

The chauffeur was waiting in arrivals. It had been eight hours since he had had the call and the chauffeur was respectfully silent as he negotiated the early evening rush hour to drive to the hospital.

His chest tightened when he saw her. She was in a private room, hooked to a drip of clear liquid and one of blood. The ventilator was pumping up and down and there were tubes from her nose and in both arms. It looked as if a tube was draining from her chest. Strangely she didn't look any different. She didn't look as though she was so dreadfully injured. Her hair was splayed on the pillow framing her pale face in a ghostly halo. Her eyes were closed and she looked so peaceful.

He took her hand and squeezed. "Sarah, my darling, it's me, Clive." He desperately searched her face for any sign of recognition. "My poor darling, Sarah, you will be fine sweetheart." He held her hand and caressed her face, gently telling her he loved her and she would be OK.

"Mr Cook?" a voice enquired as the door opened.

"Yes, how is she?"

"My name is Richards, we spoke on the phone. Your wife has done remarkably well so far. The ventilator is breathing for her and the force of the impact of the airbag has damaged her chest cavity. Her neck has suffered severe whiplash and we cannot yet do a scan because to move her could cause damage to her spine."

"Dad, oh my poor Dad." Adrian entered the room. He had stepped out for a cigarette. He hugged his father. He held on and they sobbed together. "It's a miracle she is alive Dad. She was cut out of the car; everyone was going so fast, braking too late. Oh my God. Dad, will she be OK?"

"The doctor has told me her vital signs are good. It will take time to assess exactly what has been damaged and how it can be repaired. We must have faith that she will come through this." They both sat down either side of the bed, holding her hands, both completely exhausted.

5

Mavis Dunwoody was a shopaholic. She would go to the supermarket for the weekly shop and come back with 'some real bargains'. Two tops, a pair of shoes and a handbag to match. She would rush home to try them on, and after an hour remember to put the food in the fridge. She would go to the sales, see a pair of shoes reduced from forty pounds to fifteen pounds and my word, what a bargain, and buy three pairs in three different colours. They would be just so comfortable. If she didn't go shopping for a couple of days, she worked part-time in the village Post Office three days a week, when she did, she would start to shake. Literally shake. A bit like a glutton salivating over a gourmet banquet. Insatiable.

Unfortunately, it was a case of champagne taste with a beer bottle budget. Stuart Dunwoody was a sales representative for a telephone directory. He had to initially cold call, drop into the businesses and persuade them to advertise in the directory. He was good at his job but the recession was biting, competition was stiff and it was becoming more cut throat by the day. Twice he had cut up Mavis's credit cards. She was sorry, she would only buy when she had the cash in her hand, no more credit. But Mavis never had the cash. Three days' work in the Post Office did not amount to a bag of beans in her lifestyle.

Stuart strived to get more contacts, trying different approaches. He worked twelve hours a day to try and work off the debt while the interest seemed to double overnight.

He went to a loan company. It was the only way even though the interest rate was ridiculously high and this only served to assist Mavis into thinking now they had money — she could spend. Stuart had no idea that Mavis was like this before they married. They both lived in council houses on the same estate, they liked the same things and he always thought she looked lovely, beautiful clothes, lovely hair and nails, yet he never dreamt it was all on credit. Now things were dire, and he was grasping at straws in a never-ending downward spiral.

He was driving to his next appointment, worrying thoughts crowding his brain, when a car in the middle lane suddenly pulled in front of him in the fast lane. He tried to brake but he couldn't avoid it. He hit it at seventy mph, shunting it into the wall of the central reservation, his car spinning round and round. The airbag saved his chest from being crushed by the steering wheel as he finally came to a stop facing the oncoming traffic, which was desperately trying to stop. He felt a tremendous pain in his side and as he blacked out, his mind tried to grasp what was happening. A large red stain was spreading from his groin through his suit and it would not stop.

Mavis was half in and half out of a blue dress in the changing rooms of John Lewis when her mobile phone rang. She was trying to choose between the blue or green dress, both looked good so she would take both. She fished in her bag for the phone. Just as she reached it, it stopped. She pulled the dress off and sat on the bench. She always found she was either in the loo or had left it in another bag when it rang so this was true to form. She didn't recognise the number but called it back anyway. "Hello, I have a missed call from you."

"Is that Mavis Dunwoody?" a woman's voice asked.

"Yes, who is this?"

"Mrs Dunwoody, is anyone with you?"

"No, I am in the changing rooms in John Lewis, what is going on?"

"I am Geraldine from your husband Stuart's office."

"What?" interrupted Mavis, "Is Stuart OK, what has happened?"

"Mrs Dunwoody, I am sorry to have to tell you that Stuart has been in a car accident near Heathrow airport. He has been taken to Hillingdon hospital."

"Oh my God, oh my God, what shall I do, I need to get there."

"Are you in the store near Oxford Circus tube station?"

"Yes, yes I am."

"Please get a taxi to take you to the hospital. Did you drive to the store?"

"No, I came on the tube."

"Mrs Carlisle from HR will meet you at the hospital. Tell the driver to go straight to A & E. It will take you about thirty minutes from Oxford Street and Mrs Carlisle will be there to meet you. Please try to keep calm. We do not have any information on Stuart's condition. We only know he was taken to the hospital about eleven a.m. this morning. Do you understand Mrs Dunwoody?"

"Yes, yes, I get a taxi to Hillingdon hospital and Mrs Car someone will meet me there. I am on my way." She hurriedly dressed, grabbed her bag, and for the first time in her life, Mavis Dunwoody left a store without a purchase to her name.

Katherine Carlisle was waiting by the entrance to A & E when the taxi pulled up and she recognised Mavis Dunwoody from when she had been at office dos with Stuart. Expensively dressed, she noticed the cut of her coat, but her whole demeanour was one of anxiety and as she tried to run to her, her legs kind of crumpled and Katherine just managed to catch her and get her through the door.

6

Teresa Fairchild was having coffee with her friend Serena when a policeman knocked at her door to tell her that her husband had been in an accident on the M4 and he was in Hillingdon hospital. His Land Rover had jack-knifed and overturned. Serena immediately said she would take Teresa to the hospital. The policeman said there was a car outside to take them. Teresa asked the policeman how he was, how was her Don and the policeman said he just knew he had been admitted to the hospital and it was a matter of urgency that they get there.

Teresa and Serena had been friends for over twenty years. They had had their children within months of each other, shared the worries of babies, and the challenges of bringing them up through the terrible twos to the raging hormones of teenagers and Teresa had had more than her fair share of teenager troubles. They had laughed and cried together, always there for one another, loyal and true and it was only right that Serena would be at Teresa's side at this dreadful time. Serena helped Teresa pack some pyjamas and toiletries and was holding the case as they were ushered to a private room.

"What is going on, where's my Don?" Teresa asked. Serena held her hand and a man with a stethoscope around his neck entered the room. Serena thought he was far too young to be anyone important. These days policemen looked like lanky teenagers.

"Mrs Fairchild," a voice interrupted Serena's thoughts.

"Yes?" Teresa said, obviously very agitated. They sat on three chairs in a stark bare room. Serena held Teresa's hand.

"Mrs Fairchild, I am so sorry to say your husband has been in an accident. He has suffered severe injuries and is currently on a life support machine."

"What do you mean, a life support machine? Does that mean he is dying, or living, what life is being supported?" Serena gripped her hand.

"Mrs Fairchild, life support refers to a spectrum of techniques used to maintain life after the failure of one or more vital organs and your husband is being kept alive by the machine." Teresa felt her head was giddy, her mouth was dry and she couldn't speak. She kind of slipped in the chair she was sitting on and if Serena hadn't held her tight, she would have fallen to the floor. The doctor got some water from a machine in the corner.

"Is, is he dying then?"

The doctor shook his head. "I am sorry Mrs Fairchild, there is nothing further we can do. Is there anyone else in the family?"

Serena said, "Charlie is sixteen at college and Miranda is eighteen and at her boyfriend's."

"Is there an older relative, brother, sister?"

"I am the sister she never had," said Serena. "There is no one else. Don was an orphan, he never knew his father. I am a widow otherwise my Joe would have been here for Don. Cancer took him a year ago."

The doctor stood. "This has been a terrible shock. I am so sorry Mrs Fairchild."

"I have to see him," Teresa said. "He will know I am there and he will hear me. He cannot go on alone. He is my life. Why would I not be able to see him?" Her tiny voice, full of determination caused the tears to stream down Serena's face.

"I will take you to him." There was an eerie quietness in the room. Teresa ignored the bank of machines, the tubes, and the sterile whiteness. All she saw was her Don, lying on a big bed in the middle of the room. Don was a hard-working honest man who loved his family. He loved his wife with an unspoken devotion. He couldn't understand his children with all their new-fangled electronic stuff. They had come along when he and Teresa least expected them, in their forties. In his day it was reading, writing and arithmetic. You learned your tables and did the sums on paper without a calculator — and you learned to spell proper words not this funny texting they did.

Right now, he didn't understand what was happening to him. He didn't hurt, but he couldn't feel anything, couldn't see, only black. Teresa took his hand. "There, there lamb. It's me, Teresa." He wanted so much to tell her, tell her he loved her and he was sorry, sorry he couldn't stay. He knew he would be leaving her and he was sad. He wasn't afraid, he was just wondering. Never been here before you see, never had a way with words. "Don, you have given me a wonderful life and two great kids." He wished he could let her know he could hear her but nothing seemed to work any more. "I know you can't stay here Don, but you are going to a much better place and the first hand you hold will be your father's, Don. He will be waiting for you so don't be afraid, please don't be afraid. You will meet in heaven, or whatever that place is where there is no pain, just love and a kind of peace. I will be strong Don. I will be strong for the kids and they will grow up good and fine because you are their dad." A sudden *beep, beep,* sound came from one of the machines and people rushed in. They took Teresa from the side of the bed and tried to resuscitate him. Teresa looked at the doctor; his face was compassion and sympathy.

"I am sorry, he has gone."

Teresa went to the side of the bed, kissed his poor bandaged head and his hands. "God bless you my darling, I will miss you more than you will ever know." Serena rushed to the door when she heard the most dreadful scream and caught Teresa as she fell into her arms.

7

Dave Samson was gradually regaining consciousness. He was aware of a searing pain in his left leg and he couldn't feel his foot. He was sitting upright with the deflated airbag against his chest. This had probably saved his life. The front of the car was embedded in the front of a black saloon that was facing him. He desperately tried to move but he couldn't free his foot and he was aware of a loud noise, he couldn't think what it was, a horn blaring, what was happening? He was wedged tight as a sardine in a tin and gradually he remembered. Where's the phone? He was talking on the phone. He was not really talking, he was shouting, 'where are you?' to his wife and she was saying she was between sessions at her beauty therapist course and she couldn't talk right now and would call him back. He knew she wasn't. That was why he was so angry. She could lie just like that, because she knew he was on his way to Heathrow and he had no way of knowing where she was or what she was up to.

He had a way of knowing she knew nothing about. Susie, his daughter had said Mum had been acting funny and she had seen a car leaving the drive when she had got a lift with Helen to get home early to go riding. He couldn't believe anything could be going on. He got hold of a private detective to follow her and report back, with whatever he had found out. He was good and Julie never saw the tail on her car. When Dave saw the photographs, the hard evidence against his wife, he was gutted. Totally gutted. He never thought she would do this, not after twenty years of marriage. He had thought they were solid, no messing, and he knew he had to confront her, but there was never the right time. That's why he was calling her now. He didn't want to believe she would lie, but lie she did.

He didn't tell her he was going to sell the frigging villa in Cyprus. A Russian wanted it; one million cash and that would be one million Julie would never see. Had he been concentrating on his driving he would have seen the accident happening right in front of him and the car spinning round and stopping dead as his Range Rover ploughed into it. It was the crash bar that had prevented the front crumpling up and crushing him.

Where was the phone, oh my God, please help me, someone please help me, but when he went to shout out nothing came out and he began to sink back down into oblivion. He didn't hear the firemen shouting, 'we got a live one here', and he didn't hear the splintering glass as they broke open the passenger door and the paramedic thumping a syringe into his leg. His foot was trapped under the pedal that was firmly stuck and they used cutting gear to cut away the steering column to cut through the shaft of the pedal and lift it away. He was freed from the wreckage and another ambulance was on its way, two anxious faced paramedics in the back so determined this man would not die, not on their watch.

He was quite a short man, tight curly black hair, and toned muscular body, his work keeping him fit and at forty-eight he looked a lot younger. He was a demolition man. He had started work in the steel works in Scunthorpe and came south when they were closing down. He had found work with a gang of labourers knocking buildings down. Sounded so simple didn't it but he learned fast. The trick was getting the contracts for the big jobs, and you needed to know people to do that, people in the right places and his boss did. He had two councillors in his pocket and he told Dave it was so easy to find them. They were always up for a backhander those smarmy bastards in their smart suits, looking so clean and so ready to do good works for the public, as long as they got their cut.

His boss liked him. He always went the extra mile and he sent him to another of his yards to manage it because he trusted him. Not many you could trust in his line of work, mostly gypsies worked for him and he saw something more in Dave and he was right. He wheeled and dealed, and landed a big job taking down an old hospital, clearing the land ready for a housing development and there was a lot of cash involved. He didn't spend it, he stashed it. His boss was in failing health after a heart attack and asked Dave if he would be prepared to take the business on. Dave said he would, but he wanted total control and the old man was happy to take the generous wad Dave offered him in return for both yards. He went from strength to strength. Nothing so true as where there's muck there's brass and he got his hands very dirty, but he had certain standards and had not crossed too many boundaries, just made sure that people knew he didn't take prisoners, the odd beating here and there so people understood him.

He was twenty-six when he was offered the job of taking down an old mansion house in Hertfordshire. He looked it over and thought it was not in that bad a state and he decided he would renovate, rather than demolish it. His reputation ensured he had a good team working on it, the architect from the council was only too pleased for a cash job and the drawings he produced impressed Dave. All the builders were cash in hand and Homeoaks was finally completed a year later. An enormous house which just needed a family to fill it.

Dave didn't mix in the kind of circles where you met gorgeous women, but he had the money to impress his young secretary. She was a petite blonde, eighteen years old, with huge breasts that all the men used to ogle and when she walked down the yard in her ridiculously high red stilettos, carefully picking her way through the puddles, she had the rapt attention of every worker there. Dave took her out in his shiny black Mercedes and the deal was as good as done. They went to the pictures and he took her to the dogs, brought her first saveloy and you would have thought it was caviar. She fell in love with him and he thought she was a bit of all right and they made it legal a year later and she was pregnant in the first month.

Julie was a good girl, her mum Susan always said it, and was most impressed at the lifestyle her daughter was leading. She told her friend Eileen you would not believe the size of her kitchen and she kept it lovely. She was a good mum, always had a hot meal on the table, nothing fancy, just good plain food like she had been brought up to eat and Susan loved going there to stay. Julie's dad had left ages ago and wouldn't he be surprised at how she had turned out now. Two more babies and their little family seemed complete and Julie always found ways to make sure Dave never needed to go elsewhere for anything. She had been a 'goer' before she married Dave, but nothing would tempt her away from this man. Her mum said it's hard being a wife because you had to be a good listener, a good mum, a good cook and a whore in the bedroom. She was all of these and more and Dave was amazed at how she would dress for him, and he couldn't get enough of stockings and suspenders, even when he thought he just wanted to go to sleep.

The kids were growing fast and he enjoyed seeing them do so well. They all went to the private school, posh blazers and clean white shirts and kept up with all the other kids in the school because money opened an awful lot of doors. Julie adapted well too. She shopped and dressed for all the occasions at the school, and Dave didn't feel comfortable at the receptions where you stood and nibbled funny bits on toast, and chatted about nothing at all. Don't do that small talk lark he had said to Julie, but she excelled and with her perfect figure and shapely legs she drew many appreciative glances from lots of husbands. This didn't go unnoticed by the wives and she wasn't invited to the lunches they organised between themselves. She didn't mind at all. Dave had brought her the latest Mercedes sports car and she would drop the kids off at school and then go to collect her mum to go to the shopping mall. Dave had offered to buy her mum a new house near them in the village, but she was happy where she was with her mates and just loved being part of the family and staying over whenever she could.

Dave's work took him away more and more. He looked at demolition work in Cornwall, the mines had ceased to work and there were large contracts up for grabs and he even went to Scunthorpe to dismantle the old steel works where he first started.

Money was no object but he found it very hard to switch off. Julie brought loads of travel brochures home, always asking him if they could have a holiday, the kids would love it, just to get away. He couldn't understand why anyone would want to go away from Homeoaks. They had everything there, a pool, a gym and huge snooker room. There were ponies in the paddock, his daughter loved her pony and was good at mucking out and poo picking and all in all they had no reason to go elsewhere to some hot place with lots of toffs sitting round pools drinking cocktails.

Julie didn't push it but gradually she realised they were spending less time together, mainly because he was always after the next big job, and her mum was a sweetheart but she was missing something. She was missing excitement, something a little out of the ordinary. Basically, she was bored. The daily did the housework and a girl from the village did the ironing. She was beginning to feel as if she really wasn't needed. The kids did their own thing. They were always off with their mates at the weekend and Susie had her friends over and they would ride and go on hacks and she would do her nails and wonder why.

Dave was oblivious of course. He didn't see how sad she had become. She made all the right noises but he couldn't see how lonely she was. He thought she was happy as Larry, going here and there with her mum, but her mum was getting more and more tired and when she was diagnosed with cancer it was a bolt out of the blue. It pulled them all up sharp and Julie now had a purpose. She insisted her mum move in with them, there was the guest suite and she could keep her eye on her, take her for her treatments and it never occurred to her that her mum might not get better.

The consultant called them in and Julie just stared at him when he said that, unfortunately, the drugs were not working, the cancer had spread to her liver and there was nothing more they could do.

Dave immediately sought a second opinion. What was money for if you couldn't sort stuff like this? He couldn't believe that this was happening and in two months she was gone.

Julie went into a kind of depression. She was mortified. At least Dave was around more, he was worried about her and didn't want her to be on her own. He did his best to make sure he was there as much as he could be, moving his secretary into the house to work from there so there was always someone around.

It was the kids that saved her. Susie was completely bereft her nan was dead and she needed Julie. She needed her mum as Julie had so needed hers, and they both went to the doctors to see if there was anything he could give them. He was a kindly man, but of the old school, and he didn't believe in pills but suggested a counsellor who Dave immediately employed to help both the ladies in his life.

They both found that by talking things through things got easier. You never forgot. Julie thought, you could never fill that space, but she put the photos back that she had taken down. Susie gradually pulled herself back up and Julie was so pleased when she heard her laugh for the first time in a long time.

Dave's work was expanding. He brought a huge area of land, supposedly green belt but a few nods here and there and it became brown land and he moved in his heavy trucking equipment and cranes. He really had the whole lot covered.

He suggested Julie and the kids go on holiday to Cyprus. He would go with them because a mate of his had said there were good investment opportunities there, lovely villas on the coast, which you could buy and rent out. Julie didn't need telling twice. The estate agent showed them several properties but the one overlooking the sea with its own beach and huge infinity pool was the one they settled on and everyone was happy. Dave did the business and returned to the UK and Julie and the kids stayed for the whole six weeks of the summer break. Julie thought they would miss their mates, but Dave had planned a surprise and organised that their mates could go for a couple of weeks, paying all their costs.

It was very hot but the air con did its work and although Julie missed Dave she enjoyed the pool and the beach and the kids seemed to enjoy having her around so that was fine.

The nearest villa was a mile away and Julie was surprised one evening when the maid showed a very handsome, dark-haired man into the lounge. He introduced himself as Gary Peterson, your neighbour from a mile away. He had just brought the villa and was excited to know his new neighbours and introduce his children. Julie explained they were just going to use it for their holidays but would they all like to stay for supper. He was delighted to accept. She explained her husband was back in the UK and he said he was a widower but he likewise wanted this for his family to enjoy. The kids chatted away and after supper they organised a taxi to go into Paphos, which meant they wouldn't be back until the small hours. Gary thought this might worry Julie but she said they were a good bunch and would look out for each other and it was what kids did these days.

Gary and Julie chatted away like old friends. They were roughly the same age, she thought, and he told her he had been alone for two years now and felt he could move on. She empathised telling him about her mum, and just talking about her made Julie well up and he held her while she just sobbed.

It was one o'clock in the morning when Gary said he was so sorry, he hadn't noticed the time and he better be on his way or he would meet the kids coming in as he was going home. He asked whether Julie would mind if he took her for a drive the next day, he had been exploring on his own and it wasn't much fun and to her surprise she didn't hesitate. He said he would pick her up about eleven and they could make a day of it.

The kids were surprised to find her still up an hour later and she told them she was going sight-seeing the next day. Susie thought and had said that was odd without Dad and Julie had laughed and said for goodness sake, she would be enjoying adult company for a change and so she did.

They had a wonderful day visiting the touristy bits but he also knew of a wonderful restaurant in the hills where whatever was cooking in the clay oven was what was on the menu. They enjoyed the most delicious meat and fried potatoes washed down with ice-cold wine and Gary cracked up at Julie's face when the man told her it was goat. The day went far too fast and Julie insisted he stay for supper totally ignoring Susie's glare and she and her mate went to their rooms saying they weren't hungry right now. The boys chatted away about going on jet-skis the next day. Gary asked whether would they mind if he came with them? He secretly thought it was a rather dangerous thing to do without an adult around and they had said great, and asked their mum too.

It became a regular occurrence. Gary and Julie and the kids, and he was sad when he had to return to the UK. He had invited them all over to his villa, which was similar to theirs but not quite as large, and no sea views. He was a good host and mucked about in the pool with them organising a volley ball competition, which exhausted them completely.

Julie was surprised at just how much she missed him. She had told Dave all about him and what fun he was with the kids and Dave was glad she had someone to go out and about with because he really couldn't spare the time.

Julie settled back into the routine of school runs but she felt so lonely particularly after such a full, busy, happy summer holiday. Dave had told her that she just had the after-holiday blues, and just laughed it off but she wondered if it was something more. She wouldn't admit to herself that Gary had actually made a huge impact on her. Maybe it was the timing; she had finally been able to enjoy herself after her mum's death without feeling guilty. She knew she was giving just a bit too much of herself to a man who was really quite vulnerable. Not physically, but she was on his wavelength, could anticipate his thoughts and she decided it was probably just as well he had left when he did.

The secretary moved back into the new offices Dave had had built to house the considerable admin staff that was necessary now his company had virtually quadrupled in size. Julie decided she really needed to do something with her life. She had been a secretary before she married Dave and hadn't worked since and she fancied a change. She enjoyed her trips to the beauty salon, for company mostly, but she thought it can't be rocket science to put gel on nails, do the facials, pedicures and seaweed wraps.

Dave wasn't impressed she wanted to work. He had said that she had everything; they didn't need the money and found it hard to understand she was 'unfulfilled'. However, she said that she had enrolled at a college that did a one-year course in health and beauty and he realised he stood no chance and did not stand in her way.

It was a month after her return from Cyprus when she was totally gobsmacked to open the door to Gary.

He was holding an enormous bouquet and presented her with a bottle of scotch for Dave as she asked him in.

He told her that he was working on a project half an hour away and did she mind him looking her up? Of course not, she was totally blown away. He looked amazing, tanned with his sleeves rolled up to his elbows and his open neck shirt tucked into his smart navy chinos.

She made him a coffee and he had asked if he could meet Dave, if he was here. She was sorry; he was away for a couple of days but if he was around for a while they would surely arrange to meet. She was so pleased to see him. He was obviously thrilled to find her in and she told him all about her course and how excited she was to be actually doing something positive with her life. He had said she was already doing positive things with her children, they were always a challenge. His were staying with his mother while he was away but he hoped they would all meet again possibly in Cyprus.

He looked at his watch. She apologised for keeping him but he had said that was fine and she made him lunch and they had wine and she knew, she knew they would make love. She just didn't expect it to be so intense. He was a good lover, he teased her and his tongue was exquisite and she gave herself completely, desperately filling an empty void, it had been such a long lonely time. They lay there. In her marital bed. In the bed she shared with Dave and he held her and murmured in her hair that he loved her and they were soulmates and he had wanted to do that since they first met, on the very first day.

She had sat up looking down at him and said she had too, she had felt the chemistry but she had been stronger then and now she was weak and he had asked where they went from here? She wasn't at all sure. She knew she wanted him, she knew he excited her and she knew she was married.

They dressed and he poured them coffee and there was a silence between them that spoke volumes. He had to go, but he had to come back. He couldn't leave this here. She felt the same but she needed to think. She needed to realise what she had done and what they had done. She needed to try and rationalise that it was a one off, that was that and he just looked at her and touched her and she knew it was never that simple.

He typed his mobile number into her phone. He said he wouldn't call, he wouldn't be in touch, and it would be up to her. She protested that wasn't fair, but he was adamant. He had nothing to lose and everything to gain and she had everything to lose. It was weird to be thinking all of these things after one brief encounter he thought, but he knew all along how it might pan out and he felt she did too.

His car went down the drive and she went inside in complete and utter turmoil. She hurriedly made the bed, showered and put on her make-up to collect the kids. They all had something on after school, as was the norm, so she had time to try and compose herself. The ball was in her court and she had an awful lot of thinking to do.

She was surprised to hear Susie in the kitchen. She had turned the radio on and hadn't heard Julie calling to her. Helen was with her and Julie wondered how long they had been there. She asked whether they had come back early, apparently, Helen's mum had given them a lift and they had gone straight to the stables to get the ponies sorted, still in their school uniforms. They changed and rushed out of the door as she drove to get the boys.

They were full of the matches they had both played after school, Wayne was pleased his team had won against a rough lot at the neighbouring school and Charlie, the younger boy, had scored the penalty in his match. Julie was aware she was not her usual self. She smiled at her sons but her mind was elsewhere. She busied herself with the supper and jumped feet when her phone rang. She half expected it to be Gary, even though he said he wouldn't call she hoped he would, and Dave said he was sorry but he would be one more day before he could come home.

She lay in bed that night and her mind was in a very strange place. Her life no longer seemed straightforward; it had changed in one single act of passion. Lust, that's what it was and you couldn't break up a marriage just on lust. She did feel he loved her, no she knew he loved her, and that both thrilled and scared her. She wasn't sure how far she could go with this. She couldn't bear to lose the children — funny it didn't occur to her that she couldn't bear to lose Dave. She could never leave them, not now, not ever. She had been a fool, she had let her desire lead her heart and her head knew it was wrong. But was it wrong? If no one found out, it couldn't be wrong. No one would get hurt but she would put herself first for a change and she would enjoy this thing, this affair — for that is what it would become.

She called Gary at midnight. He was wide awake, desperately hoping she might call. He agreed they should meet, she needed to talk to him, and she needed to say face to face how she felt. He wasn't sure which way it would work out but they parked in the station car park and he got into her car and they drove to the common, parked the car and walked, hand in hand.

He couldn't wait to kiss her, to pull her to him, take her face in his hands and kiss her, his tongue probing and lingering and she kissed him back. She tried to be matter of fact but they both knew they both wanted each other and further into the woods he spread his jacket on the ground. She lay down and their love making was an urgent need until they reached that place where ecstasy meets oblivion. They lay there, he sat up resting on one elbow, staring at her, saying how much he loved her. They gathered themselves together and walked on. She told him she couldn't leave her family, her children were everything to her. He looked at her, held her by the shoulders and told her he never expected her to, it had all been so sudden, but he hoped they could meet. The project he was working on would mean he would be in the county for a good year, and he would love it if they could meet as often as both their schedules would permit. He knew an hotel in Tring, he used it many times for business meetings and it would be a perfect rendezvous if she felt she could do this. Her course ran with the school terms so it would be easy in term time, and that for now was how they left it. Holidays would be sorted another time, it was the here and now they both wanted.

She had just come out of the shower in the Green Dragon Hotel when her phone rang and Gary handed it to her. She saw it was Dave and he was shouting at her, where was she, what was she doing and she told him she was between classes and would ring him back. Before she put the phone down she heard an enormous bang and the phone went dead.

She looked at Gary in alarm. "Oh my God Gary, he sounded so mad, do you think he knows about us, do you think he knows I am here?"

"Sweetheart, how can he know, we are always so careful, you park in the station and I meet you. Your car isn't here, how would he think you are?"

"Gary, there was a terrible crashing sound, then the phone went dead. He is on his way to Heathrow. Do you think there has been some kind of accident?" She tried his phone but it went straight to answerphone. Gary turned on the computer in the room and poured her a glass of wine. The computer whirred and he went on to

Google and checked the BBC news. There had been an accident on the M4 at the Heathrow junction. He just stared at the screen. Julie looked at him. "What?"

"Julie there has been an accident and it could be Dave is involved if what you heard was a crashing sound. Did he say anything more or did the phone just go dead?"

"It cut off, that's all I know Gary. We need to find out more, is there any more information? Find out exactly what has happened."

She was dressing all the while she spoke. Gary found the crash on the screen and it looked very bad. Cars were strewn across the carriageways and emergency vehicles were everywhere. There was a helpline number flashing at the bottom of the screen and he wrote the number down. It was an incident room and Julie asked to be put through to anyone who would know if her husband had been involved. The very calm voice on the end of the phone asked an increasingly frantic Julie the name of her husband and the make and model of the car he would have been driving. "Mrs Samson, is anyone with you?"

"I am OK, just tell me what you know, is it my husband?"

"Mrs Samson, a Mr Dave Samson has been taken to Hillingdon hospital, its three miles south of Heathrow airport. His condition is serious but he is stable. Is it possible you can get there right away?" She said she would and put the phone down. She was white as a sheet and her enormous brown eyes looked terrified. Gary hurriedly dressed and they left the hotel.

"There is no way you can drive, not in this state Julie, I will drive you. We will leave your car at the station."

"But how will that work Gary, I will need my car, the kids need to be told, I need them to be there." Gary was remarkably calm.

"OK, we will go in your car but I will drive. You can park it in the hospital car park and I can get a taxi from there. I don't think you ought to contact the children until you know a bit more. They are about an hour, tops, away from the hospital and you need to assess the situation before you get them involved." Julie sighed. She knew he was right. Thank God Dave had phoned her, if she hadn't heard that bang sound she would never have known. Never mind how he had shouted, she would cross that bridge, right now she had to get there and her head was all over the place while Gary drove her car to the hospital.

"I must call his work, they will wonder what is going on. Wonder where he was going, obviously flying somewhere, may be Manchester again." She dialled the number and was touched by the genuine concern in Trudy's voice.

"Oh, poor Dave, oh goodness, will he be OK, what's going to happen?" Julie told her that she was on her way to the hospital but until she had spoken to the doctor, she had no idea what state he was in. She

50

thanked her for her concern and would be in touch. The look on her face as he left her in the car park broke Gary's heart. He wondered if he would ever have this woman, in the way he wanted her, completely, entirely, and that look told him that right now he couldn't have her at all.

There was a team of volunteers taking people to the special room set up near the hospital entrance and Julie was escorted by a very genteel lady with steel grey hair. "Right my dear, the hospital have designated staff to help you, they will take you to where your husband has been taken, after you have spoken to one of the consultants. Would you like a cup of tea, coffee?"

"Thank you but I am fine." And Julie hoped this kind lady wouldn't smell the wine on her breath.

The consultant explained that really Mr Samson had been very lucky, mainly due to the make of car and the fact that the firemen had been able to free his foot, that would probably be instrumental in their being able to save it. His hip had dislocated and he had been given morphine for the pain, and fortunately, the airbag had prevented serious damage to his chest, although he had suspected broken ribs. He was conscious but very sedated and would she like to see him?

Julie looked at Dave, so still, so pale, tubes all over the place and she felt so sick, so sad and so sick. She went to the side of the bed and stroked his hand on the sheet. He didn't move, his eyes didn't respond, his head stayed very still. "Does he know I am here, does he know it's me?"

"Mrs Samson, he is very sedated, the morphine has done its work and he is not in any pain, but we must monitor the pain relief and he must become more stable before we can operate. We will be reinstating the hip if there is not too much damage and where the foot was trapped there is massive trauma. He will remain in this state for at least twenty-four hours. He is out of danger, but he must remain in ICU." The consultant looked at her and saw what he had seen for most of the morning. Confused, sad and some panic-stricken relatives who had been going about their normal daily routine when, out of the blue, the people they loved the most in the world were fighting to stay in it. "Mrs Samson, I suggest you go home. There is nothing you can do here, Mr Samson really needs to rest, and he cannot have you or your family around him right now. We will call you if there is any change but for now it will be best if you get home for the family."

The volunteer lady appeared from nowhere and took her hand. "Now my dear, a good strong cuppa will sort you out. You have had a shock and you cannot drive until you are calmer. We have sandwiches and cake prepared and we won't take no for an answer." Julie was grateful for this kind person who was completely taking charge. She sipped the hot sweet tea and tried a piece of cake but she really couldn't swallow it. The tea did help though and she was glad she had been persuaded to have it. She felt a bit better and thanked the lady as she made her way to the car park and edged out into the lunchtime traffic to drive home.

As soon as she got indoors, she called Gary. He was glad she was safely home and obviously very concerned about Dave. He refrained from asking if he was going to pull through, although since the accident that had been foremost in his mind. If he didn't make it he would be there for Julie, and he hoped they could make a future. It was getting to that point though. He may pull through and the time it would take for him to recover would be the time he could lose her. "How is he Julie? Is he in pain, did he know you?"

Julie was crying. Her silent tears were streaming down her face wetting her arm as she held the mobile. "Gary, he looked so poorly. So frail. He isn't a big man but he seems to have shrunk. He is not in pain, drugged up to the eyeballs with morphine and I don't think he knew I was there, at least I hope he didn't because if he did, he didn't attempt to look at me. The doctor said he will remain in ICU for at least twenty-four hours and so I will go in tomorrow. I will phone first and I will obviously keep you in the picture. The kids won't believe it, they will be devastated. I will call you after I have told them. It's Susie I worry about, ever since mum died she has been so vulnerable."

"Julie, I wish I could be there with you. It's going to be tough but you will cope. Tell them when they are all together, at supper when they have got in and settled." Julie thought that would be best but as soon as they got in they were all over the place, Susie going to meet Helen and Wayne had an exam and Charlie wanted to play his latest game on the computer. When she spoke it was not her normal voice. It was shrill, hollow, and it grabbed their attention. They all stared at her.

"Mum, what's wrong, what's going on?" Susie asked.

"It's Dad, he has been in an accident." Before she could go on Susie screamed and her hand flew to her mouth.

"Is he OK? Oh, Mum, where is he, what happened?" Julie told them exactly as she had Gary, that he needed rest and they would assess it all tomorrow but for the moment he was out of danger. All of them broke down and cried. It was inconceivable their dad, the strong head of the family, had been hurt, was in hospital, was fighting to stay alive.

Wayne put his arm around Julie. "You OK, Mum? Did he speak to you? Did he know who you were?" Julie held on to him, she felt weak and very tired.

"He is having pain relief and that makes him very sleepy and no, he didn't speak because he couldn't, Wayne. He has tubes all over the place, but they will get him through this. He is a strong man your dad."

"I need to see him," Susie said, flopping down on the sofa. "He's got to know we are all there for him, even you eh, Mum?" The iciness in Susie's voice cut the atmosphere like a knife.

"Susie, what the bloody hell are you talking about?" Charlie glared at his younger sister.

"Ask her, why don't you? I told Dad she was acting funny and I think it was that Gary. He invited himself on to our holiday and I saw the way he looked at Mum and how she was with him. Not like she is with my dad."

Wayne just stared at Susie. "Look mate, I know you have had a shock, we all have, but don't take it out on Mum. She and Gary are nothing, they just met in Cyprus and he lives up north anyway so just calm down, OK?"

Julie was still reeling. "What did you tell your dad Susie? You had no right to talk about such things. You need to be very sure of your facts before you dare to say anything so evil as this."

"Well, me and Helen saw his car driving away when we came home early weeks ago. I don't know about the car actually, but it was him, I would know him anywhere."

"You are right Susie; he did visit some weeks ago. He was down this way and called in. He brought Dad a bottle of scotch and me some flowers. We talked about old times and he left. You have added two and two and made five Susie, you are so wrong about this."

Suddenly the whole impact of the day hit her and she staggered slightly as she found a dining room chair to sit down. Her thoughts were racing. She couldn't believe her daughter hated her so much as to tell Dave about what she assumed to be going on. She knew she resented Gary, she had said as much in Cyprus, but to go this far. What if Dave had believed her, even worse, what if he had had her followed and found out about her and Gary? Wayne kneeled in front of her. "Mum, don't worry, Dad knows you far better than that. Susie, that is a lousy sense of timing, when Mum is so worried and upset. Now Mum, phone the hospital and see how Dad is. If there is any change, we can all go and visit, can't we?" He looked at Susie as if she was a piece of muck under his shoe.

Julie got the consultant's card from her bag and called the number. It went straight to answerphone but the kind lady had written the number of the incident room and she called it and asked if there was any news on Mr Samson. She was passed through and someone asked her identity and was able to tell her there was no change and that he was comfortable.

Wayne brought Julie a cup of tea and they all sat around the dining room table. "He will be OK, won't he, Mum?' Charlie's worried voice broke the silence and said what they all wanted to know.

"I am sure he will be OK Charlie. His body has had a tremendous shock and he needs to rest before they can begin to put it right. He will need an operation on his hip but they can't do that until he is more rested. He is very lucky to be alive. The car chassis saved him, and the airbag. He was actually on the phone to me when it happened. I heard the crash down the phone."

"Oh Mum, that's terrible. Good job you were here and could get to the hospital quickly." Wayne looked hopefully at her, he knew she wouldn't muck about, not do the dirty on his dad.

"I don't think you will be able to visit tomorrow, not until we know a bit more about the operation. I will call the hospital in the morning and find out what kind of night he has had and when I can go in."

"Well, I am going, for defo," Susie piped up.

"Susie, we are in the hands of the consultant. If he says no visitors, we do as he says. It could be that he has a really good night and they will operate sooner rather than later." Her voice was tired, she was tired.

"Let's get a takeaway," Charlie who was always hungry made the practical statement.

"Good idea, Charlie boy," said Wayne and they ordered an Indian and that seemed to make things a bit more normal.

Susie phoned Helen and told her about her dad. She really didn't feel up to going out now and Helen said she would come over if she liked but she said it was OK. Charlie cancelled the football kick about and Wayne knew he still had to study for his exam. Helen's mum called Julie to see if there was anything they could do and to say how very sorry she was to hear about Dave. Charlie's mate's mum did the same and this made Julie feel a lot better. She missed her mum at times like this. Times when she really was lost, not sure what to do. She had often wondered what her mum would think of her being with Gary. Her mum had never judged, never interfered but she thought on this occasion she might have had a word or two to say.

She called Gary when all the kids were asleep and he was concerned for her and she immediately felt his warmth down the line. Someone who actually cared for her, in her own right. Maybe that's why she had gone with him. He was always complimenting her — on her hair, her figure, her legs. Always saying the right thing at the right time and it wasn't an act. She knew he genuinely cared about her, genuinely loved her.

It is so sad when you are swept along in a heady rush of lust and attention that if only you had actually stopped, thought of the impact this would have on everything, your whole life, there is nothing to stop you. Your conscience doesn't interfere because you don't let it. Selfish, whereas before you were selfless. Lust is never predictable but then, is love? Hindsight is a wonderful thing, and no person in the present time can have it. If only she had been able to have these thoughts, this realisation, she would not be about to lose the one true love she ever had, the love that had been desecrated by thoughtless lust.

8

The paramedic was able to wrench open the driver's door of the Astra facing the oncoming traffic and thumped the syringe into Stuart Dunwoody's leg. He stemmed the flow of blood but the man had lost a lot. He had been lucky. The wound in his leg had missed the artery in the groin, but for that he would have bled out even though he was the third casualty to have been reached. They transferred him to the ambulance over the central reservation and moved on further down the line of cars desperately hoping that people could have survived in the tangled wrecks.

Katherine Carlisle was holding Mavis's hand as they followed a lady in a pale blue uniform along a corridor to a small room off the main drag. The lady asked them to wait, the doctor would be there as soon as possible but obviously casualties were arriving all the time.

Mavis just couldn't stop talking, nonstop verbals about how she decided she was going to have the blue and the green dress, but of course, she had left them behind. How could this have happened, how was it Stuart was involved, he was such a careful driver, did so many miles each week. Katherine knew that shock could affect someone in many different ways. Some people were silent, some weepy and some, like Mavis, just talking about anything rather than there be silence. She put her arm around this vulnerable young woman. She was quite attractive and seemed remarkably smart and it was only her nonstop talking that showed how nervous she was. Naturally so. All she needed to know was Stuart was going to be all right. He just had to be, because she had got herself into more debt with the store credit card he knew nothing about and her only way of getting out of the mess she was in would be for him to be able to carry on working to pay off all the debt he would never have been in if he hadn't married her.

The door opened and a small man with white hair and a white moustache entered carrying a clipboard, followed by a nursing sister. "Mrs Dunwoody. I am Professor Bailey and I have been attending to your husband. He has suffered a heavy blood loss and is heavily sedated. He has a deep wound in his thigh, we believe it was caused by a piece of metal from the base of the seat penetrating with the impact of the crash. That aside, he is having a blood transfusion which can take up to four hours, but this will get his bloods up to the level they should be. He has been most fortunate not to have suffered more serious injuries considering the damage done to his car. He is not conscious at the moment, the morphine will keep him under, probably for the duration of the transfusion. Would you like to see him?"

Mavis had listened to the professor but had not really taken anything in. She just needed to hear he would be fine but he hadn't said that. "He will be all right won't he doctor?"

"As far as we can tell, at this moment in time, he is holding his own. We have not X-rayed, it is more important to get his blood levels sorted but he is a young man and we do not believe there are any head injuries. The most critical injury is the leg wound, it may have caused irreparable damage and then we would have to discuss what course of action to take. However, for now, we must concentrate on replacing the blood loss. Please follow me Mrs Dunwoody."

Mavis gripped Katherine's hand as they followed the professor to a ward with four beds. Stuart was over by the window. She looked at him, he seemed the same. His face was a funny colour grey and the drips going into his body made a whirring sound. His body from his waist down was under a kind of tent, so no pressure was on the wound and she reached to touch his hand resting by his side. "Stu, it's me, Mavis. Can you hear me? The doctor says you are going to be fine, take a little bit of time but you are going to be fine Stu. I am so sorry this has happened to you, I really am. I am going to be here for as long as it takes. Katherine from your office is with me, but now I am here with you I will be fine to stay with you." She turned to Katherine who was quite alarmed to see the state of Stuart and Mavis had appeared to be oblivious of the situation. She felt she had not grasped just how dangerous it could be. She kissed Mavis on the cheek and said if she was sure she would be all right she would go, but only if she was sure. Mavis said she would be fine and thanked her very much for being there for them both. Katherine gave her, her mobile number, and said as soon as she needed to go home, or wanted anything, she was to call and she would arrange whatever was necessary.

She looked back at the bed as she left the ward. Mavis was talking to Stuart, nonstop like before, and she wondered just how this poor woman would cope if things did not work out well for Stuart. She didn't wonder for long. She knew. She would falter and fall and that's when she would need all the support she could get. Even in that short space of time, being with Mavis had made Katherine determined whatever the outcome, she would be there for her, to do whatever she could.

9

Jane Carmichael had been looking forward to the weekend for weeks and she hadn't been disappointed. The St George's High School reunion was held every year and this time the venue was a hotel in the Buckinghamshire countryside. Set in manicured lawns with deer roaming in the fields and wonderful walks to enjoy the spring flowers that were at last poking their heads up, was the perfect setting with the magnolia tulip-type flowers so beautiful against a clear blue sky.

She had flown from Edinburgh on the Friday, leaving work at lunch time to catch the flight and get the hire car, a grey Volvo from the airport to arrive at the hotel for five p.m. She registered at reception and made her way to her room. She hoped she wouldn't meet anyone until she had unpacked and freshened up.

The planned weekend was a shopping trip to Ollerton in the morning, lunch in a local bistro and the reunion dinner in the evening. Sunday was spa treatments in the morning, a light lunch and a walk in the afternoon, weather permitting, and the farewell dinner in the evening, departing Monday morning.

This was the tenth annual reunion and she had only missed two when she was out of the country on business. She was a successful fashion designer and was often called in by large companies to refresh their range of clothes as the fickle fashion industry could change overnight. A celebrity would wear a certain dress and it would fly off the shelves and online shops would run out. Many times, it had been Jane's design that had earned the retail outlets millions of pounds.

She had chosen her outfits carefully. She knew the other girls would be watching to see what she was wearing and for the drinks reception she wore a knee-length grey jersey dress of her own design with a single strand of pearls and pearl earrings. Her long legs were shod in Christian Louboutin black slingbacks — with the obligatory red sole.

She had never married. She had had several long-term relationships but commitment seemed to suddenly waver and disappear. Sometimes on her part, sometimes not, but she had always put her work first, striving to be the best and that meant something had to give. She had no regrets. She had never yearned for children and it seemed to her that her married friends were not over-the-moon happy, the first flush faded and the humdrum getting on with life automatically followed. This wasn't for her, she had to be at the cutting edge.

She looked at her reflection, adjusted her necklace and wished she could call James. She couldn't of course. That was one of the drawbacks of being the mistress of a married man. He was the one person she had met in her life who ticked all of the boxes, but he was married and she knew he wouldn't leave his wife. He had two boys at boarding school and she had been introduced to him at a work conference. He was the managing director of one of the retail outlets Jane designed for and there was an instant attraction. He made it very plain he wanted her. His blond hair and grey eyes were a strange mix, and his long strong fingers knew every inch of her body. They met whenever they could and lately it was becoming more and more regular. Deep down, deep, deep, down, she desperately hoped that maybe, one day, their relationship would be too strong to ignore and when his boys were older, now twelve and fifteen, he would break the tie and they could be together. But that was a long way off, and for now the weekends in Paris at the fashion shows and the New York fashion week were the times she lived for, and the odd one-offs if he was in Edinburgh.

She went down in the lift to reception and there was a blackboard and easel with the notice, St George's Tenth School Reunion, at the entrance to a huge panelled lounge. The sound of excited chatter greeted her and she took a glass of champagne from one of the waiters circulating around the room.

"Jane, Jane darling, you look fab — as usual!" Brenda Hay air kissed her and she did the same.

"Brenda, you haven't changed a bit."

"Well, if you don't count a few inches around the waist darling — too many lunches and not enough exercise but I love it." She led her to a group of friends, so pleased to be all together again, laughing and exchanging photos and lots of oohs and aahs. Jane gravitated towards Pauline. She always liked her, down to earth, not over the top drop dead gorgeous but so easy to be with and so honestly interested in what you had to say. She was divorced. She had been devastated two years ago when she realised Tom was playing away — with her best friend. They had been at it like rabbits, she had told Jane, and she knew she couldn't stay in the marriage. Strangely Tom and June had not lasted long after the divorce, she said, in her book, it was the illicit thrill that kept them together. Once he was free, the thrill had gone. That wouldn't have happened with James and me, Jane thought.

"How are you Pauline, I have to say you look stunning." She kissed her friend.

"I return the compliment, Jane, you look younger each year. Must be a man I think?"

"There is someone, he is a bit special but he is married." She immediately wished the ground could swallow her up. "Oh Pauline, how thoughtless of me to say such a thing. Do forgive me."

"Don't worry Jane, I believe it's better to be a rich man's darling than a poor man's slave!" And they laughed together.

"Does that mean you have someone Pauline?"

"I do, and I thought, sod it, if you can't beat them, join them and he spoils me rotten." They chatted away, another glass of champagne and it was announced that dinner was served.

Lyn Wood had organised the seating plan. She was the core of the reunion committee and took great pride in making sure all the events of the weekend ran like clockwork, from the menus to the treatment appointments. Jane sat next to Carol, she couldn't remember her name until she glanced at the name on the place card. They exchanged greetings, and Jane was very aware Carol was checking out the lines as Jane liked to call it. "Is everything going well Carol? You look very well." That was actually far better than saying you actually look worn out and you could have made more of an effort.

"We are surviving really. Alan lost his job, made redundant after fifteen years and he just cannot find another job. He was a city trader, I know it was really intense work and now he has nothing. Just like that, cut dead. He is job hunting all the time and I have gone back to work part-time. Sorry Jane, not the kind of thing you want to hear really, is it?" Jane was mortified at her first impression of Carol.

Of course she would look worn out, how could she afford to come to this weekend, oh my goodness. She would be far too proud to accept any money which Jane immediately thought she could do for her. "Carol, I am just so sorry. It must be so hard."

"We are thinking of emigrating. Alan has been on a plumbing course and he is now qualified. Australia needs tradesmen and he has some family over there. It's a huge wrench though, my mum is horrified at the thought. She has been a huge help with the children, sorting them after school and cooking their tea if we can't get back. It will break her heart."

"I know people in Australia too, couldn't your mother go with you? A huge step for her I know, but at least she could be with you."

"Trouble is, her mother is in a home and I don't think she could leave her dad. He is already lost as Alice has dementia and he wouldn't really cope without my mum."

There was a silence as they ate their seared scallops with cucumber and salsa verde, a delicious promise of a great menu. Jane tried hard to find words of comfort for Carol. Fortunately, Iris was on Carol's left and she started a light conversation. Jane actually thought she was telling a joke, that would be brilliant. Susan was on Jane's right and looked sideways at her. "Gorgeous Jane, you just never change. Must be no children, they put years on you, you know".

Her mouth was smiling but her eyes didn't. Jane wasn't sure if it was meant to hurt, but she rose above any such thought. "Susan you are amazing. Don't know how you do it juggling work with the children and having a successful marriage. Well done you, contentment is written all over you."

"Thank you, Jane, it's hard work but it's worth it."

There was a wonderful buzz of happy chatter, laughter and really a kind of abandonment, Jane thought. Everyone had left whatever problems, dreary routine, arguing children and normality to escape to an unreal bubble type atmosphere to be pampered and cosseted. She was really glad she had come and when Lyn clinked her glass for quiet as she stood to speak, everyone was relaxed and eager to hear her words.

"Dear friends. Thank you so much for coming to celebrate ten years of St George's High School reunions. It is quite staggering to think that we are from all corners of Great Britain and yet we can make the time to spend wonderful times together. Old memories shared and new ones to be made. We are very fortunate to have this bond and long may it continue. As always there are a few thank yous to the committee." She paused, a round of applause and here heres — "and to the management and staff of this superb hotel. Thank you from all of us. I hope you will enjoy the planned events, the spa and of course the great shops of Ollerton. We will meet tomorrow night for our celebration dinner — and again many contributions to the suggested menu were received, thank you. In the meantime, please enjoy the rest of the evening and we look forward to enjoying a fantastic weekend. Thank you." Slightly flushed Lyn sat down to table thumping and applause.

Jane opened her bag and discreetly checked her phone. Her heart flipped when she saw she had a text from James. She excused herself after coffee and went to the powder room. She opened the text and read:

Darling, I have some wonderful news for you. I will be at the car hire office when you bring the car back on Monday. Please remember I love you very very much. James xx.

Jane lent against the cubicle door. Could it be, no, that was not on the agenda. He was staying married, she knew that — but what could it be? Something wonderful, wonderful news? Her head was spinning, not least with the champagne and Sauvignon Blanc, but this had thrown her. His texts were always brief, love you, take care etc. It was his own mobile and she felt she could text without alerting anyone else.

James, how curious, how exciting. Now I have to go two whole days without knowing, can't you text me about it?

She pressed send and realised she hadn't even said I love you. It buzzed back.

Darling, I have to tell you face to face. Enjoy your pampering sweetheart and meeting your old friends. I will text when I can but you know I love you and will meet you on Monday. Text me when you think you will be at the car hire. Love you.

Oh, my goodness me, thought Jane. That's typical James. Always full of surprises. A weekend away, a holiday together? Hopeful thoughts crowded her brain.

The party was breaking up, many had travelled a long way to the hotel and a busy day beckoned on the Saturday so she bid goodnight to her friends and went to her room. She went to bed without showering, just taking off her make-up and fell asleep dreaming happily of what might be.

The day was perfectly planned and enjoyed by all. She was thrilled to see one of her designs in a small but very expensive dress shop. Wow, didn't realise smaller shops could carry them. The bistro was just perfect for a light lunch complemented by a chilled glass of Pinot Grigio. She had chosen a full-length creamy silk dress over which there was a layer of chiffon dotted with tiny black beads and she knew she had turned heads as she enjoyed the evening banquet. The food was excellent and they had all contributed to a bouquet and a pair of gold earrings for Lyn as a thank you for all her efforts in organising the reunion.

Sunday, she thoroughly indulged herself with a stones massage and a pedicure and manicure. Moisturised to within an inch of her life, her facial was the final touch and she felt wonderful. They all convened for drinks before lunch, and she tried to make eye contact with Carol, but she was involved in another conversation. You sat anywhere for lunch and she found a table with three others and within minutes they were remembering old times and laughing at their various antics.

The farewell dinner was poignant and fulfilling at the same time. Many old memories had resurfaced, slightly embellished but still such fun and they all stood and laughed and clapped as the flaming pavlova was brought in, the grand finale to a wonderful weekend. She said her goodbyes before going to bed. She deliberately approached Carol and managed to slip her, her card. "Carol, I am so sorry for your troubles and I hope they can get resolved soon. If you go to Australia, I have contacts there so please don't hesitate to call me, for whatever reason and I will do my best to try to help. She squeezed her arm and kissed her goodbye. She wanted to leave early, just to get there, just to get to James. She had a coffee and some orange juice, cleaned her teeth, closed her case, settled her account and checked out of the hotel.

She put the case in the boot, took a deep breath and drove out of the grounds onto the main road. The traffic wasn't too bad and she turned off the M25 on to the M4 towards Heathrow. Her head was full of different ideas as to what the surprise could be. She had always done this. Tried hard not to pre-empt a situation but always embroidering facts in her head and this sometimes led to disappointment. She tried to hold back, not to be too hopeful, although he had said it was something wonderful. She drove in the fast lane, keeping to a steady seventy mph and was glad the traffic wasn't too heavy. She saw the lights flashing above the motorway, *slow down accident*. She had seen the warning signs before and everyone just seemed to keep driving at the same speed. She did begin to slow as she saw the traffic ahead, but she left it just a little too late. She saw flashing blue lights and slammed her foot on the brake, skidding and bouncing off the central reservation and the car travelling behind her was going far too fast, had not attempted to slow down early enough and crashed at sixty mph into the back of Jane's car. The impact lifted the car into the air and it landed on its side slewing to a stop across the two lanes, wheels still spinning as the sound of screaming tyres braking too late reverberated across the motorway.

Jane was held by her seat belt, on the side of the car upended, her body crumpled, her neck thrown back, her mouth open, her eyes gradually closing, fluttering, shutting down as her heart could no longer pump the blood, pierced by her broken ribs.

A grotesque caricature of a twisted marionette and the puppeteer was death.

10

It was an ordinary Monday morning on an ordinary day when Kevin Whittaker's life was about to change in the most extraordinary way.

He lived in a room in a house in Dalston, a twenty-minute tube ride away from Canary Wharf where he was a very successful chemist in the laboratories of the John Bartlett Corporation. His specialist field was pharmaceuticals and he had carried out his research striving to create a cream that really did what it said on the tin — banish wrinkles. He couldn't find that elusive ingredient, one enzyme that could react with another to stimulate collagen production, smoothing away the wrinkles that so many ladies referred to as 'laughter lines'. He had been working on this aspect for nearly four years and finally the breakthrough had come almost exactly one year ago. He had discovered the use of stem cells, taken from plants using them to stimulate human cells. He found that the plant cells could influence the behaviour of human cells and made them act younger than they were. He had extracted them from the plant and grown them on in the laboratory. Crushing them in a saltwater solution released the active ingredients which could then be processed into the skin cream.

John Bartlett was ecstatic. The product could revolutionise the cosmetic industry and he had it first. It was his baby and would bring millions to his already successful empire. In Kevin Whittaker's eyes it was his. The product went through the extremely thorough testing processes and was being produced under the code HXP5 and the brand name was Impactus. The marketing team were working on the design of the container, tube or bottle, or both, to present it to the public. The patent had been applied for which ensured that no one globally could file the same application and it be granted. The legal department had applied for the Patent Cooperation Treaty which covered the patent in one hundred and forty-two countries globally and also the European Patent Convention covering the majority of Europe and some extension states. They had consulted a patent attorney, aware that the patent law could vary from country to country to make sure they were applying correctly. The John Bartlett Corporation trademark protected the logo and name of the product. Although it could take up to four years for the patent to be granted, they had taken all the necessary precautions to protect their product.

To his boss, Kevin was the best cosmetologist he had ever known, but unknown to John Bartlett was the fact that Kevin had an addiction. He gambled. He was never sure when it changed from being just a bit of harmless fun to a full-blown need. Maybe it started because he was a loner, living alone in a flat where you could lose yourself and be totally unaccountable.

He once had a semi-detached house in the suburb of Enfield where he lived with his girlfriend, Susan, and they had a future. His salary easily covered the mortgage and living costs and he had a fair amount of spare cash each month. He and Susan were saving to get married. Their savings amounted to nearly £20,000. He had been frugal and Susan was contributing from her job in the typing pool.

He had begun to place the odd bet and it seemed to him he just couldn't lose. First of all, it was a whim, a flight of fancy and he began to get known in the local bookmakers. He also subscribed to the *Racing Post* and studied form. The bets became larger and his winnings were becoming seriously large. He was on a roll. Any money he may have had left after the regular payments dwindled and the wedding fund remained static.

He studied the form of one particular horse and knew it had to win. It was a 'racing certainty', couldn't lose. He had backed it before and this time it wasn't the favourite, odds of ten to one. Amazing. He used £2,000 from the wedding fund and made £20,000. It was ridiculously easy. Susan was blissfully unaware of 'their' good fortune. She knew you had to save and plan for at least a year. She knew what she wanted, the full monty, the dress, the flowers, the venue culminating in a wonderful honeymoon in a faraway place — a dream come true.

Kevin opened an account at the bookmakers and could study form without moving from his newspaper to place the bets. His account was nearly always credited with his winnings, the odd loss deducted, but that was rare. He upped his game. The limit on his bets was £200,000 and the bookies would lay the bets off with others if Kevin's odds were not so much in their favour. He knew it had become an obsession, almost as if something had a pulse he would bet on it, the outcome of football matches, Liverpool to win the cup, on and on. He cared for nothing else but the next rush of adrenaline when he won — and all the time no one knew, not Susan or his laboratory assistants.

Of course his luck did change. They often say you don't normally see a poor bookmaker. He placed £50,000 on an odds-on favourite and it was pulled up lame a furlong from the winning post. Sadly, this loss occurred just when Susan had booked the venue for the wedding, needing £2,000 deposit from their savings. She had organised the date and had been lucky to get both the church and the manor house for six months ahead. She needed money for the dress and the cars — only the Rolls would do, she didn't want those strange VW van things that seemed to be advertised all over the place. Kevin took out a loan to cover this unexpected urge from Susan to spend money, for God's sake why now? Luckily there was enough money for an accumulator bet, but the third horse didn't come in and he lost the lot.

He fell behind with the mortgage payments. He asked the building society if he could defer the payments for six months but they could see no reason for this as he had not lost his job and the economy was no longer as buoyant as it had been when he took out the mortgage. They foreclosed on his mortgage and the house was to be repossessed.

Susan had absolutely no idea of his predicament until she came home one Friday night after work and Kevin was completely out of it, drunk as a skunk and totally incoherent. She managed to sober him up. She thought someone had died, although she couldn't think who as he was an only child and his parents were dead. Maybe he had lost his job. He was totally exhausted and told her in a dull monotone broken voice that he had not been able to meet the mortgage payments, the house was being repossessed and they were homeless.

"No, no, we have the wedding fund, we can get married in a registry office, I can cancel everything, everything." She just could not grasp it, until he told her there was no wedding fund, he had gambled it away and there was nothing. She was stunned, as though she had been physically struck. "When, when could you gamble. If you are not at work, you are with me, and you do all the overtime on Saturdays. What about your salary, have you lost your job?" Her mind was working overtime and she was struggling. He just stared at her, he couldn't say anything. The sordid truth gradually dawned. Gambling meant more to him than she did. She was nothing in his life. She obviously couldn't compete with the thrill of the chase — and that was what it was for him. She really didn't come anywhere near, she couldn't fulfil this sick need of his.

She put what she could in a suitcase and walked out, not even slamming the door, she was drained. She walked to the train station. Her month's salary had been paid into her account that day that was all she had. Everything else had gone to the wedding fund. She called her mother who heard the great sadness in her voice. "Susan, darling, whatever is the matter?"

"Mum, can I come tonight?"

"Of course, but what is it, what has happened, is Kevin all right?"

"We have split, Mum I can talk to you when I see you. I can get to Liverpool Street then come out to you from there. I will call you when I know which train I will be on."

"We will be there to meet you darling, but please try to be calm, you sound awful. We will wait to hear when you know the time. Please take care." Susan closed the phone. She was in shock and she really did not know what on earth she was going to do. She just focused on getting to her parents, her life as she had planned it was not going to happen. She was back at the starting post and the going was not good.

Kevin sat in the house, staring into the huge void he had created. He kept seeing the look on Susan's face, the shock, the horror and finally the disgust. He had ruined her life, he had taken her dreams and trashed them into the gutter. He tried her phone but she cut it dead. Just like their lives, cut dead. He was now totally alone. He had no friends, his 'overtime' on Saturdays was the bookies.

He left the house the next day but he didn't go to the bookies. He went to the internet cafe and searched for rooms to rent. He found one fairly near the tube station at Dalston. It was a house share and they wanted two months' rent up front and one hundred and fifty a week for the room. The man who opened the door was about forty something and showed him up the stairs to quite a large room sparsely furnished. The bathroom was on the landing and downstairs the kitchen would be adequate for four to share. He would just use the microwave. He had the money, just, from his salary and collected his few things from his house and moved in. On the Monday when he went to work no one had any idea he had split from Susan and moved house. They had no idea the only money he had to his name was what was left after paying the deposit and one month's rent on a single room.

For the first time in a long time, he had time to reflect and he realised that he was at rock bottom. He could not get any lower. He avoided the bookies, his account was closed. He concentrated on his work, working all hours to avoid having to pass an open bookmaker, and he didn't gamble.

Seven months after he had lost his house John Bartlett called him into the boardroom and the directors stood to a man to applaud the star of the show. Kevin was totally taken aback. "Kevin, Impactus is going public at a launch in Manchester in four weeks' time. As a small token of the appreciation of the company we would like you to accept this cheque as a bonus for your dedication and hard work in creating Impactus. We will of course, raise your salary accordingly, but in the meantime thank you very much Kevin." There was applause again and Kevin held a cheque in his hand for £25,000. John congratulated him and said that obviously the confidentiality agreement he had signed was still in place and this would cover any future work he undertook for them.

Kevin went back to his laboratory and sat down. The work he was currently applying himself to was to find a way to banish 'sun spots' on mature skin. His studies had shown that stem cells taken from mammals were far more effective at stimulating human cell renewal than those taken from plants and he was confident that a breakthrough was imminent. However, today he had £25,000 and no real debts. His salary covered his rent and his needs were minimal.

He knew there was a bookmaker's around the corner, five minutes' walk away and just walking through the door brought a wonderful feeling of expectancy, of hope that he could win again. Just a small bet, on a horse he had not heard of before and it won.

He realised he needed to get back to studying form, not just pick a horse because he fancied it. That had been a lucky break, but he was now back in the saddle and he needed to feel that adrenaline rush again. He was amazed at how quickly he could switch his brain into concentrating on the odds and the ground, soft, hard, and began to build up his winnings.

He was happy in his modest room. The other housemates seemed to have regular jobs and just used the house as a base. He left for work early so that he could use the bathroom and be away before anyone was around. He used his lunch breaks to place his bets and would collect his winnings after work, but found himself staying on to bet on evening events until the bookies closed their doors. He was content in his own addiction. He didn't actually see it as that, it was just he was only happy when he was studying form and placing his bets. He was completely unaware that he was being watched by a team of three men, observing his movements from when he left his room to when he returned at night.

He was breaking even, but a £5,000 bet on 'the most promising runner in the race' which didn't even come in, put him in deep trouble. He bet to win, not each way and the horses didn't come in. His last bet was on a horse that had won for him before, the going was good and it came from fourth to third and he felt a surge of hope, he needed this win to survive. Unfortunately, an unknown horse came from the back of the field and streaked past the winning post and won by a length.

He began to walk back to work when a man came from behind him and tapped him on the shoulder. He spun round. "Not having much luck are you mate?" Kevin walked on, now very aware that the man was very big and seemed to know exactly what he had been doing.

"Get lost, I don't know you so piss off," he said in a voice which didn't seem to carry much conviction.

"Listen mate, we all do it. We all think, this is the one, this is the money. I know someone who would be able to help you out you know." The man drew level with him.

"I said go away, leave me alone."

"Just have a chat with him. He knows your boss, Kevin. You wouldn't want John to know what you do now would you, not a man with your knowledge, know what I mean?"

Kevin stopped dead. "Who the hell are you, what do you want? What I do in my own time is nothing to do with my boss, he doesn't own me."

"You underestimate your importance, Kevin. You are not really in a position to argue, are you?"

"I am going to my office. If you persist in following me, I will call the police."

"And tell them what? We were having a chat, that's all mate." Kevin hurried into the revolving doors and down through security to his lab. He sat down and realised he was shaking and sweating. He felt sick. He reached for his lab coat and tried to study his notes. He couldn't read them, he couldn't concentrate after his encounter with the man. I cannot go to John and tell him that I don't have any money until next pay day, not after the bonus. He will realise what I do. Did this man follow him everywhere, did he know where he lived? He went to the water cooler and filled a tumbler. He took a sip and put it down. Think man, think. What is this all about? I am just a chemist. OK, not just a chemist. I create formulas that make people a lot of money. Luckily the other lab assistants were working at the other end of the laboratory and were unaware of the wreck Kevin had become. He called his secretary and told her he did not feel well, must be something he ate at lunchtime. He was going home. She wished him better, but had she seen him she would have realised that something was dreadfully wrong. He changed from his lab coat, shrugged on his jacket and walked out through the security doors and out of the revolving door. He was shaking and very scared.

The big man was leaning on the railings outside the building. "Hey, Kevin, what's up mate, leaving early?" He kept walking but another man appeared and blocked his path.

"Leave me alone, I will shout out, go away."

"Hold on Kevin, think about it mate. Who is going to help you out of this one eh?" He couldn't breathe, his legs gave way from under him. The two men held him up and frog-marched him to the nearby underground car park. To anyone watching, it looked as though he had had too much to drink and his mates were taking him home.

Kevin's eyes could not adjust to the darkness, the dim lights only serving to create shadows against the walls. The headlights of a large car switched on, dazzling Kevin. The men pulled him to the car and a door opened. He was bundled in, one man getting in next to him and one in the front with the driver. The car moved slowly out of the car park into the bright sunshine and was soon joining the early afternoon traffic. Kevin could not see the face of the man next to him, only his neatly pressed trousers. He could not place the accent, not French or German, but deep and devoid of any emotion.

"Kevin, you are aware of the situation you are in. You must face facts. You are a gambler, that's fine. But you are in a position of trust in your work, and that makes you a rare commodity. A gift to me actually. You see, you cannot go back to Bartletts. You have compromised your position. John gave you a generous bonus, in his eyes. We could give you so much more, Kevin. He has not treated you with the respect you deserve. You have made his company a massive amount of money and what does he do? He gives you £25,000 and you have managed to lose that in under four weeks."

Kevin turned his head but still could not see the face. "You must be mad, I will tell John everything, he will not let me go, we go back years and he knows what I can create and what I am working on now — he knows I can make him a huge fortune."

"Kevin, we know you have developed Impactus. We know the formula is in your possession."

"Wrong, so wrong. It's under lock and key, they are not stupid."

"But you are Kevin, you have the formula in your brain. You know the vital ingredient that you just couldn't discover until one year ago." Kevin's mind was racing. Who could have betrayed him? Who could know that the formula was discovered a year ago, he even knew the name, and it hadn't been launched yet. Someone on the inside of the company was working for this man. But that someone could not get the formula, no way. That's why he was here in this car and if he had not gambled, if only he had not been a gambler, he would not be in this predicament. But he was, he had, he realised, betrayed himself, yet again.

"Kevin, we have had you in our sights for a long time. We know where you live, we know you have no friends, and of course, we know your habit. I want you to come and work for me in Switzerland."

"Switzerland, just who are you, what is your company?" Kevin actually had an idea of which company it was. There was always rivalry between the various cosmetic companies and he was aware of the Ellenberg Corporation based in Geneva.

Kevin had never been abroad and to be honest had been dreading the exotic location that Susan had wanted to choose for the honeymoon. On the rare occasions they had been out to restaurants he always chose the meat and two veg option.

"Switzerland," he repeated.

"It is not so far away Kevin, one and a half hours on a plane. My laboratories are unique. They are equipped with lasers and technology that John Bartlett could only dream about. You can only imagine the facilities which will be available to you Kevin. Your weekly salary will be what John would consider a bonus. We are aware of your addiction. You will not have to hide it from us and we will make sure you have adequate funds to enjoy yourself on the racetrack. All we ask is that you apply your brain, you convert the numbers in your head to paper, you deliver the formula of Impactus and you complete the work you have started on the age spots. You will be short of nothing and the facilities for you to create your formulae will astound you.

"We are going to go to your room in Laburnham Road. We have suitcases in the trunk and you will be able to pack your bag and get to the airport for the evening flight to Geneva. Your passport and tickets are in the attaché case in the trunk. So Kevin, what do you say?"

He could not believe what he was hearing. All he really heard was, not the amazing laboratory facilities, not the salary, what stood out was 'enjoy yourself on the race track'. He would no longer have to hide his addiction. They knew. Nothing to be ashamed of. "What if I refuse to do as you ask?"

"Should you decide you cannot accept our generous offer, John Bartlett will become aware that his treasured chemist is a gambler who had amassed huge debts and the only way out was to commit suicide. A terrible tragedy when the man was at the pinnacle of his career having created the most amazing product to have ever come out of his corporation."

Kevin's heart sank. He wouldn't commit suicide, they would kill him. The car turned into the motorway services at Heston. The man sat forward and Kevin saw a man with almost black eyes, piercing his. His skin was whiter than white. Had his eyes been pink he would have been an albino. He was totally bald, except for a yellowish pony tail at the base of his head which hung over the collar of his jacket. "So Kevin, have you arrived at a decision?"

"You are Allessandro Degen of the Ellenberg Corporation aren't you?" He had seen him before at various conferences in the profession.

"Kevin, you really do not need to know about that until you are in the air. Now, will you be joining us?"

"I don't seem to have any choice, do I?"

Allessandro Degen smiled. "Driver, proceed to Laburnham Road. Kevin packed his few clothes. The cases were put in the trunk and he opened the attaché case. He opened the passport. It was him in the photograph but it was not his name. "Welcome to the first day of the rest of your life Adam Jones." Degen settled back in his seat. It had been a long wait, to snare his prize, but he had him now and his mission was accomplished. Kevin — no Adam — tried to relax, tried to take on board what had happened in one day, but he was exhausted and watched the evening traffic as the car drove to the airport, having to take a diversion ahead of the Heathrow junction where there had been a dreadful crash earlier in the day.

11

As soon as John Bartlett had checked into the Grand Hotel he called Adrian Cook. The call went to answerphone and he assumed he would not have it turned on due to the possible interference with the hospital equipment. He calmed himself with the thought that if there had been any change he would have been contacted.

He freshened up and met Andrea in the reception and they went to the conference suite. He was delighted with the decor, the soft peach chiffon drapes perfectly complemented the colour of the packaging to launch Impactus. Each leather chair was at an individual table with the name of the guest in elegant peach script. Behind the rostrum was a table laden with the gift bags containing a small bottle of champagne tied with peach chiffon ribbon and a selection of the lotions for bodywash and shampoos surrounding the Impactus cream which lay in a tiny casket of peach silk.

There were thirty invited guests representing the major cosmetic companies from around the world. The head of the New York operation greeted John. He had arrived the night before and shook John's hand warmly with both hands. "John, it looks great, perfect. We are all so excited, can't wait to see the reaction. You scored John. It's your baby and we are just so proud to be a part of it. Where is Sarah?" John returned the warm greeting.

"I am so sorry to say, Brian, that she was in an accident on her way to the airport this morning. She is in hospital and holding her own as far as we know, but it's serious, Brian, very serious."

"John, that cannot be. I spoke to her last night and she was all geared up and ready to go. How dreadful, is she conscious, can she speak?"

"She is unconscious and on a ventilator. Her son is with her and Clive is in the air as we speak. I deliberated as to whether or not I should come, but she wouldn't have had it any other way. She has been with it from the inception and will be rooting for us now." His voice betrayed his emotions and Brian hugged him.

"Sarah is one of the strongest women I know, she will come through John, I know she will."

"Yes, yes she will," and his voice strengthened with the power of his conviction. "Well, the show must go on as they say. The guests will be gathering in the lounge. Let's go join them. Oh, how rude of me, Brian, you know Andrea?"

"Of course, we have met before. How are you Andrea, you look wonderful."

"Thank you, Mark, I am fine, just obviously concerned about Sarah. However, we are in control and everything is set to run smoothly. Did you receive the list of attendees, Sarah said she was going to send them to you last evening?"

"Yes, I have them thank you Andrea. The usual crowd. It will be fascinating to say the least. Let's go."

They followed John into the lounge where there were many familiar faces. John mingled among the guests, warmly greeting his peers, complimenting the ladies and cajoling the men. The waiters were circulating with the champagne and canapés and there was a general feeling of camaraderie mixed with expectancy and excitement, as the various representatives of global corporations wondered exactly what was going to be revealed.

At a nod from John, the master of ceremonies announced that the guests should please make their way to their seats in the conference suite. John had been surprised that Allessandro Degen was not there in person. A Dario Gonthier introduced himself as the representative from the Ellenberg Corporation in Mr Degen's absence. Otherwise, everyone he had hoped to be there was there. A sea of expectancy met his gaze as he stood at the rostrum to open his presentation.

"Ladies and gentlemen, thank you for travelling from near and far to witness the latest innovation from the John Bartlett Corporation laboratories and welcome to the most exciting breakthrough in the cosmetic industry. You are about to witness the future of skincare in the present day. Our cosmetologist has created a product derived from various enzymes from different origins to produce a tried and tested serum that will revolutionise the industry. The formula is such that the skin cells are re-energised, therefore, the aging process is slowed down.

"My friends, six months of chemical trials and the following process of rigorous registration for the recognition of the formula has proved beyond any doubt that the product does what it says on the label. Mother Nature, we cannot beat you but we can slow you down. Ladies and gentlemen, we give you Impactus, the future of beauty in the present day."

The lights dimmed and twelve beautiful young women dressed in elegant peach chiffon evening dresses came from either side of the rostrum to distribute the gifts, placing them on the tables in front of the guests.

They stood, applauding the man and his product, he had done it, he had found what they had all been searching for and would go on searching for, a way of holding back the years, the most lucrative essence of the cosmetic industry.

John was ecstatic. He had hoped the reception of this breakthrough by his peers would be a success, and it was, everyone was smiling and he knew everyone would want to take this product to distribute through their own outlets. The formula was protected but the product was not exclusive, it was marketed to appear on every cosmetic counter in the world.

Brian shook his hand and Andrea gave him a hug — a kiss would have been the true mark of Judas. The guests were opening the gift bags and there was a buzz of approval and excitement as the perfectly presented Impactus saw the light of day. John was engulfed by so many people wanting to shake his hand. He had created Impactus and they would sell it on, their profits would soar and each sale would boost the coffers of the John Bartlett Corporation, no small achievement in a global empire.

The master of ceremonies announced lunch was served and they made their way to the banqueting hall. John approached Dario Gonthier. "Dario, I have not previously made your acquaintance. Tell me, is Allessandro well? I felt sure he would want to be here on this occasion, in fact I believe he had accepted the invitation personally."

"Mr Bartlett, please forgive me for not explaining earlier. Mr Degen has had to attend to an unexpected development which has prevented his presence on this occasion. However, I feel sure he would wish me to congratulate you on Impactus. It is an incredible achievement, and your cosmetologist is to be congratulated, as is your corporation."

"Thank you, yes, we are most fortunate to have him, he has been with us for many years and it is his creation, all credit to him."

"I am sure he has been well rewarded Mr Bartlett. I will not join you for lunch as my schedule is tight and

I must make my way, but thank you for a superb presentation and I am sure Impactus will bring your company much success. I bid you goodbye and thank you."

The menu did not disappoint, adhering to the high standards of the hotel and Sarah had been meticulous in her selection of light but delicious food, complemented by a superb selection of wines. John hardly ate, making sure he spoke to as many people on his table as possible, and then taking his wine and circulating, ready for any questions people may have. There were a few, easily dealt with by John who was well aware of the statistics and although he didn't bury the answers with too much data, there was enough to alleviate any concerns.

Brian was a great ambassador for the company and people were keen to hear what the American market would make of the breakthrough. He was able to say without hesitation, that is was a unique and very special product which would dominate the American market, and those worldwide.

Andrea was also able to extol the virtues of the product. She had been in at the inception through to the final presentation and found several of the men gravitating towards her, and not just for her input. She was a good-looking woman, elegantly dressed, slightly understated but that was her charm. She laughed at the compliments and she felt her confidence soar. She had secured a very good future for herself, purely by biding her time. She had diligently covered her tracks, blameless. The bank account in the Cayman Islands was in the name of Amanda Barrett and she couldn't wait to become that person.

Finally, the coffee and liqueurs were served and John stood once more to thank everyone for their attendance and raised his glass to Impactus, the future of the cosmetic industry in the present day.

Brian wanted John to stay for the evening and leave Tuesday morning, but with the accident he guessed it wouldn't be happening. John apologised but felt he had to get back as soon as he could. He had tried Adrian and this time he answered. Clive would be at the hospital at around six thirty and Sarah was stable and as comfortable as possible. He mentioned that the doctors may induce a coma to try to combat the trauma, but they were waiting until Clive arrived.

Andrea had organised the return flight and had thanked the staff, reassuring them that Sarah was in the best possible hands. The account would be settled in the normal way and she was waiting in the lobby for John to appear. The manager offered his sympathy to John and conveyed his best wishes for Sarah's recovery.

John thanked Andrea for stepping into Sarah's shoes with such expertise, he felt it had gone very well, in spite of the distressing events of the morning. They sat in silence on the plane and the chauffeur was waiting in arrivals. John turned to Andrea. "Can I offer you a lift, Andrea? I plan to go straight home but I can drop you to the station?"

"Thank you, John, but I will make my own way. I need to pick up a few things. I will see you in the morning?"

"Of course Andrea, and thank you for today." They parted company and Andrea made her way to the taxi rank. She took a ticket and was advised the taxi number Twenty-four would take her fare. She instructed the cabbie to go to Wimbledon, where she had an apartment in a block of flats. She settled back in the taxi and finally began to unwind, to relax, although she still had one important item to confirm. She flipped open her iPad and checked her online banking. She regularly changed the password, you just couldn't be too careful. It finally connected, she typed in her identity code, her pin number and the letters randomly picked from her password. An amount of one million pounds had been deposited in the account of Amanda Barrett two hours ago. She closed the iPad. So, Kevin Whittaker was no more, he was on his way to Geneva. She had no reason to run. She just knew that she could if she wanted to. Right now, it suited her to keep calm, play out the rest of the plan, that is act normally, go to work, be the efficient Andrea and then, when the time was right, she would become Amanda Barrett. This had all been part of the deal and Mr Degen would not let her down.

12

Andrea Harrison had grown up in a leafy suburb of London, progressing from a gawky skinny schoolgirl into a lovely young woman. You couldn't call her beautiful but her red hair and green eyes always turned heads, and she played every asset to its maximum advantage. She had had a good friend, Brenda Mason, and they had done each other's hair, gone shopping on Saturday afternoons and decided they ought to learn to smoke because everyone who was anyone seemed to smoke. They brought a packet of ten No. 6 tipped and went to the cinema. They wanted to copy Helena Carter. They both thought she was so beautiful and when she smoked the smoke came out in a stream as she removed the cigarette from her mouth. When they tried to imitate her, Andrea and Brenda disappeared in a cloud of smoke. However, they sat in the front row, trying to perfect getting a clear stream and Brenda whispered to Andrea that you had to take it down to make it do that. They both felt a little lightheaded as they left the cinema and upstairs on the bus, trying the last one, they were both sick and got off two stops before home in case the bus conductor came up the stairs.

They decided they could both smoke 'properly' now, and they progressed from the youth club to going to dances in London, just making the last tube home and then having to walk the rest of the way as the last bus had long gone. Brenda had 'done it' with Freddie Burrows when she was thirteen and told Andrea it was amazing. Andrea had always envied Brenda's boobs. She had worn a bra for ever and she had gleaming white teeth and the boys were bees round a honeypot and Brenda just lapped it up. Andrea decided that she must have something wrong with her because Brenda was always saying, 'blimey, did you just see that', as a boy walked past and Andrea actually hadn't noticed him at all. Brenda gradually dropped off the scene as her Saturdays were taken up with the different boys she had met and Andrea was her alibi if her mother called asking where Brenda was.

Andrea had a job in a London chemicals firm and in return for her doing the basic filing and photocopying she was taught shorthand and typing. She excelled at this and passed the Pitman exam with good speeds in both. She progressed to the typing pool and was always in demand and the particular favourite of Mr White. He was a tall slim man, always seemed tanned and obviously very married. Andrea took his dictation and he would look at her as if he could eat her. She was leaving the office to go to the tube station when he came out at the same time and offered her a lift, it was not out of his way and she would get soaked getting to the tube.

As soon as she got in the car, he pulled her to him. She was surprised but secretly pleased. "It's a beastly night, let's go for a drink before I take you home."

"Oh, Mr White, well, I suppose so."

He laughed. "Andrea, my name is Simon, just relax." They went to the nearby pub and she asked for a gin and tonic. She hadn't actually had one before but Helena Carter had one in the film and when he offered her a cigarette, she was very glad she knew how to smoke it. "Are you in a hurry to get home Andrea?" Simon White asked.

"No, not really."

"Good, then we can go for a drive." The rain was hammering on the roof of the car when he pulled up in a leafy lay-by near Epping Forest. He had been chatting away to Andrea, asking her about herself, what she liked to do and she had enjoyed talking to him telling him where she wanted to be in life, what she hoped to achieve. "Andrea, you are a very beautiful young woman, you know I am attracted to you, would you like to make love?" Although she was hoping something might happen, when it was kind of said in black and white her heart skipped a beat. "We will be more comfortable in the back sweetheart." And they both got a little wet getting into the back. She looked at him and he kissed her and she opened her mouth and it felt so right. She unbuttoned her coat and he kissed her neck, unbuttoned her blouse and she shrugged it off. He was out of his jacket and put her hand on him as he gently eased up her skirt and slipped his fingers inside her panties. She parted her legs, and rubbed him, hard, and he undid his belt and pushed his trousers down. She fumbled and then held him and stroked him and he was hard and she lay back and pulled her panties off and he knelt down and she felt his tongue flicking, licking and she wanted him so much. He laid her on the back seat and guided himself into her. She shuddered and he moved against her and against her until he entered her and she pulled her legs up and he was pumping her. She felt a kind of breathless ache, a need, and he exploded and she was still wanting more, not quite there and then she was and she thought she was floating and it was the most amazing feeling she had ever experienced. He moved to sit up and she put her legs to the floor and they both said nothing at all. Her head was swimming and she thought she would never ever forget this moment, and the smell of his aftershave mixed with the feel of leather on her skin was unforgettable.

"That was your first time Andrea, I hope you are OK?"

"Simon, it was wonderful," was all she could say and he drove her to her house. She thanked him for the lift, sounded silly really but she could hardly say thank you for taking my virginity so beautifully Mr White, and went indoors.

That was the beginning of an intense relationship. Simon had a friend who had a flat near the office and they would go there after work most days and Andrea felt so special and he obviously adored her. Unfortunately, the company decided that shorthand typists were an expensive overhead with the advent of Dictaphones and Mrs Goody was told that the girls in her typing pool would now use Dictaphones. Andrea was horrified. She loved using shorthand and she would no longer be visiting Simon's office to take his dictation. She got the evening paper on her way home and got a job as a secretary to a managing director of an advertising company in Holborn. She and Simon realised this would not work for them, basically Simon loved the arrangement, so simple for him, but all good things come to an end.

Andrea worked hard for her boss, she missed Simon's attention but soon found that actually, she could attract other men, and she was earning enough to find a flat in Wimbledon, small but suitable to her needs. She applied for the position of personal secretary to John Bartlett of the pharmaceutical company of the same name. With her skills and obvious good looks, she soon became his number one, progressing from secretary to more of a personal assistant. She set about making herself indispensable. Anticipating events before they happened, making sure she had organised meetings down to the minutest detail, making herself always available, staying late, coming in early. She was making a name for herself and when John confided in her that they were making great strides in the development of a new skincare product, breakthrough technology, she was excited to be in at the beginning.

She was introduced to Kevin Whittaker, the cosmetologist responsible for the work on this new product, and although she thought he was a bit of a loner, a bit strange, he welcomed her into the lab and showed her around. She had absolutely no idea of what he was doing with stem cells or whatever, but made sure she was bang up to date with any progress made.

Things were going really well. She had several relationships, but nothing that really made her stop and think this could go further. She was giving her undivided attention to getting to the top in John Bartlett's world. Then Sarah Cook arrived. John had heard of her event organising and had headhunted her from the company she worked for in north London. She was introduced as Andrea, my secretary, to Sarah Cook, my personal assistant in charge of event organisation and public relations. She will be an unbelievable asset to the company with the advent of our new product.

Andrea was devastated. Why on earth did he need this woman when she was perfect for the job? He could easily get someone to do the secretarial duties and she could concentrate more on what she had been doing for the past two years and he did not need Sarah Cook.

She had met Allessandro Degen on several occasions at various conferences and he was instantly attracted to her. They were not intimate, although he would have loved it, but Andrea was aware of where her loyalties lay. She felt she could be more useful to John by being friendly with Allessandro rather than be his lover. It was almost two years ago when he sought her out at a product launch and immediately became aware of her unhappy demeanour. "Andrea, my dear girl, where is that sparkle? Is something wrong, you look stunning, you always do, but you are not right, are you?"

"I'm fine Allessandro, things just haven't quite worked out for me though."

"Whatever do you mean darling, things haven't worked out?" She didn't hold back. Everything just poured out, how she felt she had been pushed to one side, after all she had done to promote the business and be devoted to John, all because of Sarah Cook, she was in the place she felt should be hers. Allessandro listened intently to the outpouring of pent-up frustration. He said nothing but asked if he could take her to dinner that evening.

It was in a discreet Italian bistro in Covent Garden that he suggested to Andrea that he was in a position to help her if she could help him. He told her he was aware of the cosmetologist working on the advanced technology, but he needed someone to feed him the information of what was actually happening in the laboratory. She had access to this information. Would she be willing, for a princely sum, to work for him in getting this information to him? Andrea was completely taken aback. She had not expected this. "Allessandro, I don't know, what if I am caught, will I go to prison?"

"My dear girl, firstly you will not get caught as you put it. You have told me many times you go to the laboratory but you don't know what is going on. From now on you will go to the laboratory and observe, take note and be aware of what is happening. It is not illegal, it is probably immoral, but business is business my dear. Now, what do you say, will you do this for me?"

"If I do this, what will you do for me?"

"I will open an account for you in the Cayman Islands under a different name and when our business is complete, I will deposit one million pounds. I will then pay you £500,000 annually."

Andrea thought, only for a moment. "Allessandro we are relying on an awful lot of trust here."

"Yes, my dear, it is mutual trust. At any time, you could tell John what I have asked you to do, but, what I am going to pay you could go a long way to creating a new life for you, a more fulfilling life away from the Bartlett Corporation who do not appreciate your hard work." She nodded. Why not? She had given her all for that company and for what. For Sarah Cook to be brought in to do exactly what she was more than capable of doing.

"Allessandro, we have a deal." He kissed her hand and ordered champagne, and that, as they say, was the beginning of a beautiful friendship.

13

Melanie Stammers saw the hazards flashing and the sign across the motorway, slow down, accident, reduce speed and as she slowed the car right down, she saw what appeared to be utter carnage. She turned on her hazard lights and stopped the car praying that anyone coming up from behind would see she was stationary, already having taken notice of the warning signs. She saw the taxi cab coming at speed in her mirror and knew she could only sit there. Luckily, at least for her, it swerved just in time to miss her but ploughed into the car two up in the fast lane and the sound was quite dreadful. A very loud bang and then silence.

The driver of the car in the middle lane jumped out of his car to try to wrench open the back door to get to the passenger but it was jammed and he could see the person slumped forward, wedged in the foot well, obviously they had not been wearing a seat belt. The airbag was slowly deflating and the driver was sitting upright but his head was slack, down on his chest. The man ran back towards Melanie. "Oh my God, it's bad. My battery is dead, can you phone for help?" He could see then that she was already on the phone, she signalled to him that she was trying but she couldn't get through.

Someone had though as the scream of sirens sounded nearer and nearer and Melanie knew that someone had been watching over her because she was alive by a whisker. The driver of the car behind Melanie had been aware of the warning signs and managed to stop but there was the sound of skidding tyres as cars were trying to come to a complete halt from sixty miles an hour to zero in a very short space and another car rammed the taxi. Luckily the man who had asked Melanie to phone had gone to the hard shoulder and was just standing there in complete shock.

Melanie finally got through and was told it was being dealt with. Was she OK? Could she get out of her car and go to the hard shoulder and then get as far away from the side of the road as she safely could? She joined the man on the hard shoulder and they both clambered over the rail to relative safety.

"You all right? What a bloody disaster, pardon my French. It was just so fast. I was just going along and not really speeding, well keeping up with the traffic as you do and then bang, out of the blue." His voice trailed off.

"I am OK, just feel a bit wobbly, it's horrible, it was so nearly you and me." She took the cigarette he offered. She had taken her bag with her phone but her suitcase was still in the car. "I am supposed to be meeting my husband at the airport. Funny, I always leave plenty of time, just in case I have a flat tyre or there is an accident, but this looks a very big mess doesn't it."

They had both been very lucky and they were both more shaken up than they realised. A paramedic was approaching them from the hard shoulder. "You will be safer if you can follow me and move more to the start of the accident. There is an ambulance at the scene and they will check you over. Come with me please." As they were escorted past the accident, Melanie took in the whole scene of total devastation. She couldn't believe there were so many cars involved, smashed up and at odd angles. She didn't want to see casualties. She didn't want to look at the firemen trying to free the poor souls who had been going about their business and she knew some would not be alive any more. You couldn't survive in that tangled mess of metal.

The lady in green shirt and trousers sat her down. Another similarly dressed man took her companion to another bench and they were both assessed. "You will experience a reaction, shock has a way of creeping up on you," she said to Melanie as she shone a torch in her eye, then the other one. She moved her hands gently over her head and neck, all down her right side then her left. "Can you stand for me please? What's your name please?"

Melanie was quite surprised she didn't immediately say her name. "Melanie, Melanie Stammers. I am going to meet my husband at the airport, I have plenty of time though, I always allow plenty in case of an accident." As she spoke, she started to cry. Why on earth am I crying, I am OK, I am not hurt.

"Melanie, I can see you have not suffered any physical injury and I do not think you will need to go to hospital. I will give you some paracetamol, can you take them?" She nodded. "The road is obviously closed and they have closed the other side as well. It will not be possible to drive anywhere. The diversions have been set up but that's the exit well behind where your vehicle has stopped. My job is to check people over who are in a similar situation to yourself and I will check with my colleague, to see if there is a way we can get you to the airport. What time is your flight?"

Melanie checked her watch. "That can't be the time, it's been over an hour since it happened."

"What time is your flight. Melanie?"

"Twelve fifteen. We are going to Barcelona to join the cruise ship. Is there any way I can get there do you think?" The paramedic got on the radio to her colleague and said they could organise a police car to take her back to the diversion but it would be at least an hour before that could be arranged as obviously, they were deployed elsewhere right now.

"It will be tight, it depends on how soon they can get here. You had better contact your husband now and explain. He may have heard about the accident on the radio and will be worried about you anyway."

At that very moment her phone rang and Laurence's voice almost shouted. "Melanie, is that you?"

"Yes, Laurence, I am sorry I haven't had a chance to call."

"Melanie, are you OK, there has been a dreadful accident, it's all over the news and I guessed that you could have been in it because you always allow so much time."

"I am OK Laurence. I was just so lucky. I had stopped but so many didn't and the car behind me missed me but went in the back of the one in front and, and—" She couldn't stop the tears and the lady sat her down.

"Can I talk to him?" she asked Melanie. "Mr Stammers, your wife is fine but she will experience a delayed reaction. She said your flight is at twelve fifteen. We are trying to get a vehicle to take her back to the diversion to get to the airport but it could be a while before we can do that. Rest assured we will do our very best."

Laurence thanked her profusely. "You are so very kind, with everything else going on there you must find this a bit insignificant, and I quite understand if it doesn't work out. That is the least of our worries, at least she is OK. Can I speak with her again please?" Melanie listened to his calming voice and she relaxed a little. She would keep in touch with him, she just wanted to be with him. She thanked the lady and moved to a seat further down as a paramedic brought two more people into the ambulance.

She would need to get her case. Oh no, she couldn't walk back through that dreadful scene. What about the car? Do you just leave it there, does someone come and drive it away? The keys were still in the ignition. She tried to stay calm. The man who had come in with her was shaking and had been sick and she thought she couldn't ask all these questions when people around her were in a worse state than her.

The lady came up to her. "Melanie, there is a car approaching the scene from the other side of the motorway. It will be taking you and two others to the airport. We will need to get your case and you will need to secure the car."

Melanie had been dreading this. "I don't think I can walk back there, not past all that, that dreadful awful—"

The lady interrupted her. "When the policeman gets here you can tell him your car details, where the case is, etc. Do you have the keys?"

"No, I left them in the ignition, I didn't think. The case is in the boot. What will happen to the car?"

"Was the car damaged, hit in the accident?"

"No, no, at least not while I was in it."

"If you can tell us the registration number the policeman will go and get the case and he can secure the car. Nothing will be moving for a very long time and the car will be driven to the compound about three miles from here. It will stay there until you come back from your holiday. Should it be you don't go, it will be there probably by late tonight."

Melanie gave the details to the policeman whose face was white and drawn above his navy uniform. He got the case, he could only just lever open the boot, a car had hit the back of it, and the dent prevented it from opening with the automatic locking system. The blue Peugot Estate that had hit it had the passenger door wrenched open and was empty and he couldn't believe the tailback of cars that just hadn't stopped in time. He didn't tell Melanie about the car, she really didn't need to know about that right now. He took her and two other men in business suits to the other side of the motorway and they set off.

Two and a half hours since the accident and she was on her way. No one spoke. There wasn't much to say, just a gradual realisation that they had been spared a terrible fate. Thirty minutes later she arrived at terminal one. She had never been so happy to see Laurence and he wrapped her in his arms. That hadn't happened in a very long time. She desperately hoped that this would bode well for the cruise. She wanted so much to show him that she was better now, no more paranoia, no more pills, she had finally made it — it was all behind her now.

The experience of not going mad, beating the odds, weaning herself off the pills and facing an unknown adversary had changed her, but for the better. She would be fine. She would cope. She was determined she would never go back. Never.

It had begun three years ago. People thought she was a very capable woman, coping with whatever life threw at her. It seemed to Melanie that some families went through life with no worries, children didn't disappoint, marriages were fulfilled and happy and nothing actually went wrong. She had had her fair share of worries but she hadn't complained, just got on with it. Her son, their beloved Sam, had been killed in Afghanistan. They had coped with that. He had died doing what he loved, but he was far too young. He hadn't made his mark on the world. He wanted to achieve great things in the army. He had said he may have to go there, do a tour or two, but he was nineteen. Surely, they should send more experienced soldiers, he was hardly out of training.

Laurence coped remarkably well while she was crumbling. Their daughter, Christine, took it very badly and Melanie had had to be doubly strong for her. Grief was a strange thing. You go through all sorts of stages and the anger hadn't left Christine. She was just so bitter, why did it have to be her brother in that bloody war. Melanie tried to look at it that they had been so lucky to have had him for nineteen years. He was such a good boy, never any trouble and he adored his family. He was the perfect army cadet and he really did love the army. He joked he would be brown in December when he came home, sporting a tan and fighting fit. Two weeks into his tour he had been blown apart. That was probably the start of Melanie's heartbreak. She tried to grieve, her friends rallied round, they all tried but she didn't grieve herself. She was trying so hard for Christine and for Laurence.

Christine's marriage didn't survive. Melanie wondered if her daughter had married Daniel wanting him to be like Sam. She so adored her brother and really Daniel was anything but the free, fun-loving, happy-go-lucky, Sam. He obviously adored her, but he couldn't cope with the way she changed and he didn't have the experience of age to give it time, to let it work out. He assumed she would stay in this bitter state, and although it was her brother she mourned, she didn't give one thought to her husband, and after a year he said he couldn't take it any more, and he left.

Laurence was a determined man and that probably helped him get through. He was working his way up the ladder in the Civil Service. He didn't have time for time wasters. He was in it to get to the top and he trod on a few shoulders to get there. He was not Mr Nice Guy. Well, you couldn't be could you? He never broke a rule, he always adhered strictly to the letter of the law and no fault could be found with his work, not in any respect. He was going for the post of chief executive of the Staff and Pensions branch of the MOD and he had actually used a colleague, actually a good 'friend' to get him the information he needed to get the interview. It was more 'the dirt' on his competitor. He had dug deep and found one little flaw and that proved fatal to the man who wanted it as much as he did. That flaw altered the balance and Laurence got it, the pinnacle of his career. He had to hold it down though and this meant a lot of hours had to be put in and Melanie was asked to become more involved, to accompany him on various functions, to be seen as the chief executive's wife, and she was not managing this very well. He wasn't aware of it, he just thought she was a little uncomfortable. They attended many black-tie dos and she always looked the part, but inside she was a trembling wreck.

When you get to the top through fair means or foul, it's the foul methods that are remembered, particularly by the person who has been fouled. They become determined to make the fouler pay and there are many ways to do this.

Geoffrey Palmer was a very disillusioned man. One tiny mistake, one misplaced expense that he shouldn't have claimed for, years ago, had cost him the job he wanted more than anything. More than being with the man he adored, who had left him when he realised he didn't figure in the future equation. He had hidden that fact very well. His personal life had come under scrutiny, but he had covered his tracks. Marriage had never been on the cards for him, not when you are pursuing a career and not when you are gay, and no one had even hinted that maybe he did bat for the other side.

He had money and he wanted revenge. He knew it was via a contact known to both Laurence Stammers and him that he had been exposed. They had dug very deep, but they had found it. He saw Laurence on many occasions, they were openly friendly, the show had to go on, and Geoffrey took the time to talk to Melanie whenever they met at the various dinners. He noticed she was ill at ease, not at all relaxed and he could sense her reluctance which gradually turned into a loss of purpose. He could see that she was vulnerable, and no doubt, after the death of her son, in depression.

Revenge was a dish best served cold, and he took his time to select the various ingredients he would need. He would get his own back on Laurence by hitting on Melanie, dragging her down, capitalising on her depression. He had researched this, he knew how to drive someone mad, in the most subtle way.

He actually didn't have to drive Melanie mad. Her depression was finally diagnosed by her doctor. Christine had realised just how bad things were, seeing that her mother had dropped out of life, she couldn't get up in the mornings, what would she get up for, and gradually people had stopped phoning. One very unkind 'friend' had said it was about time she got over it and pulled herself together.

She was sent for a brain scan, in case there had been some trauma in her head, but that was clear. She went for counselling but found it very tiresome that she had to do all the talking and the man just listened and so she stopped that — she thought it far too expensive anyway. So the pills were upped and she disappeared into a kind of foggy haze where she heard what Christine said but didn't really take it in.

She knew she was losing control, and finally Laurence had to acknowledge that she was very ill. He paid for a private psychologist and he had told Laurence that a chemical reaction in her brain had been triggered and she was clinically depressed. If someone breaks their leg they have a crutch and it is recognised as unfortunate. If you are mentally ill, there is a stigma that makes people shrink away, they cannot deal with it and although Laurence and Christine did their best, Melanie was not responding.

Luckily the correct balance of pills was finally prescribed and very gradually she did respond. She had lost an enormous amount of weight, she really didn't enjoy food or the pleasure of having a special meal. She knew the fuzziness in her brain was gradually going away and she eased off the pills, until six months down the line she was no longer reliant on them and things seemed to be getting back to normal.

Laurence was relieved Melanie was more like her old self, but it had taken its toll on him and he was hanging onto his job by the skin of his teeth. He had explained to his colleagues that she couldn't accompany him for a while, she had finally had a reaction to losing her son, and they were tolerant to a point, but that point was coming closer to when they would have to move him to the sidelines. However, Melanie forced herself to attend one function, then gradually it became easier and she was ninety-nine percent up to speed.

The cruise was the icing on the cake. She was delighted when Laurence said he really needed a break and it would do them both good to get away.

Finally, they were on the plane. She looked at the lines on his face and realised he had been through the mill. She felt incredibly grateful to him, for him. She would do her utmost to be there for him, to be the wife she used to be and let all her misgivings go away. Their love would carry them, they had come through too much for it not to be so.

14

Stan Roberts had had a busy night in the West End of London. He was a cabbie and had done the Knowledge, thirty-five years ago, and knew London inside out and he loved it. He had adapted to the one-way systems and knew the back ways to avoid the traffic and many famous celebrities from film, sport and television had been in the back of his cab. He liked the night life and normally would have stopped around six a.m. but his mate, George, asked him for breakfast at the Mile End Cafe, his son had graduated from Leeds University and he was as proud as punch and wanted to tell Stan all about it. They had a full English and Stan thought ruefully, that Dorry wouldn't be pleased about it one bit. She was always telling him no fry-ups and he was normally able to resist but on this occasion with a beaming George, there was no chance.

Stan and Dorry didn't have children, they had tried but after five miscarriages they decided that if God wanted them to have children, he would have organised it. They had created a very happy and busy life without them, being favourite auntie and uncle to several nieces and nephews. It was eight a.m. when Stan warmly shook George's hand and headed for his cab. He didn't turn off the hire sign as he drove down Oxford Street and stopped dead when he saw a young woman frantically flagging him down. She looked in and asked if he could take her to Heathrow, and here was fifty pounds if he could get her there in forty minutes. He smiled to himself, should be a doddle and where these young people got their money, he had no idea. Mind you he had a pretty good idea about this one. He read the papers and she was always strutting her stuff, some model or other and nearly always walking out with some pop star or film star. "Right, you are love, hop in and I'll do my best."

He glanced at her in his mirror and she really was very beautiful. Dorry would have said classy, good bone structure but he was stunned by her enormous brown eyes and she didn't seem out of it, not like some of the rich and famous who crashed out on the back seat of his cab. He liked the way she was dressed, an elegant navy suit with the palest pink blouse and her sleek auburn hair fell forward as she settled into her seat.

Cressandra was so pleased she had managed to get a cab and it looked as though they could make the airport in time. She hated being late, but Tommy just wouldn't let her get out of the bed, and she had been easy to persuade. He was so unlike the other men that had shared her bed. He was down to earth, funny, came from the same background she did, wasn't impressed by all the glamour and the hangers on. He had come from nowhere, winning a talent show, and wrote his own songs and performed them with his guitar. She had been spotted out shopping with her mum, how amazing was that. A photographer was snapping away in Regent Street as she was coming out of one of the stores, laughing with her mum and he caught her on film. He had approached her, ignoring the suspicious looks from her mum, given her his card and asked if he could take her number. The rest, as they say, is history.

She wasn't a stick-thin insect type and didn't go to any modelling schools. She was snapped up by an agency that found her work all over the world. The complete surprise was that she had taken to it like a duck to water. She actually loved it and she was a natural beauty. Impossibly long, was how her agent described her legs, and she had always only eaten when she was hungry. Her stamina stunned many who worked on her photo shoots. Her real name was Naomi Watts, but there was already a famous Naomi and so they changed it to Cressandra.

She was looking forward to this trip to the fashion week in Paris. Her good friend, Carol, would be going and they were meeting in the airport lounge. They always found something to laugh about, normal stuff, like who was doing what with who. There had been a lot of bad press about models being too thin, and to a certain extent, things had changed, but she still knew of models who would eat tissue paper to make their stomachs feel full. How they managed on no food amazed Cressandra, but they had other means to get their energy and they would never last the course. You couldn't abuse your body to that extent and survive and she was eternally grateful that she could eat sensibly and still wear the clothes. She had dabbled in drugs at the beginning. Everyone did, but she found it was the company she was keeping. She had still kept in touch with a couple of her friends from school. They were not impressed by people who took drugs. They had careers to make, they wouldn't be a part of it and their determination is what saved Cressandra from becoming more dependent on a substance to give her a high. It was the coming down that made her realise it was not worth it.

She often thought how lucky she was, how far she had come, from the depths of despair. Her stepfather had abused her from when she was eight. He told her, if she said anything to her mother, he would hurt her very much and so she said nothing. Her mother would not have believed her anyway, she adored him and that's why she put up with the beatings when he had the drink inside him. Strangely enough, when he had a massive heart attack that killed him stone dead, she didn't miss him as much as she thought she would. Cressandra was thirteen and her mother noticed that if anything, she blossomed after he was dead, and together, they moved on with their lives. Cressandra was scarred. She couldn't bear the thought of any man coming near her and when the boys tried it on at school she would lash out. She couldn't let those feelings go, the anxiety, anger, the sheer terror that he would maybe come into her room again, even though he was dead she was haunted by what he had done.

Her mother thought she was just shy when it came to boys and even though her friend Lisa had a boyfriend Cressandra was happy enough to be with her mum or go shopping with Lisa when she wasn't with her boyfriend. Lisa told her all about her sex life, how she got her pearl necklace which was nothing like the pearls her mother wore! Once she was with the agency, she did have a friend who was a boy. Stuart was gay and he adored her as she did him. He was a beautiful looking young man and they made an amazing couple to the outside world. However, it would take a very special man to show Cressandra that a man and a woman could make love, could cherish and enjoy being together. It was her agent, Max, forty years old, that guessed something in her past had made her almost frigid and he coaxed and teased her, never ever in a sexual way. He made her laugh, he would take the mickey out of her and himself and the other girls who took themselves far too seriously. When they finally got together, he used all the experience of his past years to make sure she would remember the joy of sex, and she did.

She always thought of Max with great affection and when they were no longer lovers, they were friends. He had given her the confidence to believe in herself, to realise she was as good as anyone in this world and she embraced her beauty with a grace that was far beyond her years.

The cab was making good progress, and she thought they would be in time. She took her mirror from her bag and pushed the hair off her face and noticed the lapel of her jacket was crumpled under the seat belt. She released the seat belt to smooth it out. The red light shone on the dashboard and alarmed Stan. He turned to say 'are you OK love', but the words didn't leave his lips. In that split second, just turning his head, and then turning back he saw a stationary car, stopped dead in front of him. He swung the wheel to avoid it and hit the car in the middle lane head on and a car behind him smashed into the cab. Cressandra shot forward, her head cracking on the glass which splintered into her face and she collapsed into the footwell of the cab.

The airbag exploded and stopped the steering wheel from crushing Stan's chest but his head went forward and then back on the headrest of the seat and to all the world it looked as if he had fallen asleep at the wheel.

15

Martin Taylor was talking on his mobile phone. It was an important call. He didn't have hands free in this car and he was concentrating on the conversation. He was just about to finish by reassuring the caller that everything would work out, it would be OK, when he hit the back of a black cab in the middle lane of the M4.

If he was lucky, he would come out of it with severe whiplash and maybe some broken ribs where the airbag had pushed into his chest. If he was unlucky, he could have broken his neck. Either way, he was unconscious but breathing, and the emergency services were doing their best to work back through the wrecked cars to reach the casualties as soon as they possibly could.

It would be ironic if, after all the times he had cheated death by self-imposed destruction, he should meet his maker when he was clean, no longer drug and drink dependant, but a man dedicated to helping addicts to kick the habit.

Many years earlier when he was a teenager, he experimented with cannabis which progressed to crack which progressed to cocaine. He could manage his job in the warehouse, driving the forklift truck and no one had much contact with him other than at break time.

They all went out for a smoke and he did the same, except he went separately so he could snort some coke to get him through his long shift.

It was surprising how easy it was to get stuff, it wasn't expensive, he could easily afford it on his wages and he still lived at home. Well, if you could call it that. His dad left years before and his mum would take her first drink with her cup of tea in the morning and no one really cared who was around or what was going on. She was compos mentis but expected Martin to manage his own life and he paid the rent and her job in the launderette kept her in drink. She could walk to work and to the shop for her drink and cigarettes and Martin would bring home takeaways but she rarely ate. She permanently smelt of drink but the people that brought their service washing just left it for her to do and apart from the odd thank you when they paid the money, no one got too close.

One of Martin's friends said he could get some meow. Martin had heard of this, mephedrone, and it was not that dear. Instead of going to the pub he went to his mate's house and a four-day binge ensued. He called in to work sick on the Monday morning. His mates actually didn't work, and he had an insane feeling of empathy for the people in the room, nonstop talking, telling his deepest secrets, so surprised they didn't meet before because they knew each other so well, when they had only known each other for five minutes.

The comedown from meow was totally horrible. He was depressed, anxious and he desperately needed more. When he did go home his mum said his boss had been on the blower and where was he if he wasn't at home if he was so ill? He said he had been vomiting all weekend but would go in the next day. Luckily, he looked absolutely dreadful so his boss let it go this time, and he hoped he could stop the cravings as he drove his forklift truck.

His mate got back in touch, for forty pounds, he could have a gram and he had it now. He couldn't resist. Other 'mates' turned up and the whole thing started again. He was euphoric, confident, he could take on the world, but he didn't go to work. His mum said his boss had phoned and he could forget working for him any more, just collect his wages and sling his hook.

He moved in with his mate and his descent into dreadful comedowns after ecstatic highs began. He totally dropped out of any social contact with anyone who had been a friend — in fact when they saw him, they really didn't want to be in his company.

His wages soon ran out and he went home to see if his mum had any money in her bag but she didn't and she was totally out of it on the sofa.

It was an obvious next step when the meow had lost its intensity, its appeal. It didn't quite hit the highs it had and you needed more and more to get that high. Heroin is a drug made from morphine which is extracted from the opium poppy. 'Street' heroin was sold to his mate as 'brown' and they started taking it by smoking it. His mate said it was tooting, putting it on foil, warming it till it melts into a ball of fluid which rolls along the foil leaving a trail of black residue. They inhaled the fumes with a roll of foil. The hit was amazing, more than they had ever experienced before, but they needed more, and Martin didn't have any money any more.

The old man in the corner shop knew Martin. He knew what druggies looked like, they came in all the time and he watched them like a hawk. He saw him put some chocolate in his pocket. "Going to pay for that are you?" he said to Martin.

"Naah, what you going to do about it then?"

"I'll call the cops, son." But Martin was gone, and he knew exactly where the old man had put a wad of cash out of the till. He waited till it was dark and he and a mate smashed the pane of glass above the door handle and wrenched it open. The old man was losing it, he had left the money under the counter and it couldn't have been easier. The old man hadn't called the cops, what for, they would laugh at him, taking bars of chocolate, but he did when the next morning the money was gone. Martin's mum was at the launderette when they knocked on her front door, and Martin was long gone.

He had moved into a squat and was stealing anything and everything to fund his habit. They had all walked into an electrical store and walked out with stereos while the frightened shop assistant turned away, in case they hurt her. They went to the computer shop and came out with two and gradually they stole enough to feed their habit.

They started to inject heroin, it hit the spot faster and you didn't need as much of the drug, mixing it with citric acid held over a heated spoon, sucked up through a cigarette filter to get rid of impurities, into the syringe, into the vein and a feeling of intense ecstasy.

Martin's personality had completely changed. He was distant yet anxious, mindless yet concerned to make sure he could get his next fix. His mate had moved on, he was dealing, he could fund his habit. He said to Martin, he could get him in, and so he became a dealer. People knew where to go when they needed a fix, and large amounts of money changed hands but Martin made sure he had enough left over to pay his supplier, until he nearly overdosed and needed a quick fix to get himself back to normal. No one would know whether they were heroin addicts until they couldn't get it because they sweated with dreadful chills, stomach cramps, all sorts. He used more money to get himself back on to it and did not have enough for the supplier. He just didn't have the money to pay him.

He woke up in a back alley, covered in filth and his own excrement, his head beaten black and blue and both his legs broken. The pain from his injuries was excruciating, but the withdrawal pains were worse.

He was lucky, someone saw him, and although they didn't go near him, they phoned for an ambulance and he was taken to hospital. Unfortunately, this was not uncommon in the area he lived. He told them he was homeless and they cleaned him up, put his legs in plaster and he was in traction on a hospital bed. His nose and eyes were running, his body was riddled with tremors and he was sweating. For the first time in his life, he called for his mum.

She didn't come. He told them her address but she didn't come. The doctor gave the nurses a prescription for methadone. He felt it might reduce the dreadful cravings, he had seen people go 'cold turkey' and he knew this young man was in agony. He had to sip it in front of the nurse, for her to know he had taken it, and he had to do this every day for weeks while he was in hospital.

He was very fortunate that he was in an area where the protocol was between the hospital and the Salvation Army early intervention and prevention team. They worked with the local authority to make sure any homeless person who was discharged from hospital would not go back on the streets.

It was eight weeks before he was ready to leave hospital. He could walk with crutches and the plaster on his legs had been cut away. He was in support bandages and his habit was controlled by the methadone.

He was taken to a hostel where he had his own room. The hostel had his medical records and were aware of his addiction. They got the prescription filled and he had to take it in front of them each morning and evening.

He began to realise he had had a very narrow escape. He had come down from bad trips before, had been unconscious and in a coma for a week on his mate's sofa yet still survived. The beating he had taken was one beat away from murder. Had he not been seen, and it was only a miracle that someone had walked down that dark alley, he would have died in his own excrement.

He was making it through the day, his legs were healing and his trips back to the hospital were less frequent. He was making good progress and he got his breakfast from the shelter and an evening meal at the Salvation Army.

He was seeing a counsellor at the drug abusers clinic and he was gradually turning a very big corner. He asked about getting some kind of work. He had actually wasted eight years of his life, thrown them away but the counsellor gave him hope. There was hope, he was reliant on methadone but he was coping and he was gaining confidence, enough to walk down the street looking straight ahead instead of his head down, his face hiding under his unruly hair.

He asked the counsellor, if there was a way he could come off methadone. There was a way, but he would have to be ready to want to do it, ready to put himself through the agony of going cold turkey. He needed to be in a safe place, away from any temptations, any chance meeting with an old mate. He had to make a cocoon for himself and live in it for a long time.

The counsellor spoke to his manager. He had been impressed with Martin. He had worked hard in every aspect of the tasks he had set him. He seemed to be ready to get back into society, and he asked if it would be inappropriate if he could take him in, to live in his flat while he went through the process of finally becoming clean, free of all traces of drugs. The manager was concerned but he knew this counsellor, he had had success before and he knew it was essential that there should be no temptation in Martin's way.

It was all down to that kind act. The counsellor suggested to Martin he move in with him. There was a bed in the spare room and he would be there for breakfast and evening dinner. It was the daytime that they would all worry about, when he was on his own but he set him some simple tasks and asked him to keep a journal. Write down his anxieties, when they hit, his sense of loss and dependency, and if ever he knew he was sinking, he must phone, get to the phone and he would be on the other end.

Martin knew it was now or never. He had been shown kindness he had never before experienced and he knew he couldn't let this man down, or himself. But it took so much. He couldn't believe the sheer agony of not getting a hit and his body craved just the one, just one to make it all better. He phoned Barry five times on the second day, and Barry organised it that he could be there at lunchtime, doing his computer print outs and arranging his appointments outside that time. Martin put on a lot of weight. Chocolate and sweet things were his cravings and they helped combat the craving for methadone.

Barry could see the difference and he desperately hoped that Martin would not relapse. He didn't. He strove to achieve, he worked on the projects that Barry set him and he was succeeding. Nine months later the fearful cravings had gone. The test would be to see if he could settle into the routine of daily life without Barry's watchful eye.

The work that he had been doing for Barry had proven to be a very useful dossier. He asked Martin if he would like to carry on producing information and learning how other drug addicts had shaken the habit. He jumped at the chance and for the first time in nearly nine years he was in work and his self-respect was beginning to grow.

It had not been an easy path, but he was determined he would never go back. He attended evening sessions to help him, talking to others about his addiction while they off loaded theirs really helped and it was a vital element in keeping him clean.

He wondered about his mum. He had let her down so badly, she had a problem, he could see that now but in a different light and he resolved to go and see her. A little old lady answered the door of his old home. No dear, she died you know, so sorry son, but she was a drinker and her liver gave up. Martin didn't really feel any great sorrow, he felt sad for the loss of someone who once really must have cared about him, but struggling on when his dad left was not easy and he could see how drink could help her through.

Barry's manager asked Martin if he would like to become a counsellor. Martin was totally stunned. All the counsellors he had met had come from university, big qualifications and big words and he felt inadequate to say the least. The manager said he had the best qualification of anyone — experience, and that was the wisest teacher. And he was the wisest teacher. Martin sat in on various sessions with Barry and two other counsellors and he knew he could make a difference. He wanted to reach out to the clients, to say, look at me, I was worse than you and look at me now. I have my life back, but he knew it had to come from them. They really did have to be nearly dead, no money, nowhere to live to realise they didn't want to be in that place any more. They had to find the motivation to climb back up out of their slough of despond.

It was one such person he was talking to, begging them to hold on, he was on his way, just hold on, when he felt the enormous thud in his chest and he blacked out.

16

James Hardcastle was becoming concerned. He ran his fingers through his thick grey hair and again walked up to the reception of the Executive Car Hire office. "I am expecting a friend of mine, Jane Carmichael. She was hiring a Volvo from you for the weekend and should be returning it this morning. She should have been here by now, is there any way of contacting her, I can't reach her on her mobile?"

The receptionist scanned the computer. "Yes, Ms Carmichael should have returned the car by now, she was getting a flight to Edinburgh at noon. I am sorry, I haven't got any way of contacting her, but I can check the route organiser if you know the direction she would be coming from." James said it was from Buckinghamshire, so the M4 to Heathrow would be the route once off the M25. The receptionist typed in the route and immediately her hands faltered on the keys. She picked up the phone and asked to speak to the road traffic control officer for the M4.

"Hello, it's Executive Car Hire, can you tell me if there have been any incidents on the M4 this morning?" She turned to James. "Are you a relative, sir?"

"No, she is a work colleague, we were going to fly to Edinburgh together this morning." He didn't tell her they actually were not going to fly to Edinburgh, they were going to Paris, to their favourite hotel and he was going to ask her to marry him.

"I think you may need to sit down sir. There has been a serious road traffic accident on the M4 near the Heathrow turn off. It is actually on the news. There are many casualties and it happened at nine o'clock, or around that time. I have an emergency number for you to call and the number of the hospital the casualties have been taken to."

James tried to compose himself. "Please give me the numbers." The receptionist took him into an office where he could use the phone in private. The emergency number confirmed that there were many casualties, some had been taken to Uxbridge hospital and some to Hillingdon. He tried the Hillingdon hospital number first and asked to be put through to the department dealing with the accident on the M4.

The voice was professional and calm. "Are you a relative of Ms Carmichael sir?"

"No, I am a work colleague, we are due to fly to Edinburgh this morning at noon and she has not arrived to return the hire car. I am at their offices at Heathrow."

"Mr Hardcastle, do you know her next of kin, a relative? We cannot impart any information to you unless you are a relative."

James racked his brain, think man. "Her mother lives in Newbury, in Berkshire, I don't have the number but please tell me, is she, all right? Can I come and see her? Is she at the hospital?"

"Mr Hardcastle, I am so sorry I cannot give you any information until I have contacted her mother. I will try to source the number and if you leave me your contact number, I will be able to get back to you shortly."

James just sat and stared at the phone. His mind was racing and he was trying so hard to be rational. Not to jump to conclusions but the hospital didn't say Jane was there, they didn't say if she was being treated. They had told him nothing. He was more a relative than her mother, he thought, I know her better than anyone. He was becoming angry. Unreasonable and angry. He was very used to getting his own way and he had been thwarted at every turn. The receptionist asked if she could get him anything, a tea or coffee. "Thank you but no. May I stay here, the hospital is going to phone me back?"

"Of course, sir, and please let me know if we can be of any help in any way." He thanked her. His voice was flat, resigned.

The mobile vibrated in his pocket. "Mr Hardcastle?"

"Yes, yes, have you any news?"

"I have contacted Mrs Carmichael, her daughter lives with her and was there when I had to inform her that she had been pronounced dead at the scene of the accident. Mr Hardcastle, are you with anyone, can anyone help you, can you hear me?" James found it very hard to breathe. He dropped the phone and his head went forward onto his chest. The receptionist came in and another man and they helped him to sit up and she retrieved the phone. "Hello, hello, Mr Hardcastle?" The voice was not as calm now. The receptionist said Mr Hardcastle was in their office and they would assist him as she cut the call.

James was crushed. He was completely crushed and he couldn't speak, couldn't voice his pain, was just numb. The receptionist made him a cup of hot sweet tea. "Please drink this sir, you have had a dreadful shock. I am so sorry, is there anyone I can call to help you, someone in the company?" James couldn't move, couldn't respond. He wanted to be dead. He wanted to be with his Jane. They should have died together. Dead, how could she be dead, this wonderful vibrant clever woman who had waited so patiently for him, never called the shots, only was there for him and now he was free, free to be with her, and she was dead. Just dead. Not injured, not being operated on, could recover — dead.

The receptionist asked if they could take him to the airport. "What for, where would I go?"

"Sir, you said you were going to Edinburgh."

"Oh, Edinburgh. No, no I won't go there. I can't go there you see, she won't be there. Not now."

The receptionist looked at the man in the office, her eyes pleading for some direction, some response. "Sir, you have had a dreadful shock. Can I call someone in your company, someone based down here who could come and collect you — your family, your wife?"

At the mention of the word wife James howled. He actually howled, the sound of a wounded animal in dreadful pain. His wife? She who never really cared for him, oh she was a dutiful wife in all things business, keeping up appearances, the perfect marriage, two wonderful sons and the golf club. Always the friggin' golf club. Captain of the ladies' team for the third year in succession and such a socialite. She wouldn't be in anyway and he really couldn't speak to her now, not after his parting shot — I am divorcing you, Michelle, there is no point to this sham of a marriage."

The man offered him a cigarette, took him outside for some fresh air, anything to try to ease such a dreadful situation. "Is there anyone sir, anyone we could contact to come and be with you?"

James stared at the man. "Do you know what, she was coming to be with me. She didn't know it, but I was going to ask her to marry me. We weren't going to Edinburgh. I had made arrangements with her company that she was taking leave, we were going to attend a fashion show in Paris and I was going to ask her to marry me in our favourite restaurant. I loved her you see. I thought I couldn't leave my wife but I could, I did. I left her last Friday."

The man looked at James. "Oh, I am just so sorry, sir, but there must be someone I can call, someone from your office?"

"Thank you, but no. I will be OK. You have been more than kind. I think I need to be alone for a bit. I can go to the hotel, I left there this morning, I can go there. Need a bit of time, need to…" His voice trailed off. The man rang for a taxi. The taxi came and James gave him the London Heathrow Hilton address and he sat back for the short ride to the hotel.

The receptionist greeted him warmly. "Why Mr Hardcastle, didn't expect you back so soon — would you like your old room?"

"Yes Tania, thank you." James put his suitcase in the hall and sat in the suite and poured himself a large scotch.

He really couldn't take it in. On Friday, he had felt his life was just beginning, a new life with a woman who had mesmerised him, occupied his whole world for three years and who would be his whole world until he died. But she had died. She had died coming to meet him, coming to hear what he had to say, his secret.

He thought back to last Friday. It had actually been so easy. He had summoned the courage to talk to Michelle, to calmly discuss their non-existent marriage. She was just back from a game of golf, happy that her team had won and mixing herself a martini when he came into the lounge. "You're back early, good job, time to shower and change." was all that she said. "Where's the damn olives?"

"Michelle, can we talk?"

"Us, talk, don't be silly darling, we never talk. We never see each other and what you do and what I do — we don't need to talk about because we have nothing in common. Now, don't forget we are at the Hunters tonight, I made it tonight thinking you were going away in the morning. James, are you listening to me?" He looked at her, flounced on the sofa, stirring her martini. "Well don't just stand there, and don't forget we need to impress the Hunters, they know the Williams and they are talking of a party going away on their yacht — and that includes us."

James sat down on the sofa. "Michelle, you just about summed up our marriage. We have separate lives. We come together at weekends, sometimes, and we never really talk. You have your golf and I have my job. We hardly see the boys. They seem content with that, but sometimes I do wonder. You see, Michelle, I have met someone. For the first time in my life, I have found someone who I have tremendous—"

"You what, you have met someone, how, don't be so ridiculous, you, what have you got to offer anyone? Don't be stupid James, we have a perfectly good life. Just because we aren't together every minute of the day. We are just like most of my friends at the golf club. Their husbands are away and we play golf. Their husbands come home James, they do not play away, so just stop talking nonsense and go and get changed. Whoever it is you have met you can just forget about. Your life is here with me and our social circle. Can you pour me another drink?" As she handed him her glass.

James put the glass down with surprising restraint. "Michelle, I don't give a flying fuck about your social circle, your golf club or your yacht holidays. Did you hear one word of what I have said. I have met someone who is very special and important to me. Michelle, I cannot spend the rest of my life living a lie. Marriage isn't all about your precious social climbing. It's about being together — and for that I do take responsibility because I didn't expect the business to take off in quite such a way and I obviously have to travel."

"That's where you met this woman isn't it? On your travels. Is she a trolley dolly on a plane?" Michelle was gradually realising that James was being very serious. She was beginning to panic. "James, darling, please don't do this. We may not be the perfect couple, but how many perfect couples do you know, do I know? You see, you make the best of it. You have provided a very comfortable lifestyle which I adore, in fact I love it James and I really cannot understand why you are doing this. Now please, get rid of the woman and come to your senses. I don't care if you have 'been' with her, it's over now and you must realise where your responsibilities lie." James really did wonder what planet Michelle was on. All his revelations about finding someone else seemed to have fallen on waste ground. It wasn't him she cared about, or the fact he had 'been' with someone else, it was the impact it would have on her. Her social climbing would not succeed if she was a woman on her own. She needed an arm to guide her into her glitzy glamour world, never mind if the arm belonged to someone who was actually beginning to despise her.

"Michelle, I am incredibly sorry it has come to this. You will be well provided for, you can keep the house." Before he could say any more, she flew at him, clawing at his face and forcing him back on the sofa.

"Keep the house, keep the house, you bastard. By the time I have finished with you, you will be lucky to still have the suit you are standing in. How dare you do this to me. Do you know what this will do to me, to my social standing, to my position in the golf club? Have you any idea of just what you have done to me? I am down to be the first woman president of the golf club — never been known James, never been known — and now what?" Suddenly she flopped. She sank back into the sofa, completely and utterly exhausted. She wasn't even angry. She was baffled. How could he do this to her, didn't he realise just how important she was? He would pay though, if he was seriously going to leave her, he would pay. She would never let this lifestyle go, she couldn't. She would have to make up something. She wouldn't tell anyone, no, that was it. She could tell them James had gone abroad to float a new company in America and would be gone for a while, but back to see the boys in the holidays. Oh, thank goodness, a plausible plan, a reasonable course of events. She visibly relaxed at the thought of it, a plan of action, face will be saved, no one will know he has left her.

"James, if you are going to divorce me it will be a long process. I don't want anyone here knowing about it. I don't want any solicitors from within thirty miles of here. I want you to organise that. I will be represented by my uncle Thomas, he is a solicitor in Lincoln's Inn Fields in London. The boys are to know nothing. I will tell everyone that you have gone to America to organise a new branch of the company over there and you will be back to see me and the boys as and when time permits. You will have to do this for me. I have standards James and I will not have them lowered, not at any cost."

James just looked at her. "Michelle, people will know, these things have a habit of coming out."

"Never, no one will hear a thing. They won't hear it from me and they won't hear it from you. The boys will be told about America and that will be that. You have your flat in Edinburgh, don't you? Well, you go there or find somewhere and no one is to know at work. I don't want anyone from there contacting me about anything." James did silently wonder why on earth anyone would ever contact Michelle from his work. His home and business lives were totally separate, but he realised for the moment, he would have to go along with this. He would instigate divorce proceedings and he knew Uncle Thomas and his firm so he could give his solicitors his contact details.

Just like that. A marriage ended. He didn't feel sadness or remorse. He felt that they had drifted apart for all sorts of reasons, and after she had rejected his attempts at love making — we don't need to do that now darling — he realised his place in her world was merely the provider of the cash. That all important commodity that enabled you to open doors and meet other shallow people who were doing exactly the same as you. Climbing to the top and when you got there, it was an enormous merry-go-round of lies and deceit and there was not one ounce of genuine feeling from all the air kissing people that inhabited that sphere of inconsequence. No one really mattered.

He had gathered a few clothes together, he had a wardrobe in the flat anyway. There was nothing more to be said really. He poured her another martini.

"Did you ever love me, James?"

"Oh yes, Michelle, I did and nothing can take away our two wonderful sons, I think we should be proud of them, but for all sorts of reasons we are no longer that couple, are we?"

"People change James, you need different things."

"Michelle, I never needed anything, sounds strange doesn't it. I never needed to pretend to be something I am not. I never needed to show people material things, buy expensive clothes. I just needed to be as we were, but that wouldn't really do for you, would it? You didn't want me in the bedroom, sex wasn't on the agenda and although it wasn't the be all and end all, it was bloody important in a marriage that was so often fraught with problems. I am going to divorce you Michelle, our marriage is a sham. Don't worry, I will not tell anyone, I will get my solicitor to contact Uncle Thomas and it will be made clear that it is to be conducted with the utmost discretion."

She didn't even look up when the door closed behind him. She swallowed the martini. Oh, my goodness, look at the time. Just time to run a lovely deep bath, do her hair and select her dress. She would tell Carol Hunter that unfortunately James had had to go away on business, he had just called to collect some things for the trip — better say that in case someone may have seen the car — and yes, she thought to herself, she would be president — never say die.

James poured another scotch. There really was nobody he wanted to call, he was officially on holiday anyway and he knew his secretary knew about Jane. At the thought of Jane, he just stopped, stopped thinking. Oh, my poor, poor sweetheart. You never knew, you never knew we would marry, that I would be free, that I am now free, and where are you, please darling, please don't tell me you are hurting because if I could I would be there instead, I would take your pain and I would let you live.

He finally felt the hot tears, silent tears, not gut-wrenching aching sobs, just silent wet tears of an enormous loss pour down his face, wetting his shirt, spilling into his scotch and he knew that from now on there was no now on. There was nothing any more. No hope, no love. Just an enormous whirlpool that was a bottomless pit of empty lost love, no recovery, just endless pain and sorrow. He was lost and for all that he had, he had not. He had lived his life, there was no point to anything. He just hoped with all his heart that he could die, he had no need to be alive any more, there was nothing to care about, no one to hope about, no one to love about. An enormous void engulfed him and he was completely and utterly alone.

He must have fallen asleep because he could hear a sound, a distant ringing, and he reached for his phone. A woman's voice, one he knew, yes, it was Jane. "Jane, oh my darling Jane."

"James? James I am so sorry, I am Jane's mother, Doreen. I am so very sorry, I know we sound alike, I just wanted to speak to you. I called the hospital and they gave me your number, I hope you don't mind."

His mind was racing. He was sure this was Jane. She hadn't died, she was alive, she was speaking to him. "Jane, is that you?"

Doreen Carmichael didn't know what to say. "James, I am sorry, Jane died in the accident. She is dead James." Her voice faltered and she broke down, sobbing. She had been determined to hold herself together, but was failing.

Her daughter took the phone. "James, I am Penny, Jane's sister. We are both so very sorry for your loss, Jane had told us all about you, we knew she was going to meet you before you both went back to Edinburgh. James, she loved you very much, please be sure of that."

James was trying so hard to get himself together. He realised now that this wasn't Jane, it was her sister and she and her mother had lost the person they loved, who he loved. "I am so, so, sorry. I loved her so much you see. We were going to get married. I am divorcing my wife and Jane didn't know, it was a surprise you see, and we were going to Paris and I was going to ask her to marry me. I love her very much."

Penny spoke in a very gentle soft voice. "Poor James, we feel so sad for you, we are so sorry, we knew Jane adored you, she was just happy to be in your life." James stared hopelessly at the phone. "James, where are you now?"

"I am at the Hilton at Heathrow. I don't know what to do Penny."

"Mum and I are going to the hospital. We have to…" her voice faltered, but she recovered her composure. "We have to identify Jane. I don't know if you would want to, want to meet us there? I don't know if it might help you, give you closure, I really don't know how you would feel…"

"Thank you, Penny, yes, I would want to come. If that's all right, I would want to see her, with you. Oh my God, isn't it dreadful, it's just so dreadful." Penny said she would be leaving in about an hour and suggested they try and meet at about four in the reception. She had heard they had closed off the motorway in both directions so it may take longer but they would keep in touch by mobile.

James sat up in the chair, he now had a purpose. He could go and see her, he could say goodbye. He was in a kind of vacuum, going through the motions, not really aware of exactly what was going on. He made a coffee and sat staring at the wall, his mind couldn't think, he couldn't remember how to feel any more, because he could not feel.

He realised he had to tell his office. He called his secretary who was surprised to hear from him, although she had been aware of the pile-up on the motorway near Heathrow. "James, oh it's good to hear from you. I did wonder if you were OK because there has been an accident—"

He cut her dead. "Yes, yes, I know, Linda. That's why I am calling. I am OK, I am OK, but it's Jane, Jane is…"

"James, where are you, is someone with you?" She knew his voice was not normal.

"Jane has been killed, she is dead, Linda."

Linda gripped the phone as if the very act would make what she had just heard be wrong. "James, oh no, the accident?" her voice asked.

"I am going to meet her mother and sister at the hospital. She has been taken there. I don't know what I will do Linda."

"James, what about Keith, shall I ask him to meet you? He is in Surrey, he could get there, to be with you."

Keith was his number one rep, a good colleague and friend.

"Thank you, Linda, but no, I need to get to the hospital and then I don't know. I won't be going…" and she knew he wouldn't be going to Paris any more. She had booked the tickets for him and she was so thrilled his personal life looked like it was going to sort itself out, he would finally be with the woman she knew he loved so much. Now, how could life be so cruel? Just when it was going to be so good.

"James, please keep in touch with me or you have Keith's number. I am so sorry, so very very sorry." She put the phone down and sobbed. She felt his sorrow, because she had always loved him and when you love someone you take their pain.

He called a taxi and gave the hospital address. The taxi company told him it may take a bit longer, had he allowed for that? There had been a major accident on the motorway and the diversions were really busy. He said he needed to be there for around four and the taxi driver said they should be OK for that time.

The diversion ensured they didn't have to go past the carnage. He didn't have to see any of that and he didn't know how he would be when he saw Jane. He didn't know how he would react because he couldn't feel anything right now. He just felt hollow, nothing inside him, not even grief. He was worried, surely, he should feel grief.

He recognised Penny, she was so similar to Jane and he could see her daughter in Doreen Carmichael's sad face. They all hugged. They had never met but it felt as though they knew each other so well, united in their loss for someone they loved very much.

James put his arms around them both and a man in a suit escorted them to the morgue. Jane looked so beautiful. She looked so normal, just asleep. Her hair was brushed against the pillow and her face looked so peaceful. How could she be dead when she looked as she did when he last saw her? Doreen Carmichael smoothed her daughter's cheek, caressed her face and she kissed her mouth. Penny held on to her mum, so tight, and she was sobbing as she kissed her hair. James stared so hard through his tears. He bent to kiss her and he almost recoiled, she was so cold, her skin was so cold. He wanted to stay, to sit by her, to wait for her to wake up, and Penny gently took his hand, and he knew he had to leave her. He couldn't go with her, he couldn't be with her any more.

The man in the suit said there were some formalities that needed to be dealt with and Penny said to James why didn't he take Doreen to the canteen. The man in the suit said there was a relatives' room they could wait in, and there was tea and coffee available there. It would be more private.

Penny joined them and said they would be making arrangements for the funeral which would be in about two weeks' time. There was so much to say but no one could speak. Three people who were bound by their love for one woman who had been so tragically taken from them.

The door opened and Keith Norwood entered the room. James looked up and realised he was actually so pleased to see him, his friend, someone he could lean on when he felt so lost. "James, I am so sorry. Linda told me you would be here and I came as fast as I could." He turned to Doreen and Penny. "I am so sorry for your loss, this is absolutely awful. Is there anything I can do for you? I will be taking James with me, but can I help you, drive you?" They thanked him, but they had their car and they would be making their way home now.

Penny turned to James. "Don't be a stranger James, you have my number and we will be in touch about the funeral. We have all had a dreadful shock and I really can't think of anything to say, other than you have us, we are Jane's family and you are part of it. Take care, I will call you tomorrow." They all hugged and Keith took James' arm as they left the hospital.

Keith had never seen James look so ill. He was grey and he was stumbling as Keith supported him to get him to the car. "I think we will stay in London tonight James, and I will make arrangements to fly back with you tomorrow morning. Will that be all right?" James couldn't really hear what Keith was saying. There was a buzzing in his ears and he felt faint, he felt as if he was going to be sick. He slumped in the seat of Keith's car. He just stared ahead, not able to communicate. Keith drove to the Hilton and booked them both in. The receptionists had changed shifts and the new girl was unaware of the drama that had unfolded. Keith took James to his room and sat with him. He called the office and told Linda they would be coming on the morning flight and said he would be staying with James. He felt he couldn't leave him, he was very worried, he couldn't get any response from him, it was as if he wasn't there. James lay down on the bed, he couldn't cry, he couldn't feel anything. He just wanted to go to sleep and not wake up and then he would be with Jane.

Keith stayed in the room, nodding on and off in the chair and managed to get James up and to the airport to fly to Edinburgh the next morning. He had no idea of how James would cope with this tragedy, he only knew he had to stay with him, be there for him, until this state of shock eased and he could begin to function on his own. He was now, totally on his own and it would be a long time before James Hardcastle could emerge from his despair. He was falling, deeper and deeper into a great sadness he had never in his life experienced before.

17

Elaine Radley was a survivor. Against all the odds, when things seemed so hopeless, she found the will and the strength to pull through. It's when the chips are down you have to be strong, for the sake of the children. She was a proud mum to her twins, Charlie and Harriet and she wondered what their father would think of them now.

She was amazed that Charlie had such a clever academic brain. To be honest she didn't know where he got it from. It was almost as if his sister's brains must have gone to Charlie in the womb, not that she would ever say that to Harriet who was a lovely daughter. Their father left when they were five.

He was a builder and working at the home of some rich guy with a bored wife who relieved her boredom by seducing him at every turn. To be fair it didn't take much because he had always had a wandering eye. Always told Elaine she would have to worry if he stopped looking — something she never understood until he actually did stop looking because he was completely absorbed in this big busted rich tart. She was a tart. She didn't charge for it but she was a tart. She knew he was married — at least Elaine had assumed he kept his ring on — and she wanted him.

Bill Radley thought he had died and gone to heaven when she opened the door, her boobs just about in her blouse, short skirt, high heels and a welcoming red lipstick smile that really said, 'come in and fuck me'. Well, that's how he saw it. He wasn't a man who had a way with words and she liked a bit of rough and the fact that he was always up for it. On the first day she took him around the house and lead him to the huge frilly bed and undid his belt, just like that. He always took it if it was offered. In his line of work, you met lots of bored housewives, but this one had money. The house was a huge three-storey Victorian building which was big enough to be an hotel and he was the lucky sod who got the job. The husband was away a lot, earning the money to keep his wife in expensive lingerie and shoes, let alone the cars and the lifestyle of shopping and the gym and more shopping.

Elaine was blissfully unaware as she made his sandwiches each morning, filled his flask and kissed him goodbye, that as soon as he was on the road, he ditched the sandwiches and poured the coffee out of the window. He had always been meticulous about his appearance and she thought nothing of it when he applied the aftershave and made sure his white T-shirt and pressed trousers looked neat, his overalls fresh every day. She didn't even ask about the job, he was a good workman and never needed to advertise and as she was making her way to her job as a teaching assistant, he was enjoying a glass of champagne, lying in a huge bed with a woman with huge breasts laying back and saying, 'I want you so much, fuck me again', and he never let her down.

But let Elaine down he did. The bored housewife told the husband she wanted a divorce. He was never there for her — mainly because he was working his socks off for a woman he was beginning to resent. When she said she didn't feel the same about him any more he didn't suggest they try to make a go of it, he went to a solicitor and set the wheels in motion.

Bill Radley didn't actually think he was doing anything wrong. He and Elaine were both working hard — she thought for the good of the family, to bring the twins up with a good home — and he thought because that's what you did. They had married when she was two months pregnant although she looked a bit big for two months. He thought he should marry her because he had got her up the duff in the back of his pick-up truck one hot summers night and he thought it right and proper that he should do right by her. He was twenty-one and she was eighteen. It was a very low-key affair with his parents saying, oh well, things happen in this day and age, even though his mother had thought in this day and age with all the contraception how could it happen. Her mother's dream of a big white wedding went out of the window and her dad didn't seem to care one way or the other.

They rented Jasmine Cottage from one of Bill's old clients on the understanding he would gut and renew the bathroom and put an extension on the back to enlarge the kitchen, materials to be supplied. He did this in lieu of rent, working in the day for himself and doing the cottage up at night.

The twins were a big shock to the system. Luckily her mother came up trumps and was able to move into the spare bedroom to help with the feeds and she would go home in the day and come back late afternoon. For three months Elaine was in a permanent spin of nappies, bottles, feeding, burping, and more nappies. Bill thought they were lovely but he needed his sleep and Elaine's mum said he would have to put the extension on hold because of all the dust until the twins were a bit older. This was the one concession he made towards being a dad. He really wasn't hands on with all this stuff. In fact, his hands were huge and more used to fixing and screwing than holding the tiny twins.

Gradually feeds became less and they were going through the night. Elaine's mum came two days a week to help with the washing and cleaning and Bill started on the extension again and Elaine went back to work on the two days her mum came round.

So they had muddled along and Bill finished the extension and the cottage looked lovely. The landlord said they could carry on living there at a really reasonable rent. He knew when the time came, he would be able to sell it and the profit would be considerable.

Right now, it suited him not to sell and so Bill and Elaine were easily able to manage the rent and bring up the twins.

When he came home and told her he had met someone, and would be leaving, she couldn't believe it. She thought they were OK. Not much in the way of sex in their marriage but there never had been, not with the twins taking up so much time early on and he was always too tired if she had made a move in that direction. If you don't have it you don't miss it, and she assumed that's how it was. She didn't say anything when he told her. She didn't ask who or why. She just sat down at the kitchen table and stared straight ahead. Come on Elaine, say something, anything.

"What about the twins? You can't leave them. How can you leave your gorgeous children? They are five years old for Christ's sake." He didn't really have an answer to that. He thought she would cope and they didn't really need him. He never had time to be there with them, even weekends he worked whenever he could and he liked it that way. He liked what he was doing now, better than anything in his life before. He had no idea a woman could be so inventive in bed, different ways of doing it, getting him to please her while she teased him. He almost got a hard on just thinking about it.

"Well Elaine I am sorry about the twins but I can't live a lie. I can't stay just because of them. I will send you money for them, but I can't stay."

She looked at him and she realised she really didn't know him. They had muddled along, got the cottage looking good and she always made sure the twins were well turned out. She had a meal on the table for him each night, even though lately she plated it and he reheated it in the microwave. She had always assumed this was marriage. You had to work to keep body and soul together. There were no luxuries, no time off, it was a kind of wheel that just kept turning and you had to keep going because you couldn't get off.

But he could. He could get off the humdrum circle of their lives. He could walk away and leave them to sink or swim. That was it. Sink or swim and she knew she would never sink.

"What's she like?" she asked in a very quiet controlled voice.

"Oh Elaine, don't even go there. She is what I want. We like the same things, she makes me laugh."

"Does she know about us Bill?"

"She does now. She said she felt sorry for you but in this life, you have to go with your feelings."

That was actually the spark that Elaine needed. Anger now came into the equation. "Sorry for me, sorry for me. The bitch, the fucking tart, who the fuck does she think she is? She doesn't even know me, she only knows the fuck who married me and you fucking deserve each other. Yeah, you go, you go to your tart and leave us because we will be fine. You won't see your children, you won't miss them because you never had time for them anyway. Clear out, just fuck off and die."

Bill was completely stunned into silence. He had never heard Elaine swear, not ever, and the anger and sheer hatred in her voice stopped him in his tracks. He never knew she was capable of such passion, such determination. He picked up his jacket and his phone and walked out of the door. She slammed it behind him and started to shake. The tears rolled down her face. She couldn't be angry for long, she had said what she felt in her heart and she knew she had lost him, if she had ever really had him.

She wished she had something to drink. They didn't keep it in the house because Bill would go to the pub on his way home most nights, although she realised he probably wasn't doing that now.

She felt sick. It gradually dawned on her that she was on her own. She went up to the twins' bedroom and thanked God they were fast asleep. They wouldn't miss their dad. He was someone who came in when they were in bed and left before they were awake. Even at weekends, she thought ruefully, he was probably shagging his tart while they took a picnic to the park.

She called her mum who immediately came round. You needed your mum at a time like this. She was so glad she had hers and she hugged her and held her as she sobbed and she gradually calmed down. The tears stopped and a dull ache replaced the calm that had been in her until two hours ago.

Her mother asked no questions, not who is the woman, not how could he, not even what about the children. She never judged. It didn't pay anyway, everyone lived their lives and got on with it. That's what Elaine would have to do now. Get on with it. It wasn't ideal but no one had died, no one had cancer and every problem has a solution.

Elaine would have to find a job that paid better than a teaching assistant. She didn't have any qualifications that would help in finding work and the new superstore in Reading would only pay basic rates. She decided that for now she would stay at the school, at least she would get school holidays and her mum said she would sit at night if she wanted to get a job in the supermarket doing shelf stacking or whatever.

She saw a solicitor with legal aid to get the divorce and she knew there was no mileage in asking for much money. The solicitor said Bill would have to maintain the children and he would fight for £800 a month. Elaine did not know that this was a drop in the ocean for Bill's new-found money tree, but she hoped he would be able to manage that. The landlord said as long as the rent was paid, he was fine, she could stay and she was grateful for that and made sure it was paid on the due date every month.

She got a job stacking shelves six to ten on weekday nights. It was all extra money and she could get the bus from the village into Reading. To be honest she enjoyed chatting with the other workers and with

Bill's money supporting the twins she was making ends meet. She couldn't have done it without her mum and she thanked God for her every day. Her mum actually enjoyed being 'useful'. Her husband, Elaine's father, had had a heart attack on the golf course and died on the way to hospital. She missed him dreadfully and Elaine and the children were her reason to be. The twins were her only grandchildren and she adored them. They were happy delightful children, and she had always found time to read to them, teach them their numbers and letters and it seemed as if they were doing very well at school. No bad reports, in fact 'glowing' was the word from the teachers. They were really two very well-adjusted children, and although she realised Charlie had a very quick receptive brain, she never mentioned it to Elaine.

Charlie was seven when the head teacher asked if Elaine could see him after school one day that week and she put them in the after-school club and went along to his office. He told her that their secondary school would automatically be the one in Reading which had a very good reputation and although this move was three years away, he wanted to set the scene. He felt that academically Charlie could achieve more than that particular school could offer him and he felt they could try for a scholarship to the Kevin Brownlow Public School for boys in Berkshire. He explained that it was a boarding school and the fees were considerable but with the scholarship he felt they could possibly be affordable.

Elaine tried to take in what he was telling her. What, she wondered, did he consider was 'affordable'. He gave her a brochure about the school, the academic achievements and the fees and even with a scholarship she didn't think it was possible. She thanked him very much and he said he really hoped she might be able to do it because Charlie 'would walk' the scholarship and the doors that an education from this school would open were second to none.

She talked it over with her mum before she went to work that night and left the brochure with her. Her mum wasn't surprised about Charlie's ability, not one bit, but she was surprised that Elaine could even consider boarding school for him. However, she settled down to read the brochure and what the school had to offer and she had no idea a school could provide such a huge range of subjects to study and sports activities to enjoy.

They talked for a long time that night and Elaine was torn. She knew that Charlie had great academic ability and the head was right, he wouldn't be out of his depth in such an environment, but how on God's earth could she afford the fees?

Her mum wished with all her heart she could help with the money, but she couldn't. There had been no life insurance when her husband died and her widow's pension was only just enough to keep the wolf from the door.

Elaine went to see the head after school the next day. He explained to her that if Charlie passed the scholarship there was a bursary she could apply for. It was a means tested award for parents who could not otherwise afford the fees. The scholarship would cover five percent of the fees and the bursary could in some cases fund the remaining ninety-five percent. To enter the Kevin Brownlow Public School at age eleven Charlie would take the scholarship at age nine. Elaine would then apply for the bursary and the primary school would endorse the application. In some cases, there would also be help towards the cost of the uniform and books. He told her everything regarding the scholarship and the bursary funding was in the strictest confidence.

She went to work that night and chatted to her friend Joanne. "I am in a right pickle Joanne. I want the best for Charlie but I don't want to be the one that takes the freebie. It's a hell of a lot of money and what I earn here and at the school probably wouldn't buy his lunch for a week."

Her friend listened to her and she felt very sorry for her. She couldn't let this opportunity go by, yet she would feel the same if she had to be asking for help. "How serious are you about wanting to earn more money, Elaine?" Joanne asked.

"I am deadly serious Joanne, why, do you know of a job that pays well?"

"Now don't take this the wrong way Elaine, but my mate Gillian works for a club that's just opened in town. She is a hostess, you know, wears evening dresses and serves drinks and cigarettes to the clients. She welcomes them and sits with them and gets them to buy champagne, only ever champagne, and she can make £300 a night."

Elaine's mouth dropped open. "£300 a night for just sitting with blokes — I don't believe you Joanne. I bet she does a bit more than drinking with them and I am not into that, no way."

"I know, I couldn't do any of that stuff, but seriously she tells me she is just friendly with them, makes them feel special like."

"My mum wouldn't stand for it Joanne."

"Elaine, your mum needn't know need she? Gillian does ten to two. You could do six to ten like you do here and no one will know you don't come here. Lots of blokes call in after work, you know a bit like an up-market drinking club. You could give your notice in here and start there. They provide the clothes and stuff. Why don't you give it a go, you are a good-looking woman and you never know, you might enjoy it. I'll give Gillian a call, in fact I'll call her now and see what you have to do. It's only been open for a couple of months so they are always looking out for new people to work there."

"Why don't you work there Joanne?"

"To be honest Elaine, and again don't get me wrong, I only come out for pin money and to chat with the girls. Jim earns a good wage and he understands I need to get away from the kids for a bit and this suits us both very well. It will bring you a lot of money Elaine, you would be able to pay for Charlie's books and uniform if the bursary will cover the fees." Gillian told her Elaine could go along any time from ten the next morning.

Elaine was in more of a quandary than before. She couldn't deceive her lovely mum. She just couldn't. She could be economical with the truth though. She would tell her there was a new club opened in the town and they were looking for upmarket waitresses. That was partly true. She wouldn't say she had to sell the champagne and be friendly.

She told her mum she was going for a quick drink after work with her friend, Joanne, because it was her birthday and would be back about eleven. She could get a taxi if the buses had stopped, but she didn't want to let Joanne down.

She took a cab to the club, the Pandora, which was brightly lit with a huge entrance, bit like a private house. There was soft music playing and elegant young women in evening gowns circulating in the hall. There was a winding staircase off the hall and she could see a lounge from where she stood. A young man approached her. "Good evening madam, may I help you?"

"Yes, I would like to see the manager about a job please." Nice, thought the young man. Good legs, good figure, make-up needed a bit of sorting but she could fit in very well, very well indeed.

"Of course, I can take you to Mr Greene now if that's all right?"

"That's fine," she said as he led the way up the winding stair case to an office where her heels sank into the most luxurious carpet she had ever seen.

"Good evening. I am Mark, and you are?"

"Elaine, Elaine Radley."

"Hello Elaine, how can I help you? I understand you would like to work here."

"Yes, I haven't done anything like this before, but my friend's friend Gillian works here some evenings. She serves champagne to clients and just chats from what I understand."

Oh my God, we have a right one here, thought Mark but he liked her. She wasn't drop dead gorgeous or anything, just attractive. Hair needed sorting, but she would look good in the dresses the girls wore and she seemed friendly, if not rather naïve. "What hours could you do Elaine? The job is sometimes a bit more than just chatting, you have to be attentive and really make our clients feel special. The pay is £40 per hour, but you earn your tips. The more champagne you sell, the bigger the tips. You could earn as much as £300 a night, other nights not so much, but it does pay well and we are very busy, the only club of its kind in this area. We have a good reputation in the short time we have been open and we intend to keep it that way. The clients expect confidentiality and we afford them their privacy. They pay well and we deliver. We can give you a trial run, if you like us and we like you, we can make it more permanent. Now what hours?"

Elaine hadn't expected everything to move quite so fast. "Six until ten, if that's any good."

"That's good with us. We are open all day but after six is busy when our clients finish work, drop in for a drink or make an evening of it. How about you start next week?"

"I have to give notice. I work at the supermarket the other side of town. Can I call you and let you know? I think it's only a week?"

"Right ho, you call us when you think you can start. You look about a size twelve, is that right?"

"Yes, size ten in some shops and twelve in others." He shook her hand and she went down the stairs and into the fresh air. She got a cab home, she couldn't face sitting on the bus and her mum was still up. She had said she would stay over and they had a cup of tea.

"Did you have a good time?" she asked and Elaine smiled.

"It was nice, Mum, and thanks again for staying. I am a bit tired now, think I'll go up." They both went to bed but Elaine couldn't sleep. She wasn't sure if what she had just agreed to was really happening. She wasn't stupid, she guessed there might be a bit more of the up close and personal bit and strangely enough she didn't find it daunting. She had always looked after herself, eating sensibly and working at the school and the supermarket kept her on her toes, she hardly ever sat down, always on the go. Yet this work, if you could call it that, seemed just so easy. She was excited and nervous, but she had her goal. She had made the decision she would do all that she could to make sure Charlie went to the Kevin Brownlow Public School and she was getting the ball rolling.

She saw the head the next day and he was very pleased that Charlie would be taking the scholarship. He told her she would never regret this decision and he was very proud of her. The school would support her in any way that they could and Charlie would thank her one day because she was setting him on a path that would only lead upwards to a great education and the best possible start in life.

Elaine started work at the Pandora two weeks later. She had told her mum it was an opportunity to earn good money for doing not a lot and she was going to give it a try. One of the girls showed her how to do her make-up, enhance her eyes, and although Elaine thought it made her look a bit like a panda, in the softly lit room she looked almost beautiful. She was given a different dress each evening, always black and low cut and she had invested in a pair of very high heels. The underwear was also rather risqué she thought, but what the hell, a job's a job and she slipped into the role of Miranda, hostess at the Pandora with surprising ease. The men that came through the door were from all walks of life. She found it no trouble at all to fall into conversation with them. Some were very intelligent, but most just wanted to sit and chat and drink and touch. Well, not full-on touching, but pretty near it. She felt nothing, she acted her role superbly and came across as being completely absorbed and utterly mesmerised by the client. In the first week she had earned £60 in tips and Mark told her he was very pleased and they would be happy, if she was, for her to work at the Pandora on a permanent basis.

She opened an account in the local building society for Charlie and one for Harriet. She knew Harriet didn't have the academic ability of Charlie, but she treated them fairly and wanted Harriet to have some security for the future. She put £60 a week in each account and put the cash in envelopes under the mattress. She had regular clients, they always asked if she was available and she arranged times so that she would be, almost appointments if you like. It was very discreet. A natural progression from informal chatting to more intense and sensual conversation to the private room with a sumptuous bed and sex. She had seen it coming and had gone back on the pill and at first, she only did oral sex. She could distance herself from any emotion, you didn't have to do love and promises, it was a business and she was earning the money. Mark seemed pleased, the clients were pleased and she said to Mark she would have sex with them if they wore condoms. Mark said naturally, they were always available in the drawer by the bed and so she had three clients a night, one hour each and in the free hour she would meet and greet new clients.

It was hard to say who was the more surprised. Elaine or Dave Porter, the headmaster of her primary school when she greeted him in the softly lit lounge. She had never enquired about his private life, she thought he was married but didn't actually know. She didn't know either that once a month he had been seeing Gillian but this evening he needed a drink and Gillian had told him she wouldn't be available on this occasion.

They both stared at each other but Elaine recovered her composure. "Hello, I am Miranda, how lovely to see you." He had half a mind to turn and run, but what for, there was no point, both their secrets were out. She took a bottle of champagne to a table in the corner of the lounge. She wondered how he could afford to come to the Pandora on a headmaster's salary but hers was not to reason why.

"Elaine" he stuttered.

"Miranda, Dave." They both laughed. It broke the tension and they both relaxed. They were both adults, no need for any explanation, what happened at the Pandora stayed at the Pandora and he sipped his champagne and told her that he normally saw Gillian around eleven once a month. His marriage was dead in the water but for the sake of the children they stayed together and it would do him great harm if he should cause any kind of scandal such as divorce in his kind of work.

She told him she was determined Charlie shall not want for anything at the Kevin Brownlow Public School and she would make sure she could match any shortfall the bursary might not be able to provide. He looked at her in a totally different way. She was really quite lovely and her determination to do whatever it took endeared her to him and they chatted like old friends. It was time for her to leave and they said goodbye and she went to change. He was waiting when she came out to give her a lift home but she thanked him and told him her taxi was waiting. She had to keep this professional, she didn't want any emotional ties in her work, she could only cope if she kept it strictly business and if she took that ride home she felt she might let things get out of control.

She rarely saw him at the school, her job was just in the classroom or the playground and that suited her, no feelings, nothing personal, just a job.

She was earning an amazing amount of money. The accounts were growing and the cash under the mattress was beginning to worry her. She really needed to invest it, but she couldn't pay tax on it. She Googled offshore investments on Charlie's computer and went to see a financial adviser who advertised his services to do such work. He set up an account for her offshore and she could leave the money for two years or five and the interest rate was a lot more than the building society accounts.

Charlie sat the scholarship and passed with flying colours. Dave Porter was thrilled at Charlie's success and for her and it did a lot for the school's reputation as well.

She carried on working at the Pandora until the twins were eleven. She had been granted a bursary for Charlie and there was just ten percent of the fees to be found. She was able to pay the money directly from her account in the Cayman Islands and the money in the building society covered the uniform and the schoolbooks.

She asked her mum if she would like to go with them, to say goodbye. Harriet had been remarkably stoic about the whole thing. She would miss her twin but she knew he was way above the other children in the school and she was very proud of him. She hugged him and told him so, and Charlie loved her all the more. She was a good sister and they had been through thick and thin, always side by side and if there was a down side to the new school it would be that he couldn't share things with her like he had before. Elaine booked an hotel for the weekend and Charlie's suitcase looked bigger than him. Harriet had made a beautiful photo album which she gave to Charlie, embroidered with their names intertwining and Charlie just about held back the tears at her thoughtfulness. Elaine and her mum cried when they saw Charlie, grey suit with mauve tie, smart shiny shoes and a whiter than white shirt. He looked so vulnerable, so very young to be going away from home, but Charlie was a strong lad in many ways and they were a very tight family unit. He would be fine, it was she who was inwardly falling apart.

They hugged each other and Charlie said, "Don't cry, Mum, I will be fine. Harriet, you look after Mum and Nan, and I will do my best to make you proud of me. Mr Porter said I can call him any time and I will text you when I can. You can come and visit after the first week and I can go out with you too. Thank you for doing this for me, Mum, I know how hard you work and it's all so I can come here. I love you and I will not let you down." This of course had Elaine in floods but her mum gave her one of her 'looks' and she took a deep breath and smiled at him.

"I will think of you every day and I will be down to see you as soon as I can. Your nan, Harriet and I are so very proud of you and we love you very very much." They all walked through the enormous double doors and a senior boy came up to them and escorted them to a lounge where they were all offered coffee. Elaine and Charlie had been here for several open days and he had a rough idea of where he had to go and so, after coffee, they all hugged smiled.

Charlie smiled back and mouthed, "Don't worry, Mum." He turned around and the prefect took him one way as Elaine, Harriet and her mum went out of the door and down the steps to the car.

She had decided she would stop her job at the school. Her evening work more than paid for her expenses and any extra things that the school may suddenly need and Dave Porter was disappointed but totally understood. They had a kind of unspoken bond, each one respecting the confidences of the other and she appreciated him all the more for that.

She pulled the car over at a service station and her mum held her while she sobbed. "You have done the very best for Charlie and for Harriet, Elaine, I am very proud of you and what you have achieved. Charlie will be fine, it's just a bit raw leaving him, that's all, and he has a good head on his shoulders so you are not to worry. Tell you what, instead of getting straight home, let's get some lunch, my treat, and we will toast the future of my two amazing grandchildren." This they did. Had they travelled straight on to Reading they would have been caught up in one of the worst motorway accidents in a long time. Someone was watching over them, they both realised that when they were diverted off the motorway to avoid 'an incident at Junction four'.

18

The fireman managed to cut the side of the door away so that the paramedic could get in to the casualty. It was a miracle that no fires had broken out, with all the sparks and petrol from the cars that was one thing to be thankful for. The paramedic looked at the thick auburn hair that had fallen over the face of a thirty-something woman, and she was breathing but the pulse was very weak. He called for his mate and they managed to get a line into the vein which he had a hard job to raise, and this may help her to survive. She was unconscious and her legs had been forced under the driver's seat at a very odd angle. Her heels were ridiculously high for driving, what on earth had she thought she was doing trying to negotiate pedals with those on her feet. He guessed that was half the trouble. She couldn't have hit the brake hard enough in time to stop as she had whacked into the back of a dark green Jaguar.

The fireman proceeded to cut the driver's door away and she half tipped out but her legs were trapping her. They took the roof off and tried moving her by holding under her arms and they had to be so careful because they didn't know what damage had been done to her frail body. Her face was covered in blood from the windscreen but it seemed as if her breathing was becoming more regular and the paramedic gently pulled her legs from under the seat as the firemen, one either side balancing on the bonnet of the car, eased her up and out of the car on to a waiting stretcher.

They lifted her over the central reservation and another ambulance sped away, the paramedics working on her in the back of the ambulance.

They cut open her blouse, through her bra, and as it fell away, they both stopped dead. This was not a woman. "Bloody hell, we've got a transvestite," one of them said. "Poor bugger, probably doesn't know if he is Arthur or Martha. Still, let's get her/him cleaned up. You do the face, I'll see what damage has been done to the legs." He cut away the skirt and exposed sheer stockings and suspenders and a very tight pair of black lacy knickers. It looked as though one leg was broken, it was at an odd angle and the ankle was damaged with the bone coming through the skin. There was nothing to identify the person, it was more important to get them to hospital than gather any personal belongings. They covered him with a blanket as they moved the stretcher onto the trolley for the waiting nurses and doctors. As they whizzed him along a brightly lit corridor, his eyes flickered open, just for a minute, and he looked totally bizarre with his false eyelashes half winking as his eyes closed again.

He was trying to think what had happened. He had remembered he was driving home after a very successful tranny night. He had always loved dressing in girls clothes since he was eight. His mother thought it was just a phase, but he loved it with a passion she found a little confusing. He would borrow his sister's skirts and tops and would parade in front of his bedroom mirror, happy and excited to be a little girl.

As a teenager it was more difficult because his body was developing and he found it so annoying. He wanted breasts and watched enviously as his sister developed and when she was out he would get a bra from her drawer and stuff it with his socks and fit his penis into a pair of her prettiest knickers. He would slip a dress over his head and this made him ecstatic.

His mother was in a kind of denial. She had seen him once, he was so busy admiring himself he didn't see her looking through a crack in his bedroom door, and she just didn't know what to do. She couldn't grasp that her son was happier looking like a girl than her daughter, who was fine in jeans and a T-shirt.

He did reasonably well at school and got a job in a bank earning a small wage. He gave his mother money for the rent and still had some left to get some wigs and make-up and he would go up to his room and practice with different make-ups, and different coloured wigs. He decided the auburn wig looked good with his brown eyes. His hair was naturally sandy and he started to grow it. His manager at the bank had a word, but nowadays he could be accused of interfering with his human rights and so he let it pass.

He had perfected the art of make-up and invested over £3,000 on an auburn wig that was guaranteed to stay put even in a force ten gale. He was particularly mindful of his underwear and bought some breast forms because they gave a far better impression than stuffing your bra with socks. He so wanted to go out as a woman. He researched the Internet and he decided he needed professional help and settled for an escorting service. He made contact with another tranny girl who took him on his first tranny night out, showing him the ropes and the venues and she helped him overcome his first-time nerves. She was more of a chaperone than an escort really.

He was astounded at how welcoming the other tranny girls were. They had all been like him once, a first timer and he learned a lot by chatting to them about lingerie, fashion and shoes, what works and what doesn't. They told him what was classy and what was tacky and he gained confidence as the evening progressed.

He had had to move out from home. His need to be a woman had become so great he couldn't bear being in his suit all evening around the family and he was doing well enough in the bank to afford the rent on a first floor flat.

He hadn't known what to expect when he stepped out in public and a taxi had come with his escort when it was dark, just in case a neighbour saw him come out of his flat. He thought people would laugh at him, that he would be a source of ridicule but he had learned the art of cross dressing very well indeed and the escort found it hard to believe he was a first timer. The most difficult aspect of it all had been learning to walk in high heels. He spent about £1,000 experimenting with different pairs and once he had mastered it, he wore them all the time in his flat.

He normally changed his shoes when he drove but he was on a high, he loved his long legs in their silky nylon stockings and the high heels showed them at their best and so he decided he would keep them on. He did actually look stunning and he was humming along to the radio, his mind on the previous evening's fun when he saw the red brake lights right in front of him and he couldn't get his foot to the brake in time as the long spiky heel snagged on the rubber matting. He had no chance of braking in time and he screamed in agony as the car slammed into the back of the one in front and his legs were forced back as the car crumpled into them. Robert Mason, or April Rutherford, was another casualty who may or may not survive and it would be a difficult task for the hospital administrators to know who to contact with no identification, whether he was known as a man or a woman in his private life.

19

Pauline Collins had no idea why the car just died on her. She was on her way to work, the car had recently been serviced and she had enough petrol but it just stopped and would not start. Lucky I am not on the motorway yet, she thought and the car was tight to the side of the road, well a country lane actually. She always allowed plenty of time to get to work because you could never predict how heavy the traffic would be and Mondays were always busy with people returning from weekends away or just going to the airport to get away on business or holiday trips. She rummaged through her bag for her mobile phone and called the breakdown service which was next to her tax disc on the front window. They said it would be at least an hour before anyone would get to her so she called the office at Hounslow. Kathy answered the phone. "Hi Pauline, you all right?"

"No, the car has just died on me and I have telephoned the breakdown service and they think they can get to me in about an hour or so. Luckily I am not on the motorway and am not obstructing anything."

"Oh, poor you, hope it won't be too long and I will let Roger know."

"Thanks Kathy, I cannot understand it because it has only just had a service."

She knew she could do nothing but sit and wait, and it was quite a change for her not to be rushing from a to b. She had always had a sixth sense. When she was a little girl she had an 'Imaginary' friend. Her mother would say, Pauly is talking to her little friend again, as she listened outside her bedroom door. Inside her room a very pretty little girl in a crinoline dress was laughing with her as they played with the dolls and the pretty little girl said she was so pleased Pauline had come to live there because she had been so lonely with no one to play with. "You must come and have some tea with me Charlotte, please, you never come out of my bedroom." Charlotte said she was happy to stay because she knew they could play when Pauline went to bed and Pauline did think it very odd that her mother did not see Charlotte because she was not about to start talking to herself.

Pauline used to see lots of people that her mother didn't see. There was a little boy with beautiful golden curly hair who told her he had been thrown from his horse. She would play with him in the garden and he told her all about the grand house he lived in which had been knocked down to make room for the housing development where they lived. She told her mother about the little boy and described the grand house with pillars and steps leading to a huge front door and there was a courtyard at the back and stables and cottages for the servants who didn't live in the house.

Her mother discussed it with her father and she went to the library to look it up and sure enough there was a picture of the house exactly as Pauline had described it.

As she grew up, she realised she had a kind of gift that she could see people that others could not. It didn't scare her because they all seemed so kind and pleased to be with her. She told her friends at school which was not the brightest thing to do because they said if she did see people they couldn't she must be a witch and she found she suddenly didn't have very many friends any more. Her friend, Michael, thought she was just awesome and asked her if she could see his mother who had died two years ago. They were walking home from school and she stopped dead in her tracks. "Oh Michael, there is a very tall lady in a red suit and she has her arms around you."

"What colour is her hair Pauly?"

"It is a beautiful golden colour Michael, like yours, and she is saying she is very proud of you and your brother and your dad is doing so well. She is sorry she had to go but a horrid disease had robbed her of her future." Michael began to cry and so did Pauline, and she hugged him. She said she was so sorry for upsetting him but he said no, it was a wonderful thing to be told and reassured and comforted. Michael and Pauline became very close and he would always ask how his mum was and he thought it perfectly natural that Pauline could be in touch with people who had died.

They both went their separate ways, Michael to university and Pauline to a college of hair and beauty in London. She qualified as a hair stylist but did not take kindly to being told to sweep the salon floor and pass the rollers, she expected to be a hairdresser and didn't realise that that was what a junior did. She knew she could do far better than the stylists that worked there and her dad taught her to drive and got her a car and Pauline's Mobile Hairdressing Service was born and prospered.

Her clients always opened up and chatted away in the privacy of their own homes and on one occasion she saw a photograph in the lounge and the very person was sitting next to her client. "Who is that in the photograph?" she had asked and was told it was the woman's son. She burst into tears and Pauline tried to comfort her.

"He was killed last year in a motor bike accident, he was just nineteen."

"I am so sorry, Mrs Redbourne."

"I just know he is here, I can feel him, Pauline." Pauline made her a cup of tea and they sat down.

"Mrs Redbourne, I can see your son. He is right here and is stroking your hair. He says he is OK, he thinks you may have seen him, out of the corner of your eye, when he was in the kitchen the other day. He says he is happy where he is and often plays tricks on you, he moves your purse and puts it somewhere silly like the fridge."

"Oh Pauline, how amazing, that is absolutely true. The other day I went to get my purse to pay the window cleaner and it was not by the bed. I searched high and low and found it in the fridge when I went to get the milk for the window cleaner's tea! Pauline, you should do this for a living you know, you have an amazing gift. Oh, my goodness, I feel so much better now, I know Nick is OK, and I am glad he comes to see me." Pauline said she was happy that she had been able to help but she had been ridiculed at school and would not want to go through that again. "But Pauline that was then. You know what kids are like, if you are different you won't fit in, they exclude you and make fun of you because they do not understand. A lot of my friends believe in the afterlife, that people don't just die and that's it. You surely cannot go through all the challenges of modern day living, just to go into a black void when you die. No, there is something far better, at least that is what I believe and I now know, I now know that Nick is OK." Pauline finished her tea and combed Mrs Redbourne out. "You should advertise Pauline. I know three people off the top of my head who would pay to see you."

"Mrs Redbourne, I would not charge. Let me see how I get on with just one of your friends to start with, and if that friend thinks I have helped them, then I will think about it."

The following Tuesday afternoon Pauline went to Mrs Redbourne's house and her friend, Astrid, was there. Mrs Redbourne left the room and Astrid looked as nervous as a kitten as they sat together in the front room. Pauline said there was a lady, the spit double of her, sitting beside her on the sofa. "She has your colouring and she is smiling. She says she was taken at birth and has been with you all through your life. She is your twin."

Astrid's mouth dropped open. "My goodness Pauline, my twin died at birth and you are telling me she is here with me now?"

"Yes, and she is very well and does the name Margaret mean anything to you?"

Astrid thought for a moment. "No, I don't think so, I don't recall that name."

"She is quite elderly, she passed about five years ago."

Recognition dawned on Astrid's face. "Of course, my Auntie Peggy. Is she here too?"

"Yes, she is with your sister." Pauline went on to tell her about others that were now in the spirit world and Astrid was totally amazed.

"I cannot believe it, Pauline. You are fantastic. You must use your gift, it gives comfort and I will tell my friends and I insist I give you some money. I have often wondered about my sister and now I feel so much better."

Pauline was pleased she had been able to bring comfort to Astrid and decided that she would put a small advertisement in the local paper just to test the water. Word of mouth is the best form of recommendation and she soon found her afternoons were being booked up. She made a modest charge, only if she had satisfied her clients, and she accepted that she had been given a gift and if it could help others and bring comfort and closure, that was fine.

She earned enough from her clairvoyancy and her hairdressing to enable her to rent a small flat near her parents' house. Her reputation spread and she found she had to free up one day a week from her hairdressing to fit in all her appointments. She was determined to keep her weekends free, just doing the odd hour if the client could only see her on a Saturday. She could not foresee anything for herself and it was totally unexpected when an evening appointment with a young man caused her deep concern. She had never felt threatened by her clients, but the young man seemed very disturbed. She often found her clients were cautious when they first entered the lounge, but she could always put them at their ease, but this young man had a very bad aura around him. She could actually feel the evil that emitted from him and she believed he was possessed. For the first time in her life, she felt a dreadful sense of foreboding. She felt fear. He looked at her and said, "Do you know about me then?"

"No, I don't, and I am not getting anyone coming through." She didn't tell him there was a man holding a knife over him, with sheer evil intent in his eyes. "Mr Almond, I am sorry, I must ask you to leave. I have obviously not been successful in trying to help you."

"No, you haven't have you? You see I know your type, you are a fraud. You take people's money and you don't know nothing. You need to stop this, you need to stop interfering with people's lives. In fact, you can be absolutely sure that if you continue doing this, you will end up dead, and then see who comes to talk to you. My old man is dead, dead and buried and that's it. He used to fillet people like fish, and you should have seen the look in his eye when I turned on him. But that's for me to know and you to wonder about. No one should interfere with people and try and find out things when they are dead. They are brown bread, stone dead, end of."

Pauline was not sure how she could make him leave. Her mobile was switched off and he was between her and the door. He stood up and she shrunk back. He was beyond threatening, he was pure evil and she was trembling. He kicked the chair back from behind him and she moved behind the sofa. He came towards her, but suddenly, he stopped. He stopped in the middle of the lounge and she thought he was going to die. He convulsed, his whole body shook and he turned towards the door. He lunged at it, yanked it open and was gone.

Pauline collapsed. She fell back on to the sofa and tried to control her breathing, tried to calm herself down. She felt sure he would have killed her if he could. She also felt something other than fate had saved her. Someone was watching over her and someone had caused him to stop and to leave. She closed her eyes and recited the Lord's Prayer. She was terrified that whatever evil presence had come with him, may still be there. She said it over and over again — Our Father, who art in Heaven. Over and over and over. Finally, she felt more calm.

Three hours had passed since he had gone and she managed to get up from the sofa and got her mobile phone. Her parents were on the doorstep in ten minutes and she allowed them to hold her and comfort her and ease her fears. She realised just how lucky she had been. Her father immediately wanted to call the police, but she wouldn't let him. She felt that this man, whatever he had done and tried to do to her, must not be in her life in any way. If her father involved the police, she would have to tell them what he had said, and having seen the evil in him she didn't think he had made an empty threat. She didn't tell her parents all that had gone on, but she realised this had to end. She couldn't do it any more. Her parents tried to reassure her that he was a one off, that she had this gift and she had helped so many people, but she had been terrified and she could never let people into her home again, not for readings, not any more.

She moved out of the flat and into her parents' house until she could sort things out. She had been badly shaken and her confidence was at an all-time low. She just couldn't get that evil face out of her mind, those dreadful threats. She thought she saw him in the supermarket, on the train, wherever she went he seemed to be there. He wasn't of course, but she couldn't trust her own judgement any more. Her mother suggested she have a complete change. She had virtually stopped her hairdressing round, and she learned computer skills and applied for a job in an office, just an ordinary nine to five office job, administration, keeping diaries and making appointments. She got the job, the downside was that she would have to move away from her parents which really wasn't such a bad thing, and she rented a flat in a pretty village which you would never guess was so near the motorway. It was near to the office and she had settled into a really good routine which boosted her confidence and her parents were relieved to see their old Pauline back.

The hooting of the breakdown service van called her back from her thoughts. "Sorry I have been a bit longer than advertised mate," a cheery voice came from a young man in a huge orange and yellow coat. "Now what seems to be the trouble?"

She got out of the car and handed him the key. "It just died on me, and it's come through a service last month perfect, and it's full of petrol," she added for good measure because she felt sure he might be thinking some dimwit here — just because she was a woman. He got behind the wheel and turned the key. The car spluttered into life. "I don't believe it, what did you do, how did it start — is it because it was too hot before or something?"

"Don't ask me mate, but there it is, running like clockwork."

Pauline felt a complete idiot. "I am just so sorry. It honestly didn't work, it wouldn't start, oh, I feel such a fool."

"No worries mate, where were you going anyway?"

"I was going to work, my office is at Hounslow."

The mechanic looked at her. "Well mate, I reckon someone is watching over you. Reason I was late is there has been a really bad smash up on the motorway, and the time you called in and the time you would have been on the motorway would have put you right in the thick of it. Your little breakdown has saved your life mate, no doubt about it." He waved and got in his cab. "Lots of diversions in place now, I would check in with your office before you try to get there, it will take a long-time mate."

Pauline thanked him and waved him goodbye. She sat back in the car. She tried the key. It started. Just like that. She closed her eyes and silently thanked whoever it was watching over her. Yes, she had been lucky. She had avoided a dreadful crash and it was all down to kind souls who were there, all around her and if she could see things for herself, she would see they were holding her in their arms.

20

Dorry Roberts looked at the clock in the kitchen for the umpteenth time. Stan should have rung by now, he always let her know if he was going to be late and his breakfast with George would not have gone on this long. He also knew they had to be at the station to meet her cousin at two p.m. and he would need to get back and get some sleep before then. He wasn't going to go to work that night, they were taking Barbara to the theatre, she was coming especially, to see *War Horse* and they had booked the tickets nearly a year ago.

On the rare occasions Stan had been late without explanation Dorry had said to him, 'I had got you to the hospital about to go for the operation and in you would walk. Honestly Stan, it's such a worry,' and he would give her a cuddle, say he was very sorry and it wouldn't happen again. There she was, getting him to the hospital when the shrill ringing of the telephone made her jump out of her skin. "Hello."

"Dorry?"

"Sybil, is that you?"

"Yes, it's me. Dorry, there has been an accident, Stan has been taken to Hillingdon hospital. It happened about three hours ago and Arthur is on his way to collect you to take you there."

Dorry gripped the kitchen table. "How is he Sybil?"

"We don't know Dorry. The police called the company, they gave Stan's number and so I am calling you. I will go to the hospital to meet you and Arthur. He will be with you any minute Dorry. Get your bag and coat and I will see you there."

Dorry grabbed her bag and coat. She didn't really react. She just stood in the front room watching for Arthur's cab. Don't let him die, don't take him from me, we aren't any good without each other. Her mind was racing and all the what ifs and whys and hows came crashing around in her head. Arthur's cab screeched to a halt outside the door and Dorry opened the front door and he took her arm to help her to the cab. She got in and Arthur headed off at speed. "So sorry Dot. Don't know what has happened. Stan is the most careful driver I know, not an accident to his name but what we do know is there was a massive motorway pile-up near Heathrow and he had a fare in his cab."

"But how is he Arthur, does he know what's happened?"

"Sorry Dot, we don't know more than what the police said — that you must get there asap and then we should find out more. Sybil is coming to meet us there. We shouldn't be too long now, hold on there's a dear."

Dorry hung onto the strap at the side of the window. All she could think of was he had to be OK. He had to come through because he was strong and he had always been strong for her and they had a good marriage and lots of plans. He will not die, he can't die.

Arthur stopped the cab outside the hospital where you could park for twenty minutes and took Dorry's hand as they walked through the big swing doors. It was so full of people, all looking anxious, all trying to ask questions to a group of ladies behind a huge desk with a volunteers sign. Arthur went straight up to a man with a blue badge, explained that Stan had been brought here from the accident, and asked where they should be going.

The man took them along a corridor to a side room which Arthur thought didn't look too good for Stan. He gripped Dorry's hand which was shaking and tears were running down her face. "Now then Dorry, get a grip girl. Got to be strong for our Stan, haven't we?" The man told them to sit and wait there and he would go and find out as much as he could about Stan. It was ten minutes which seemed like ten years to Dorry before a young lady with a stethoscope around her neck came in. She shook their hands firmly and introduced herself as Doctor Waring. She had attended to Stan who was still unconscious but his condition was not as serious as was at first thought. This caused Dorry's knees to buckle and Arthur swiftly got a chair under her as she crumpled.

"He is holding his own Mrs Roberts and the seat belt saved him before the airbag went off." She didn't think it prudent to say that had his passenger been wearing her seat belt she would have lived but without it there had been no chance.

"Can I see him doctor? I just want to see him, let him know he is going to be all right."

"I can take you to him but he may not regain consciousness for some time, but by all means you can sit by his bed." Dorry gripped Arthur's arm and together they entered a small side room with a single bed and Stan was lying totally flat and very still with tubes and drips and all sorts attached to a machine and stands around the bed.

Dorry was really very brave. She absolutely hated hospitals ever since she had visited her mother every day for six weeks as she lay dying and to her they were a place where most people seemed to die. Not her Stan though. He was a strong man but the sight of him looking so vulnerable and alone, his ruddy face stark against the sterile white sheets made her grip Arthur's arm so hard. She sat by the side of the bed, she whispered in his ear that she was here and he was going to be fine. She told him he had better sort himself out and get well very soon. At the thought of this she remembered Barbara. She would be arriving at the station at two p.m. "Oh Arthur, I am so grateful to you for bringing me here but my cousin Barbara is coming today and we were meeting her at two at the station. We were going to see *War Horse* and…"

Arthur held her hand. "Hold on Dot, hold on. You have had one hell of a shock and don't even think about

Barbara. I will go outside, see if I can find Sybil who can sit with you and I will go to the station. Now, shall I bring Barbara here?"

"Please Arthur. She won't be expecting this at all, none of us were, were we? She can come here then, when we know a little bit more about how Stan is, she will be staying with me. She was staying for a few days anyway. Thank you so much, you are very kind." Arthur waved it away and saw Sybil at reception. He explained about Barbara and where Dorry was and left her to go to her while he went to his cab and drove off to the station.

21

Hazel Watts had been startled by the knock on the door and as she approached, she saw a huge shape standing behind the glass. She pulled back the bolt to ease it open and saw the outline of a large policeman. "Mrs Watts?" he asked through the opening.

"Yes, yes, I am, what is wrong, what has happened — please God it's not Cressandra."

"Mrs Watts, please can you open the door. I am Sergeant Barnes from the Metropolitan police." He showed her his identification and she slid the bolt and opened the door. A woman police constable was with him and she went first showing her ID to a very white-faced mother of Cressandra. She asked if she was alone, was there a neighbour or someone who could come.

"No, no, why, just tell me what's happened." The policewoman led her to the settee and they sat down. She explained that Cressandra had been involved in an accident on her way to Heathrow airport. "How do you know it's her? When did this happen? She should be on her way to Paris by now."

"Mrs Watts, she was carrying her passport and unfortunately was pronounced dead at the scene." A howl, a dreadful howl of a wounded animal came from her lips as she grabbed the policewoman's arm.

"It can't be, it can't be, she is on her way to Paris. She is a famous model you know, my Cressandra."

The policewoman tried as gently as she could to explain, that sadly, she was in a taxi making her way to the airport. The ticket in her handbag confirmed that she should have been on the ten a.m. flight to Paris but the crash on the motorway had prevented the taxi getting through. Unfortunately, the taxi had crashed into the car in front of it. She had been instructed not to mention that the seat belt was unfastened and the red light was flashing on the driver's dashboard indicating it was not in use.

"Did she die in the taxi then?"

"As far as we can ascertain she did, Mrs Watts, but we are here to take you to the hospital where Cressandra has been taken. Is there anyone who can accompany you, a friend, a neighbour?" Hazel called her neighbour, Zoe, who said she was about to come round after seeing the police car. She came at once and they both got into the back and Hazel sat staring straight ahead wringing her hands and muttering to herself.

They were taken to the hospital morgue, unfortunately there was no disguising this with the word — morgue — over the door. The outer room was very calming, soft lighting and at one end a large curtain. "Mrs Watts, are you ready to identify Cressandra?" She nodded, gripping Zoe's arm. Gently the curtain was pulled to one side and Cressandra was laying on a bed, covered with a white sheet. Her beautiful hair was brushed a little over her face to cover the cuts made by the glass and she looked as though she was asleep. Care had been taken to cover her throat, hiding the gaping hole where a large piece of glass had taken her life. Even in death she looked so beautiful, so calm somehow.

"Mrs Watts, is this your daughter Cressandra?" She couldn't speak. She nodded and Zoe held her tight as she finally sobbed, sobbed so hard her whole body shook. The curtain was drawn shut and they sat on the chairs while the policewoman fetched water for them both. "Please accept our deepest sympathy Mrs Watts. The doctor did tell us that death was instantaneous. She would have felt nothing, if that is any comfort."

Hazel looked at the woman. Her head was spinning. Comfort? That's a strange thing to say when she was literally dissolving inside. How could there be any comfort when her beautiful daughter was dead the other side of that curtain. "Hazel, do you feel you can leave now? You need some fresh air, you have had the worst shock any mother can have and you need to be away from here." Hazel couldn't move. She sat staring at the curtain as if she could will her daughter to sit up and say 'hello mum'. That wasn't going to happen. She couldn't grasp that though, she wanted to hang on to the thought that she would be all right after all. She tried to stand but her legs were too weak to hold her. The policewoman took one side and Zoe the other and together they took her into a corridor and a side room. Zoe looked at the policewoman, pleading as to what she should do now.

"Mrs Watts, a car will be ready to take you home when you feel you are able to leave. Zoe, will you be able to go with Mrs Watts?"

"Of course, I will go with her and stay with her. She has a brother in Glasgow, he works on the oil rigs and we will get in touch with him. Thank you for your kindness. She will be able to go in a moment or two. I will come and find you when she says."

The policewoman closed the door and went to reception. The car was still outside the morgue and she asked for it to be brought around to the front of the hospital. In her job she had seen terrible things, heard terrible things but to see such a young, beautiful, broken body made her draw on her deepest reserves to hold it together, to not break down, because if she let go now, she would weep and never stop.

22

If Harriet Harvey Smart had just had orange juice in her glass at breakfast, she would have realised it was the accelerator pedal under her Jimmy Choo. It was the vodka lacing that took awareness out of the equation and somewhere in the backwaters of her mind she felt pain, a fierce crushing pain as the seat belt crushed her chest when the steering wheel slammed into her body. She tried to open her eyes but the effort was too great. Her BMW sports car was embedded in the side of a grey Volvo. She was aware of pain yet her body was numb. Gradually consciousness returned. She could remember now, remember that the diagnosis had not surprised her, the years of downing vodka martinis had reduced her liver to a pulp, the lungs barely worked with the coating of tar and she had two, maybe three months left of her life.

She had cleared Oswald's bank account early on in their marriage and made him sign a new will leaving everything to their daughter. His children from his first marriage, whom he had loved utterly before dementia robbed him of reason, got nothing. Oswald Harvey Smart died and Harriet was knocked sideways when her solicitor informed her that his children were contesting the will and consequently her Sally could not claim what was to be her sole inheritance. This was a body blow to Harriet. She wanted her daughter to be able to continue to live in the manner to which she had become accustomed. She had never worked, Oswald kept her in horses and clothes while Harriet squirreled away various amounts of money as often as she could. Oswald was totally unaware of his bank balance as he had always had money to the extent it never bothered him. It's only when you don't have money that you are absolutely aware of who has and how to get it. Sally's money attracted drug addicted losers to her bed and they would sponge off her until she grew tired of them and moved on to the next waster.

Harriet wondered if it was because of her that her daughter had no morals, no aspirations. As a young girl Harriet was adored by her parents until the birth of her sister Imogen when Harriet was nine. Imogen was, from a very early age, undeniably beautiful. She never went through that 'awkward age', with spots and gawky limbs and horrid hormonal moods. She just seemed to evolve from a girl into a woman in one easy stride. Everyone adored Imogen. High cheekbones, sparkling happy eyes framed by her perfect natural blonde hair, laughter always emitting from her cupid bow mouth. Harriet hated her, and who could blame her. She was pushed very much into the background, and while she herself was quite attractive, everyone gravitated to her incredibly beautiful younger sister. Her father put her on a pedestal and worshipped at the throne of Imogen.

In total contrast, when Harriet was fifteen, he gave her ten shillings to feel her breasts and one pound for a suck. She had sex with her father's best friend when she was sixteen and then blackmailed him after showing him the video she had set up while they were in her bed. She made herself a lot of money and was disappointed when he was exposed in the press as a paedophile and told her he would not be paying her any more as he had nothing more to lose.

Harriet had many lovers, she enjoyed them all the more if they were married and especially when she knew their wives. It heightened her enjoyment to think her body was moving, riding their husbands while they were out riding their horses.

Imogen was pursued for her beauty and maybe it was because she was adored, she adored back, and from a much-loved little girl a beautiful woman enjoyed a charmed life.

Harriet married Oswald Harvey Smart because he was very rich and she amazed him in bed, enticing him away from his very fat, rich, boring wife. Even after the divorce he had the stables and farm in Cheltenham and introduced Harriet to a whole new life of horses and parties culminating in the four-day races. She loved Cheltenham, the wide tree-lined boulevard with the art gallery and museum and the imposing period buildings. She would go to Montpellier Walk and loved the independent shops and boutiques meeting friends in the restaurants for lunch. She actually really enjoyed this lifestyle. She was used to money and what it could buy. Oswald had inherited his wealth and enjoyed it, especially when he could have all this and great sex without paying for it.

Harriet always enjoyed the Hunters' Chase evening at the end of April when the amateur jockeys took centre stage and she took two at a time in the stables after the race. Always discreet, Oswald had no idea, and she loved the smell of the hay as they would roll her and she straddled one while the other put his manhood in her mouth. That was always a bonus and she would make love that night to Oswald in such a way he thought she was the best woman he had ever had in bed.

She indulged their only daughter, sending her to the best private schools and then to Switzerland to a finishing school which really only served to finish any thought of earning a living in Sally's impressionable young mind.

Harriet loved showing Sally off at any opportunity, failing to see what her friends actually thought of her totally self-centred, spoiled daughter. Oswald slid quite quickly into dementia. It was little things at first, not being quite 'with it'. Fortunately, the running of the estate was in the hands of his loyal friend, Joseph, possibly the only male on the estate who had not shared Harriet's bed because he had a penchant for young jockeys who enjoyed his company enormously.

She had finally heeded her doctor's advice to put her house in order and made preparation for her funeral. Sally was to hire the Squires Hotel for the wake and no expense was to be spared. The flowers were to be white lilies and the music would be performed by the Cheltenham quartet as the casket with pure gold handles entered the church. She made a list of who should be invited (although she had been told by her sister that most people attended a funeral out of respect, not by invitation) and selected the buffet and champagne. She had set aside £50,000 and had placed it in Sally's account for the purpose.

She groaned as a new pain gripped her, she wasn't sure where it was coming from. She felt desperately tired. She thought she was smiling, thinking how ironic was this. She should have two months left, but somehow, she didn't think that mattered any more. At least she had everything in hand. Everything was organised, Sally would carry out her wishes and her funeral would be the talk of Cheltenham. She would leave this world in style, as she had lived it, or so she thought. She thought she heard music, she thought it must be the quartet, it sounded soft but it was growing louder. She suddenly wanted to hear it, she wanted to stay, she didn't really want to go, not now, not when that beautiful music was playing. Very gradually she slipped into unconsciousness and the music gently floated away.

Harriet Harvey Smart would not be best pleased to know that she would be presented in a plain cheap coffin with plastic handles. The record got stuck on *Abide With Me* and the local pub ran out of sandwiches because more money had been spent on the wine and beer than the bread. Sally on the other hand looked totally stunning in a scarlet long coat, black riding boots and black Russian hat, content in the knowledge that at least she had £48,000 to help her get by until the will was finally sorted out.

23

Russell Mortimer was a junior doctor who had arrived at his shift at the accident and emergency unit at six a.m. He was keen to learn all he could and was an enthusiastic member of the team. It had been a busy weekend with the Friday and Saturday night casualties of over indulgence in alcohol which caused the fights. It never ceased to amaze him that women were more likely to be the instigators of the fight than men. There were signs all around the unit that the staff would not tolerate abusive behaviour and the police had removed several people on the Saturday night. He personally couldn't understand how people would drink themselves half blind and end up in a fight and then casualty. To him they might just as well pour their money down a drain for all the good it did them. The Sunday had been busy with football injuries and broken bones and he couldn't forget the man with the fractured skull caused when his wife had hit him too hard with the frying pan. He had just about grabbed five hours sleep before the morning shift.

He was in his fourth year and had applied to do residency training in the hospital not sure of what he wanted to specialise in. He knew from his experience in his third year of working with patients under the supervision of experienced physicians that you had to totally commit to achieve your goals. You had to learn to make decisions under pressure and he always strove to achieve excellence in his practice of medicine.

At nine fifteen the hospital was put on full alert as ambulances screamed away from the hospital to attend to casualties in a motorway crash. The first casualties to arrive were taken to the emergency rooms set up, the paramedics having radioed ahead as to the injuries and their level of urgency.

Russell was immediately embroiled in doing what he loved, trying to save lives, and his heart went out to the poorly damaged people who came into the room and he fought so hard to try and save them from death.

It was three hours into the start of the crash and he hadn't even had a drink of water, and neither had the sisters and nurses working alongside him, when he gave a cry as the air was forced out of his lungs and he became stiff and fell to the ground unconscious and his body started to jerk. Two of the nurses screamed but the sister remained calm. "He is having a seizure, give him space, do not try to help him, the spasm will pass in a few minutes."

The nurses moved the gurney away from Russell who was now perfectly still and seemed to be in a deep sleep. "I think he has had a tonic seizure," the sister said. "I think it is a form of epilepsy."

Two porters put him on a trolley and took him to a recovery room and the sister assisted the porters to transfer him to a bed, pulling the side railings up.

She had followed Russell's career thus far with interest. He was one of the most promising junior doctors she had ever worked with and she felt dreadfully sad at what had occurred.

She guessed he would be asleep for an hour and peeked in at him whenever she could to watch for his return to complete consciousness. After about one and a half hours he gradually opened his eyes and she was glad she was there at that time. "Whatever happened, where am I, I am so thirsty. Debra, am I OK?" She held his hand and said that she thought he had suffered a seizure of some kind and asked him if this had ever happened before. "No, no Debra, never. Oh my God, am I an epileptic? What about my career, what about my future?" As silent tears rolled down his cheeks.

"There, there, Russell, we don't know what happened, it could easily be a one-off, the effect of the sheer pressure you are under. Unfortunately, with the current situation there are no doctors available but right now you must stay here and sip the water as often as you can. I do not want you trying to get up, your body has suffered tremendous trauma and you must be mindful it would be dangerous for you to attempt to do anything but rest."

He nodded. To be honest he had no energy and could just about raise his head to take a sip of the water.

He couldn't think straight and he couldn't even begin to understand what had happened. All he could do was pray that whatever had happened to him could be treated. He could not bear to think his career in medicine was not to be, not after all his dedicated study and training. No, there had to be a solution, some form of medication that would prevent the seizures happening again, but right now, he was exhausted and allowed his eyes to close as he fell into a deep and troubled sleep.

Later that evening it would be determined that he had suffered an epileptic fit but that this would not end his career. Debra had researched it all on the Internet and there was a breakthrough medical procedure where stem cells are intravenously administered under the skin of epileptic patients. The stem cells travel throughout the body detecting damaged cells and tissue and attempt to restore them. The foetal stem cells can also stimulate existing normal cells and tissue to operate at a higher level of function, boosting the body's own repair mechanisms to aid in the healing process. The initial process takes one hour and there are no negative side effects. She prepared all the information in a dossier and would wait until he was fully recovered from the seizure to let him know all was not lost. She marvelled at how medicine and treatments were constantly changing and improving, and she was very grateful that this hardworking young doctor would be able to realise his dream.

24

Frances Ridgeway had turned the car engine off and was sitting in a queue of traffic that was now over ten miles long. She listened to the radio and it occurred to her that the music nearly always reflected how she was feeling at that particular time. Cold Play were singing *Paradise*. Para, para, paradise. Her little piece of paradise was India. The most amazing, talented, loving, wonderful, beautiful India.

They had met on a course paid for by her firm to learn how to create and present websites. India's company were based in Slough and the course was held in a beautiful country house venue near Taunton off the M5. It was three days of concentrating on different techniques and Frances really enjoyed the challenge. Before dinner she went to the pool to do some lengths and India looked stunning in her bikini and they raced each other and India won hands down. They showered and made their way to the bar and the chemistry was electric.

Frances had never ever made the first move. She was not confident yet something deep down told her this woman wanted her in the way she wanted her. She ordered two dry martinis and they took their drinks to sit down in the lounge. They both started speaking at the same time and burst out laughing and when India brushed her hand it was as if a red-hot needle had shot through her. India later told her she noticed Frances as soon as she walked into the room and she too was desperately hoping they would meet and talk. India explained that she was gay. Just like that in about the third sentence and Frances's eyes opened wide and the happiness that radiated across her face told India all that she had hoped for was about to happen. The conversation was animated, they had so much in common and it was completely natural that India came into her bed and they made love, passionately, giving each other all of each other, wanting, holding, stroking, entwining and satisfying each other as if they had always been together. Breathlessly they both lay back, holding each other, not ever wanting to let go and then laughing, amazed that they had found each other and each one silently vowing they would cement this relationship, they would never ever part.

When the course was over, they had made plans to meet the next weekend in London and their love making was the icing on the cake, the pinnacle of satisfaction. As India said, we have all this and heaven too. They made plans for their future. They held nothing back from each other and it was as if the slate had been wiped clean and this was a totally new life for them both. They were in love, they loved each other unreservedly and

Frances knew that she had found her true vocation and was forever grateful for that.

Frances was married to Richard for eight months before she had to admit she really couldn't do this any more. Why was it she was expected to be 'normal'. To get married to a man who she really admired, respected yet deep down she didn't love, not how she felt she ought to love him.

She was fifteen when she started to self-harm. Her mother found her in the bath and she had cut her arms with the razor blade and the blood had turned the bubbles red. The doctor was very understanding yet he really didn't have a clue. She was at one of the best girls' schools in the country, her parents ran a successful Internet business, her sister was at university and everything had gone without a hitch until now. The headmistress was concerned yet seemed to do nothing to try to get to the bottom of it. In her experience a lot of the girls had issues, and Frances was not the brightest crayon in the box — she kept this to herself of course — but suggested maybe some extra tuition in maths and English may help Frances to cope a bit better. Her parents thought it a bit much that they were shelling out thousands of pounds a term and be expected to pay for extra tuition, but they did, anxious to try to ease Frances's troubled mind.

She struggled through her exams and did not achieve good grades which didn't sit well with the school. Her parents felt that maybe it was the school that caused her unhappiness and suggested a college course. Business administration seemed the obvious choice and for a while Frances flourished, the pressure of having to achieve had gone.

Yet it wasn't the pressure of achievement that haunted Frances, it was the fact that she was unbelievably attracted to one of the girls doing street dance and tap in the media studies group. The girl could not help but notice her big puppy eyes, her eagerness to please, watching her dance and the fact she was always there. She struck up a conversation and asked Frances why she didn't join the dance group and Frances said, "Oh no, I couldn't do it like you, you are just amazing." The girl gave her a hug and Frances thought she had died and gone to heaven. They would meet in the canteen and then go out of college to be together. To kiss and fondle and when her tongue went in Frances's mouth and her hand stroked her knickers, she just knew she wanted this girl so much. They went back to the girl's house and stripped naked and Frances knew this is what she had been waiting for, for so long. They caressed each other, knowing exactly how to stroke and suck and tickle and tease and she orgasmed in the girl's face and they both laughed. Frances returned the compliment and they were an item and whenever they could they would be together.

Frances's parents were so happy to see that she seemed to be so much more relaxed and at ease and altogether more healthy, no more panic attacks. They had high hopes she would achieve in her Business Administration Diploma and then hopefully join them in their business in one of the dozen outlets throughout the country.

Their bubble completely burst and disappeared into infinity when Frances told them that she was gay, a lesbian. She was in love with a girl called Jeanette and she hoped they would be very happy for the both of them.

Their reaction to this news was not at all what Frances expected. She thought they would be surprised but not horrified, not devastated, not so angry that they both just sat there. "Mum, Dad, please be happy for me. I have found someone I love very much and I want to be with them and they want to be with me." Her father left the room and her mother didn't move, didn't go to her, didn't hug her, nothing.

"Frances, you are being totally ridiculous. You are an impressionable young girl, you have no experience of the world let alone a man. You have never met a man, never had a boyfriend, you don't know what joy a man can bring a woman." This was said tongue-in-cheek because the last time they had made love was probably the night they conceived Frances. "You have one more week at college, your results will be through and then you can move right away from this woman, girl, whatever she is."

Frances just could not take it in. She could not believe her mother had dismissed her love as something impressionable. How dare she. How could she react to something so beautiful in such an ugly way? "We are going to move in together, Mum, we are going to rent a flat."

"With what? Where is the money coming from? Does this person have a job, because you certainly don't. This just demonstrates how utterly ludicrous the whole situation is. Now your father and I are sure your results will earn you the diploma and there is an opening in the office in Oxford. As soon as we have the results, we will settle you in up there."

"You are so unfair, Mum. You have paid Charlotte's uni costs, you have paid her share in the house in Leeds and you keep her in clothes. How can you not support me the same? I told Jeanette you would help us just like you helped Charlotte."

That made her mother's blood boil. "Help you, both of you, to set up a little nest to indulge in your horrible fantasies. I don't think so. Now, the sooner you get it into your head the better, you are not a gay person, lesbian whatever. You are a girl with no experience of life who has, on a whim, decided you will be with this person without thinking anything through. Well, I have thought it through and that's an end to it. There is to be no contact with this person, she is certainly never going to grace my presence and once college is over, your life begins in Oxford in a normal way."

Frances was in despair. She texted Jeanette and said they must meet. Actually, Jeanette had been held up in a lecture and was admiring a pretty blonde girl who was listening attentively to the lecturer. She caught her eye, raised her eyes to heaven as if to say doesn't he go on, and the blonde girl smiled back.

Jeanette met Frances in the canteen. She could see she was in a dreadful state. "Franny, whatever is the matter, you look terrible." And Frances told her the reaction of her parents to her 'coming out'. Jeanette listened and stroked her arm. Her thoughts were racing. "Guess this means they won't be supporting us, eh Franny?"

"Got it in one," replied Frances.

"That's a real pity Franny. We could have been together and it would have been fab."

"Jeanette, we still can be together. You did say your mum wouldn't mind us being together in your house, didn't you?"

"That's out the window now darling, my brother and his girlfriend are wanting to move back into the house and my room is kind of up for grabs. I can sofa surf for a bit, but there won't be a chance of us being together now."

Frances was distraught. "Please Jeanette, we love each other, we will find a way, we have to, you can't ignore the feelings we have for each other." Suddenly Frances saw things in a totally different light. Maybe she had done all the chasing, she had been the one to say her parents would help out, Jeanette had been up for that, yet on the turn of a sixpence she had changed. Her attitude was not open and loving. It was dismissive.

Frances was heartbroken. She knew she had no future with Jeanette. She had no one who really loved her, no one who understood her, wanted her. She was empty, drained, hung out to dry.

Her results satisfied her parents and they settled her into a flat in Oxford and the manager of the store kept her eye on her and was told not a thing about her little 'strange episode'. Frances put all her feelings aside. She formed a barrier around herself. No emotion, just work. No room to be hurt any more, no one could ever do that to her again.

Richard Slater had noticed Frances from day one. He was the salesman for the whole of Oxford and surrounding area and came into the office first thing on a Monday for his client calls and last thing on a Friday to do the paperwork. When he first saw Frances, he was absolutely blown away. She had the most beautiful creamy peaches and cream complexion, sheer blue eyes that seemed too huge for her face and a very full mouth, a very sensual full mouth.

He sensed the wall, the 'do not enter' feeling was written all over her body language, yet very gently, in fact over a period of six months, he chipped away. They went to the cinema, then straight home and no kiss goodnight, he didn't try. The meals out became more frequent and he noticed when she eventually did laugh, she had the most delightful wide smile with even white teeth and he knew this girl was the girl of his dreams.

Her parents came to visit and they took Richard and Frances out for dinner and they were quietly stunned at how relaxed the two of them were in their own company. He was a good-looking young man, her mother perceived, and she wondered if they were more than friends. It was quite apparent after they had stayed in her flat that there was no sign of any man having ever been over the threshold but they were so glad she was 'normal' again.

Frances had decided she would have to tell Richard that she thought she was gay. He was surprised but not stunned. He privately thought she had suffered some kind of trauma that made her shrink from manly affection, but this did explain a few things. Strangely he had not wanted her in that way, he had been content just to be in her company. They made each other laugh and he said it was no big deal. Let's just see what happens, let's just carry on as we are.

Frances was gradually beginning to think that maybe the feelings she had for Jeanette were just a phase, like her mum had said. She began to look forward to being with Richard, and after a wonderful evening walking along the banks of the river after a superb meal, she asked if he would like to go back to the flat for coffee. They were both incredibly nervous. He didn't want to blow it. He had been with women before, in fact he enjoyed sex, but this woman was so precious to him, he let her take the lead. Gently he kissed her mouth, her neck and she undid his belt and laid back on the bed and very gently he kissed her breasts and stroked her sweetness and she urged him inside her and she wondered how she had ever not done this before. It was quite wonderful. They both looked at each other in awe and she thought, I am not gay, I am perfectly normal. I am a woman who has made love with a man. The fact that she had also had great sex with a woman no longer interested her, and she dedicated the weekend to catching up for lost time.

Her parents were overcome with excitement on hearing the telephone call that said they were now an item and would it be OK if Richard moved into the flat because they were paying the rent and it would be rude not to ask.

Her sister Charlotte had gone on a gap year to Asia and it seemed she had met 'the love of her life' and the wedding was arranged for three months' time. That was when all of Frances's family met her young man. He was charm personified and Frances was glad that Charlotte told her she was a very lucky girl, and hoped that they would tie the knot as well.

A new position that suited Richard opened in Basingstoke and that was an easy commute to Arlesford where the family business had begun. Frances and Richard rented a small flat in Basingstoke, their first step in paying their own rent and budgeting which went very well.

Her parents were thrilled to hear they were to be grandparents — Charlotte was two months' pregnant at the wedding — and their happiness was dashed when she lost the baby. Frances was a good sister and when her parents came back from trying to help, she went herself and tried to be there for Charlotte. It is a terrible thing to lose something precious, Frances learned that for the second time in her life. However, Richard seemed to sense that it was the right time to propose and she accepted and a kind of calm settled. Well, not calm as in plans to be made, but calm for Charlotte, something to look forward to when she had been so devastated.

The pre-wedding year was, as in any household, manic. The date was set and the selection of the venue, the church, the photographer, florist, let alone the bridal gown and bridesmaids became a merry-go-round of appointments and fittings. It seemed to Frances things were moving at a pace that was spiralling out of control. Everything had to be on a grand scale. Everything had to be the best. Cousins came out of the woodwork to be bridesmaids and the guest list was growing to over two hundred. Frances thought her mother was like a woman possessed. She arranged for them to go to umpteen wedding fairs and tasting sessions at the hotel. The table plan had to be changed three times due to two of Richard's uncles not on speaking terms (one had slept with the other's wife). Aunt Dotty really was and she needed to be near the exit for the toilet and Eleanor and

Erica were an item and not sisters. They rode in five different wedding cars from a Bentley, a Rolls to a camper van and Frances felt a little like a spectator on the sidelines. She asked Richard if he was OK with it all, all this pomp and ceremony, and he said whatever made her happy and she began to doubt if this really was making her happy.

The hen 'event' was a trip to Monte Carlo and thirty young hens, with a couple of mother hens, played at the casino and shopped and sampled every luxurious treatment at the hotel spa that was possible. Frances didn't actually think about the cost. Her mother could easily afford it and her father was just happy the event was happening at all.

Richard's stag, was a curry and a nightclub, and the stripper was more drunk than them and his mates tied him to a lamp post stark naked until a policeman took pity on him and covered his modesty with his helmet.

The wedding, as weddings go, was a most magnificent affair. Frances looked beyond radiant, her make-up (after six different attempts over six weeks) was perfection and everything went according to plan. Richard was in a kind of haze of excitement, apprehensive over his speech which he needn't have worried about, and complete and utter amazement that he had married this very beautiful woman who would make his life complete.

Needless to say, the honeymoon period didn't last and Frances found herself wondering if it had all been a ghastly mistake. She knew she loved Richard, he was the kindest, sweetest man, always bringing her little gifts and leaving notes on her pillow but something was missing. She realised she loved him like a brother and when she woke one morning and actually found his love making made her feel sick, she knew she had to end it. Richard was in complete shock. He knew they had to adjust to married life but they had been living together for a year before the wedding so nothing was out of the ordinary, except it was extraordinary. Frances didn't seem to be into sex any more. He wondered if she might be pregnant but then it would probably have had to be immaculate conception because she always had a headache and when he suggested an early night, she really needed to see the late film.

Both sets of parents were dumbfounded. They hadn't been married five minutes and now it was to end. What on earth was wrong with this generation? Didn't they know you had to work at it, you had to give and take and for goodness sake they had everything unlike in their day when you had to wait to get the carpets and struggle to make ends meet. Frances dropped out of everything associated with her family and Richard.

She hunted for a different job. She had the qualifications and experience and was successful at the interview for the administrator in an agricultural machinery company in Camberley. Richard offered to buy her out of the flat (he had secured a mortgage on his salary) and with that small amount of money she paid two months' rent in advance on a small flat and put the rest in the bank. Her parents refused to have anything to do with her, and in some respects, this attitude was the spur to make her stand on her own two feet which in reality she had never done before.

The travel announcer interrupted the music on the radio and stated the obvious that there had been an accident on the westbound side of the carriageway at junction four. Traffic in both directions was at a standstill. Diversions were being set up but it would take a long while to get things moving again. She was startled by a knocking on her window and lowered it to see a young woman in obvious distress. "Do you know what's going on? My battery has run out on my mobile and I am supposed to be at the airport in an hour." Frances told her what she had heard on the radio and at this the woman's face crumpled and she burst into tears. Frances gently pushed the door open and stood to comfort her.

"I am so sorry, look, we can't do anything, we are completely stuck, are you on your own?"

"Yes, I am supposed to be meeting my brother, we have a family crisis and we have to fly to America."

"Please sit in my car, we won't be moving for a while and I have a flask of coffee if you would like a cup."

Lucy Palmer got her bag from her car and went and sat with Frances. Her mother had become ill on her holiday in Florida and was too ill to travel home so she and her brother were going to visit her to assess the situation. While she was talking to Frances, she realised she would not make the plane and there was no way she could get in touch with him with no battery. "Use my phone, you may be able to reach him if he is in an area where there is a signal."

Fortunately, Darren Palmer received the call and the relief in Lucy's voice was so good to hear. He had heard of the accident but wasn't too worried as it was on the other side to where Lucy would be travelling but neither had realised it had closed both sides of the motorway. He said he would take the flight, at least one of them could get to their mother and Lucy would have to follow on. Finally, Lucy relaxed as she handed the phone back to Frances. "Thank you, you have saved my life — I am Lucy by the way."

"Frances, and I am so pleased you have sorted things out. It's really quite frightening how you just cannot foresee or plan for such a delay as this."

Lucy asked her what was her plan, where was she on her way to or from and Frances explained that she was going to meet her friend in Denham, just the other side of where the accident must have happened. "Do you think your friend will know what has happened?" Lucy enquired. Fortunately, she had been able to contact India and even more fortunately they had planned the ceremony for the following day so it wasn't a huge problem that she would be delayed.

"We are going to be joined together in a civil partnership. We were hoping they would pass the law so that we could marry, but maybe in a year or two they will. In the meantime, we are going to Uxbridge tomorrow and we will take our vows." Lucy was surprised because Frances looked normal. Well, you are normal aren't you, you just don't have sex with men. Her voice did not hint at how incredible she thought it was as she congratulated Frances and wished her all the very best. They heard the car engines start up ahead and Lucy thanked Frances again and went back to her car.

Frances turned the ignition key and started to gradually move forward. All good things come to those who wait, she thought to herself, and paradise will be just a little later than advertised. She knew what she wanted, and India wanted her in the same way. It never occurred to Frances that she had actually wrecked a lot of lives in her pursuit of her own happiness. She seemed completely unaware of how she had made so many people unhappy. Why would she, she was who she was and she couldn't be any other way. She didn't choose her sexuality. I am as God made me, she thought, and there is absolutely nothing wrong with that.

25

Ken and Dawn Campbell had had an exhausting weekend. They knew it would be a difficult and emotional one. Dawn's mother was ninety-one when she had died, the mother to six very different children who had all married and had children who had children of their own. One brother had died but the rest of the family were at the funeral in Kent and, as Dawn's mother had said long ago, when someone dies, watch for the vultures to descend from nowhere.

She had been a very caring mother to all her children, always having time to listen, delighting in their children and the great-grandchildren were her special favourites. You shouldn't have favourites in a family but all of them knew that Wendy was the chosen one. It was Wendy this and Wendy that and yet Wendy was the daughter who did least for her mother. It had all fallen to Dawn, because she was the nearest — until she moved to Slough — to call in as her mother got older to make sure all was well.

Estelle Cunningham had enjoyed good health, worked in the charity shop in town and went to church and that gave Dawn peace of mind because her friends in the congregation always looked out for her. One or other would give her a lift if she wanted to go to a special service, or even just to the daily mass. Her husband, Ernie, had died many years ago and she had carried on regardless, mustn't grumble was her motto. She was much loved by those who knew her, and by most of the family. It was an open secret that her daughter-in-law, Anne, was always cold towards her, and Estelle often wondered if it was because her son, Edward, would call her most days — bit of the green-eyed monster she thought.

Ken's job moved him to Slough, a good promotion, and Dawn knew she had to go with him, indeed she wanted to go with him. After a family discussion a carer was employed to go in in the mornings to get her up and one to put her to bed. Dawn wasn't too concerned because she knew the network of friends would pop in and now maybe other members of the family, who lived no more than forty minutes away, would take a turn in helping out.

It worked well and Estelle never complained about anything, always pleased to hear from the family but her hearing was going and a telephone call was becoming increasingly frustrating because she just didn't hear. Another family conference was arranged. Well, that is Dawn, Edward and Julian got together to decide the next step as Estelle was not really coping. It was after a fall in the kitchen when she had got up in the night and laid there until the carer came in in the morning, they decided something had to be done.

'Mother is not going in a home', was the voice of Anthony, the son she hardly ever saw even though he was an hour and a half away. She is not going to sit in a room with loads of old dears smelling of wee and half daft. Dawn asked him would he like his mother to come and live with him, would he be able to take care of her, he and his upmarket lady-who-lunched wife? Obviously not, but it will be over my dead body she goes in a home. Oh, for goodness sake thought Dawn, what a complete egit. None of them relished the thought but it was the only practical solution. No one could move in and just popping in now and then was not going to solve the fact that she could have another fall and lay for hours before being found.

Julian was the eldest son and he was worried about the financial side of things. Dawn had found out that the council would pay the fees and when Estelle's house was sold, whenever that would be, the council would take the cost of the care out of the estate. This calmed Julian down and he voted in favour of her going into a home and Anthony was basically outvoted. It was left to Dawn, with Edward, to go to Kent for the weekend to source a home. They found one where they didn't actually gag at the smell, in fact it was really very pleasantly appointed, a large old building that had once been a boarding school. The room they selected for her was small but with a beautiful view onto a rose garden with the essential en suite toilet facilities. Estelle obviously couldn't see the view and Dawn explained that the family felt she should come and try staying there for couple of weeks holiday, to see if she liked someone doing the cooking for her. Dawn had seen the home-cooked lunches and special teas being prepared and the family would organise the decorating of her home. It was a lie but she knew Estelle would kick at the idea of 'going into a home'. Estelle said she would give it a go but she only liked magnolia coloured paint and they were not to change the layout of the furniture.

Dawn stayed in Estelle's house for a week, visiting three days out of seven while the other days were covered, to Dawn's shame, by friends of Estelle from the church. No sign of Julian or Anthony, you would have thought they would come just to see how their mother was settling in, but then why would they when they had never bothered before? Edward had been with Dawn when they had found the home and Estelle's pension was paid directly to the home and her considerable savings would fund the £1,000 a week, fee. You could imagine the face on Anne when she knew how much of her husband's inheritance was disappearing — and it would not be necessary to sell the house to fund the home for a while.

Dawn and Ken visited once a week at the weekend, if it was possible and if Ken had to go away on business Dawn went on her own. She was pleased to see how well cared for her mother was. Clean freshly ironed clothes and always a vase of flowers on the table. She did her nails for her and the hairdresser visited once a week. All in all she felt more relaxed than for a long time and it was a complete and utter shock when the home called to say her mother had suffered a stroke and could Dawn and the family come as soon as possible.

Dawn and Ken drove immediately to Kent and the rest of Estelle's children were at her bedside when she made a kind of rattling sound and there was no more, her frail body didn't move, her chest didn't rise and she was at peace.

Dawn thanked Pat, the lady in charge of the home, for her kindness to her mother during her stay. Pat told her they would make the necessary arrangements to take Estelle to the morgue and gave her a booklet, a bereavement guide, offering her condolences and saying she would be in touch.

The family went to the nearest pub and all looked rather shell-shocked as they sipped their drinks. Dawn was shocked, but not surprised, when Anne immediately said, "Well, where's the will?"

Edward glared at her. "Mum always said Mr Pegden of the solicitors in Maidstone held all her papers and her will is with him," Dawn said. All of a sudden, she felt desperately sad, her dear mum had died and who could think of anything but loss and what she had meant to them, and then to ask about the will! Ken comforted her as the tears streamed down her face.

"We will be staying in Mum's house to sort things out, there is always a lot to do when someone dies," Ken said.

"Really?" Anne piped up. "And why you, did Estelle — she had never called her mum — appoint you to do this?"

"She told me ages ago that Edward and I would be the ones to sort things after she had passed, but it will all be in the will Anne," Dawn said in a very tired voice.

Edward could not hide his fury. "That is quite enough Anne. Mum has only just taken her last breath and you disgust me. Dawn, it's good of you to stay, I have a business to run and the rest of us are committed so thank you, and you Ken. We will make our way back now and we must all keep in touch with each other. Dawn, do you need any money to set the ball rolling, I am sure Mum will have made such provision to arrange the funeral etc?"

"Thank you, Edward," Ken replied to his question. "We will be fine and as soon as we have been in touch with Pegden we will let everyone know what is going on."

They went their separate ways and Dawn couldn't quite believe that no one seemed in any way devastated by the events of the past three hours. Everyone just seemed to have taken it in their stride, except her, who experienced a feeling of being in a huge vacuum, facing an enormous emptiness and loss.

Mr Pegden was a dapper little man in his three-piece pin-striped suit, shiny black shoes and shiny face, a pair of glasses balancing on his shiny bony nose. He expressed his sympathy to Dawn and Ken and told them that Estelle had appointed her and Edward as executors of her will. It was a straightforward division of assets between the five surviving children, James's share was to go to his widow. Mr Pegden went on to say that they may not have been aware that their mother had accumulated considerable wealth as an author. "Mr Pegden, forgive me, but my mother was never an author. Surely, I would have known, when did she write, how long ago, did she publish her work?" The questions tumbled from Dawn, completely taken aback by this revelation.

Mr Pegden seemed delighted to be able to impart such information. "Mrs Campbell, your mother was well known in literary circles, are you aware of the author, Donald P Sycamore?"

"I am," said Ken. "He writes rather good, rather graphic murder mysteries as I recall."

"Yes, a very good author. That is the pen name of your mother, Mrs Campbell."

Dawn and Ken looked at each other. "My mother, writing murder mysteries, being famous as an author. Why didn't she say? Why did she carry on living in her bungalow when, if she was successful, she could have had all kinds of help, easily affordable? Why did it have to be a secret?"

"She came to see me about twenty years ago. She started very late in life, she had a huge amount of material gathered through her own life, from when she was in the war in the Blitz in London through good times and bad. It was when her husband died, she began to write and I remember her bringing me her first book. I have a signed copy in my study at home, I feel very privileged that she chose me to confide in, and of course, she went from strength to strength. She never disclosed her true identity, she never gave interviews or had anything to do with publicity. That was her secret. She used to tell me that if people knew who she was they may see their personality in some of her characters in her books, and she would chuckle at the thought. Now she has passed, God rest her soul, her secret can be revealed. She was a very wealthy woman and all of her children will receive in excess of £500,000 cash and the deeds to the house in Scotland, well actually it is a castle. She based one of her books on it after she went there on a coach tour. She liked it so much that she invested two million pounds to buy it." Mr Pegden really rather enjoyed being able to divulge such information, not often he had had the pleasure of working for such a wealthy client and he himself had been admirably rewarded for his work on her behalf.

Dawn and Ken slumped in their chairs. It was very difficult to absorb such information. Dawn could not see how she had never seen evidence of drafts of books or writings. Her mother had learned computer skills many years ago when she worked in an office in Maidstone. She had one in the house and Dawn always smiled to herself at the thought of her mum trying to get to grips with the Internet and emails. She never did, didn't want to be connected to that kind of stuff, just happy to be able to type. Dawn felt sad that there had come a time when she couldn't see to type and had to leave the bungalow to go to the home.

Mr Pegden allowed time for the dust to settle from the bombshell. "Your mother earned a considerable amount, the standard seven percent royalty on every paperback and of late, with the advent of e-books, twenty-five percent on every five pound e-book. Authors receive royalty cheques every six months and all the money from the sale of her books was placed in a totally separate account, of which I was the administrator while she was alive. All tax matters were handled by our accountant who knew nothing of the true identity of Donald P Sycamore. There was talk of a television series of her famous detective, and that is something you will need to progress."

Dawn held Ken's hand. Nothing was making any sense. She couldn't grasp the fact, and yes, it was a fact, that her dear old mum was capable of writing books that sold all over the world, and never told anyone, not a soul except her friend Mr Pegden. "Mr Pegden, I do apologise, I am absolutely dumbfounded. Thank you so much for being my mother's confidant, for being scrupulous in your dealings with her and for keeping her confidence. She must have had a great deal of respect for you to make you the keeper of her secret. Were you ever asked about Donald P Sycamore, did anyone ever want to do an article on him, publicity etc?"

"No Mrs Campbell. When the first novel was published, and it was a shock to your mother that she was so successful at her first attempt, she made it very clear that Donald P Sycamore lived in Florida, USA, with his wife and craved anonymity. No interviews could be given and certainly no television interviews. I am not sure who the photograph is on the sleeve, but it is of a rather handsome fifty-something man." Mr Pegden smiled at the last revelation. He and Estelle had had great fun selecting the photograph and enhancing it, the publishers had wanted some information to put on the cover.

Mr Pegden buzzed his secretary and asked for a tray of tea. He would miss the banter with Estelle. He had been to see her in the home on several occasions and they would chat over old times, and he again promised her that only on her death would her secret be revealed. She had enjoyed a wonderful life and was so pleased to be able to leave such a substantial legacy to her children. She knew they would make sure their children and their children's children would enjoy the luxury of a financial cushion. Money was not the root of all evil, it was the love of money, Estelle had thought wryly and a picture of Edward's wife came into her head when she thought such thoughts.

Ken and Dawn felt sad, elated, bewildered and very tired. Ken knew her mother's death was affecting Dawn more than she let on, and although this was amazing news, it was still quite something to take on board. All sorts of questions were crowding into his head, this was a life changing sum of money for all of the siblings and he was grateful for Mr Pegden's professionalism in handling Estelle's affairs.

Mr Pegden broke the silence. "Mrs Campbell, there are a lot of things you have to do following your mother's death and I will of course be happy to administer the estate if you would wish it."

"Mr Pegden, I would be honoured if you would process the estate. I can think of no one better suited."

"I will start the procedure Mrs Campbell. Please take my card and don't hesitate to call me at any time."

Ken and Dawn left the office and went into a nearby coffee shop to try to get some semblance of order as to what to do next. "Edward must be told at once," Dawn said. "Can you just imagine the lovely Anne on hearing the news? Should everyone be told immediately, oh Ken, what a responsibility."

Ken ordered two coffees and two toasted teacakes. "I think we will have to ask Mr Pegden the correct way forward Dawn. Obviously, Edward could have been the one to have been told had he gone himself to Mr Pegden so we will have to take his legal advice. I do know, from reading the book the lady at the home gave us, that we have to tell the family doctor, sort a funeral director — wonder if there was anything in the will about that — and we have to get a medical certificate of cause of death. Then we have to register the death." They drank their coffee in silence and were both surprised how ready they were for the teacakes.

"One step at a time, Ken, I will call Mr Pegden now and ask about when we should tell the family the amazing news. Whether it should just be Edward as he is the other executor. Also, don't know what kind of funeral Mum wanted, he would know that from the will wouldn't he?" Mr Pegden confirmed that Edward should be told immediately and he would call him himself for the sake of protocol. Estelle had wanted a Church of England service with no particular order of service other than she wanted *All things bright and beautiful* and Mr Timms was the funeral director she had requested. Dawn gave him Edward's number and they left the coffee shop and went to Estelle's house to try and work their way through the list.

Edward took the call from Mr Pegden and was as amazed and baffled as Dawn had been. He immediately telephoned her and Mr Pegden had told him that once the formalities had been sorted and the funeral had taken place the other beneficiaries would be told of their inheritance. It was a straightforward cause of death and after the funeral he would arrange a meeting at his offices for the beneficiaries to be informed. Dawn and Edward felt that due to the enormous amount of money involved it would be appropriate for Mr Pegden to reveal the contents of the will to all concerned.

The funeral was well attended and two people from the church spoke of Estelle with great warmth and

Dawn managed to read *Death is nothing at all* and only faltered slightly as she looked at the wicker coffin covered in white carnations. It just looked so small.

Needless to say, Anne had gone totally over the top, a sheer silk black dress with a huge black brimmed hat and heels she could just totter around in. Her perfectly manicured nails were painted in the obligatory blood red nail varnish which Estelle would have said was in the worst possible taste. She had confided to Dawn that she was glad Anne made Edward happy, but she did wonder how much she actually cost Edward to make him happy.

The local pub had put on a very good lunch and Edward and Dawn had decided that champagne should be served for the toast. They had decided not to reveal their mother's secret, not until all the family had been told, and Ken spoke very warmly of a wonderful mother and grandmother and friend, who would be greatly missed. Anne had rather a lot of champagne and Dawn was dreading as to how she would behave. She needn't have worried. After a few drinks Anne was talking animatedly to anyone who would listen about how much she would miss her darling Estelle.

On a chilly Friday morning, the family gathered in the conference room of Pegden's, family solicitors. Coffee and biscuits were offered and the five children of Estelle sat, with their partners, and waited to hear what Mr Pegden had to say.

You could have heard a pin drop as Mr Pegden concluded the reading of the will. They stared, some open mouthed in disbelief but all completely dumbfounded by the life their mother had led. Edward physically squirmed when Anne said, "Right, what shall we do with the castle — where is it, can we go and see it — who has the keys?"

Mr Pegden had heard it all before. He had seen greed in many different forms, anxiety, desperation, hope — but this lady was one of the worst. "The keys are in my possession and I have arranged for a brochure to be made available to all of you — it was the one used by your late mother when she brought it. It is in need of some repair, she had hoped to refurbish it and use it as a kind of country retreat in her old age, but Donald P Sycamore was far too busy. You will all need to reach agreement as to what you will do in this regard as it is yours equally."

"Is it right that James's widow should have anything? She didn't come to the funeral, did she?" Anne's clipped curt tone was quite unbelievable.

"She lives in Australia, Anne, with her two sons. She is finding it hard to manage and I had a lovely letter from her saying how sad she was that Mum had died but please to understand she couldn't afford to come to England for the funeral — I am just so thrilled that Mum's legacy will help her out enormously." Edward was seriously embarrassed. There were so many things he had learned about his wife over the past year, she really wasn't the woman he had married. She seemed all bitter and twisted yet it was she who didn't want children. Dirty, messy, noisy creatures, totally interfering with your leisure time. He didn't think her outburst deemed a reply and just raised his eyes to heaven, but he knew what the rest of the family thought about her, and he couldn't blame them in the slightest.

Mr Pegden confirmed that it was Estelle's wish that the estate be divided six ways and he would inform Phillipa of her inheritance. He would keep her up to speed regarding the sale of Estelle's house and whatever was the outcome over the future of the castle.

Julian was feeling faint. He could not grasp his good fortune. He could not believe that this amazing amount of money was going to come to him, plus the spinoffs of the sale of the house and contents. It was as if his mother knew just how desperate his situation had become — but no, all were treated the same. He doubted if anyone else in that room could feel the most amazing sense of relief that was flooding over him. He wasn't a gambler as on the horses or any sport, he gambled at the casino online. He was now in real trouble yet he blamed the television with all the advertising to bet, to gamble, preying on people's weakness — and Julian was very weak. He felt as though he was anonymous, no one would know that it was him betting on the roll of the dice — very ignorant he now realised. He had been contacted at first online, a polite email, requesting he settle his outstanding account. He ignored it, he would soon win enough to get that back but unfortunately his losses accrued until he was completely stunned by a phone call at work suggesting that he settle the account today — now — right now. He actually looked around him at the people in his office, thinking it must be one of them, someone who knew about his online gambling. After he had put the phone down it immediately rang again and he was told a Mr Jones was at reception for his urgent appointment. Mr Jones greeted Julian with a firm handshake and a look in his eye that spoke volumes.

They had walked out of the offices and Mr Jones suggested they go straight to the bank. Julian had withdrawn all that he could from his account and it was a drop in the ocean. Mr Jones suggested they go for a coffee, and told him that he had one week to get the £200,000 he owed to the company. Julian put the house up as collateral, his wife's father's legacy had settled the outstanding mortgage, and he was able to settle the outstanding account. He was absolutely terrified Cynthia would find out, but when he thought rationally, she was totally unaware of what was going on. All this had happened six months ago and he now had an even bigger problem with the accrued interest on the loan. He had extended it to pay the interest, and he was in a downward spiralling hole and the light at the end of the tunnel was becoming very dim.

Thus, it was the £500,000 would completely pay off all his debts leaving £76,000 which in itself was a tidy sum to play with. However, finally, Julian had learned his lesson and would not 'play' with this money, oh no.

Anthony was already making plans. Never mind pay off the mortgage, more like a boat, a really fine boat, which he could keep in the harbour at Harwich, a few miles from his house. He had of course, not even discussed this with Madeleine which was just as well because she was planning a trip to New Zealand and a designer label shopping spree. For now, they were still in the company of Mr Pegden and it was Dawn who suggested they might like to go to their mother's house to see if they would like to take any mementos to remind them of her.

Wendy was secretly fuming. She felt they all knew she was the 'favourite', she should have been signalled out for a special bequest. She stayed behind when the others left to go to the house and spoke to Mr Pegden. "Mr Pegden, I was particularly close to my mother, I am sure she would have told you how special I was to her — and I wondered if there was a part of the will you have not disclosed? I thought she would have written an amount that I was to have, just for me?"

Again, Mr Pegden was not surprised — greed — for goodness sake they had all gone out of the room £500,000 better off and still this woman wanted more. "I am sorry, your name?"

"Wendy, Wendy Foreman."

"Mrs Foreman I have read the will, the entire will and there is absolutely no mention of anyone being singled out for any special bequest, at least not in the family."

Wendy could not conceal her anger. "I find that very hard to believe, after all the times we had together. Well, I bid you good day Mr Pegden."

"Goodbye Mrs Foreman," replied a very tired Mr Pegden.

Wendy drove to the house. The money would certainly come in very useful, but wait, let's hope the rest of the family hadn't taken anything Mother would have wanted me to have, she thought, as she walked through the door.

Ken and Dawn watched as Anne went through the jewellery box. "Have you taken anything Dawn — before we came that is?"

Dawn could not really believe her ears. "Anne, mum's jewellery is as it was left by her, in the box. I believe Mr Pegden said I was to have her engagement ring which he has in his possession. I really don't care what you think, Anne, take what you want." She was very pleased she hadn't actually told her to sod off, although the way she was feeling she could have used a much stronger word and no one would have blamed her.

Finally, everyone had taken what they thought they would like although why on earth Wendy had taken the entire contents of the airing cupboard, down to the tea towels, did cause Dawn a certain amount of amusement.

Each of the children had been handed the brochure of the castle and in it was an envelope enclosing a cheque for £500,000.

Edward suggested that they all meet in a month, a date to be agreed, to discuss what was to be done about the castle. He guessed they would all have different ideas, but they all had enough to contend with right now without getting further embroiled. He had asked Mr Pegden to appoint an estate agent and Dawn and Ken had said they would stay on until the Monday to box up anything that would be needed for the charity shop. Edward added that he and Anne would also stay on in their hotel for the weekend to help in any way they could. This had caused Anne to stop her search of the bedroom drawers to query exactly why. Edward said enough had been left to Dawn to do in the past and four of them could make great inroads in sorting the house for the sale.

It was getting late and Anthony, Julian and finally Wendy had left the house. They were going to stay the Friday night in their accommodation and drive back to their respective homes on the Saturday morning. Edward and Anne left and Dawn and Ken got some fish and chips and crashed into bed. The four of them worked all day Saturday and Sunday, and on the Sunday night went to the local pub where they enjoyed a good old roast beef dinner and delicious apple pie and toasted their amazing mum. Dawn was pleased at the way they had rallied together to get the house presentable, even though she had often found Anne rummaging through boxes, looking for some lost golden locket Dawn thought smiling to herself.

Edward and Anne were going to make an early start, they were going to Reading to see Anne's sister and would stop for breakfast en route. Dawn and Ken had decided they would leave around seven as well, but a last minute look around, reminded Ken they hadn't read the meters and he wanted to turn off the water.

They were approaching junction four on the M4 and saw the 'caution accident' sign flashing and the speed limit was reduced to forty. "I thought it was getting busier, traffic is really heavy in all three lanes. Wonder what the accident is?" Ken remarked to a sleepy Dawn.

"Accident, which way would Anne and Edward have gone Ken?"

"I am not sure, I don't even know where the accident has happened but they would have been ahead of us on the M4 if they were going to Donna's house. Try Edward's mobile Dawn, God I hope they are OK."

Dawn rang the mobile and it went straight to answerphone. "Could be no signal, out of range but then Edward always has it switched off when he is driving, he always intended to get a hands' free" Dawn replied.

As Edward finally lapsed into unconsciousness, he was trying to remember what he was shouting at Anne, what was he saying? He remembered turning to face her, his voice screaming at her, her face staring straight ahead, oblivious to his words when there was an enormous bang, the windscreen caved in and a huge fountain of blood spurted out of Anne's face and it all went dark.

They cut Anne out of the car. Her head was almost severed from her neck, the shard of glass had gone through her throat and embedded itself in the seat. Edward had the steering wheel pushed so hard into his groin they thought they would have to amputate his legs, but after cutting away the top of the car they had room to manoeuvre and lift the wheel off his body and eased him onto the stretcher. Anne's body was covered on a gurney and put in the ambulance alongside Edward who was immediately attached to drips and pads were applied to stem the flow of blood as the ambulance sped to the hospital.

Dawn and Ken sat for three hours in the traffic. They had been about half an hour behind the accident and diversions were not in place as they watched the emergency vehicles rushing to and fro. "That could have been us in there, Ken," Dawn muttered, almost to herself. "If you hadn't read the meters and taken time to find the stopcock it would have been us. Oh my God Ken, it could be Edward in that mess. Wish he would answer his phone, please Edward, turn on the bloody phone."

26

Kiri Wallace grabbed the mobile on its first ring. "Hello."

"Kiri, oh Kiri, thank God I can talk to you. How are you baby? I am so sorry I haven't been in touch, so much is going on here and I have hardly left Sarah's side."

"Clive, oh I have missed you, I can't think I can't eat, I am so worried for you both. How is she doing, is she conscious, does she know you are there?"

"No darling, she is unconscious with so many drips. There is a swelling in her brain and this can constrict blood supply and destroy brain tissue so they are going to have to medically induce a comatose state. It will mean she will be in a very deep unconscious state but the brain can rest and the swelling should decrease and this will prevent, hopefully, some or all brain damage from occurring. Believe me, Kiri, I have been there and back with the surgeon, he has been so kind and so thorough explaining the procedure to me. It will at least give her more of a chance. Kiri, she looks no different. It is so strange, apart from bruising and a few superficial cuts, she looks just the same." He stopped himself from actually saying, just like my Sarah.

Kiri cursed the phone line. She really couldn't tell how Clive was feeling, his voice was flat and it made the distance between them vast. He might as well have been on the moon. There were no 'I miss yous', no can't wait to get back. She was beginning to think this would end it. She could never bear that. Not now, not now they had it all — well almost all.

"I am just so sorry Clive, but at least it sounds as if inducing a coma will help her to heal. Are there any other injuries, the impact must have been enormous?"

"They thought she had some spinal damage and they have scanned as best they can in the position she is in, but it appears not. Broken ribs from the airbag and thank God no internal damage. At first, they thought the broken rib had punctured the lung but again she has been so lucky. It could have been so much worse, Kiri, I could have lost her." His last words struck like ice into her heart. How could she interpret that in any other way other than — I don't want to lose her. Oh my God, oh no, please Clive, please remember us, please think on all the good times we had. Her head was pounding and she couldn't find the words. She couldn't come across as needy, not as but what about me? What about us?

"Kiri, are you still there?"

"Yes Clive, there was a kind of hitch on the line," she lied.

"Kiri, I really don't know what I am going to do. The surgeon cannot give me a prognosis time wise. He said sometimes, if they have caught everything in time, and it was a matter of hours, it can be only a week and things can begin to sort out. I am going to stay at the hospital tonight and then probably with Adrian. She is not on the danger list but obviously in a serious condition in intensive care. I will at least be able to work in the London office, once I can be assured I am not needed at the hospital, and obviously then we can be in touch in the normal way. I am just so sorry this has happened Kiri, and at the moment I cannot see me getting to New York for a while. I am so sorry but I just have to be here, you can see that sweetheart?"

She tried very hard to control her voice, she wanted it to come across as warm and caring but a very brittle sound emitted when she said, "I will be fine darling, just hang on in there. Clive, I have to go, but come back when you can."

"I will Kiri, and you be strong too. I love you."

Normally they couldn't bear to say goodbye, they would hang on and hang on until laughingly one of them would hang up — you first, no you. She really didn't know what to do. She didn't know how to react, how should she react, shouldn't he be more for her, poor Kiri, we can't be together for a while type of touch. It suddenly seemed that she really was second fiddle. His wife suddenly mattered more than her. It had never been that way. They had their life, their wonderful times together and the wife word was never said and never considered. Their life together was far more important, he had made it so. He had told her they had a future.

Had he forgotten all that they had done together. All the times they had spent in each other's arms. The sex. He surely must remember and miss that. She loved sex. She honestly felt that it was the most amazing feeling to reach that point where you ached for release and the build-up, the sheer rhythm of wanting and desire to finally breathlessly reach somewhere beyond your physical body, pushing until there was no more. Just a shuddering juddering collapse into complete fulfilment.

She hoped that wasn't all there was to their relationship. It was the core. Clive said she was just so fuckable, so uninhibited, he matched her passion and maybe they both had the edge because it was clandestine, openly clandestine. At first that was what the attraction was. It was actually against the rules.

Kiri had been in several relationships before she met Clive. She was now thirty-three and until now she had never thought about her age. She had always thought her future would be with Clive. They would be together and he would give her a child. They would be a complete family and he would not travel to Europe any more. That had been on the cards for some time, the president of the company had said to Clive so many times couldn't he persuade Sarah to up sticks and come to New York. Clive had always said she had the family and grandchildren and although it was only five hours away, she also had a career of her own. It was the career of her own that had really driven the gulf between them. Kiri was quick to realise she was actually on a winner here, and then she fell in love with the man. She never intended to, or deep down, did she, was it all part of her plan to settle down, finally. She felt sure Clive loved her, he told her so many times and when he held her at the airport, she felt he truly did. Now, what a difference a day makes. How can everything that was so settled, so secure and so hopeful, be changed in a wink of an eye. That was all it was, a twist of fate that it was Sarah's car on the road at that time.

Kiri's friends had all tried to tell her she was on a road to nowhere. He would never leave his wife, they never do. They tried to include her in their special holidays, Christmas was the worst time, but he was always there for Thanksgiving and they would celebrate with her friends and their partners and it was as if they themselves were together forever.

She really didn't know where to turn. She looked around the apartment and Clive was everywhere. His clothes, his books and there was the smell of him. She threw herself on the bed and buried her head in his pillow. She couldn't cry, for the moment she was just empty and she suddenly realised that she had no rights, no real hold on the man she loved. His wife owned him and she was his lover in New York. Not partner, just someone he screwed and left and for the first time in three years Kiri wondered if he ever made love to Sarah when he was in London. For the first time in three years, she realised she maybe didn't matter quite as much as she thought she did.

Clive put the phone in his pocket. He was glad Kiri was OK about things. After all, what else could he do? He was dreadfully worried about Sarah, and maybe there was a tinge of guilt, just a smidgen, if he had been in London would it have happened? Of course, he couldn't have prevented her going on her business trip, but as she was being cut out of the car he was in bed with Kiri, and that did not sit well. Suddenly the conscience pricked. Maybe, after all this time, it had been wrong and all the while his thoughts did not once turn to Kiri and how she might be feeling. No, this was his wife, the mother of his children and a wonderful grandmother. Please God, please let her pull through and his guilty tears ran down his face.

27

Victoria Bartlett was sitting in the lounge, actually indulging herself looking at a magazine illustrating new and exciting ways to decorate your home. She leafed through the pages showing so many variations on a theme and realised their home needed none of this. It was a Georgian house, set in its own grounds with enormous windows and rooms with high ceilings and they had both fallen in love with it. The children had enjoyed a wonderful childhood there and although they both realised it was really far too big for the two of them, they loved it too much to move. Victoria was a great hostess and her dinner parties were always a great success, plus the children loved coming to stay with their little ones. It was a wonderful family home, and a far cry from their humble beginnings in the bedsit in Bristol.

Her daughter never got tired of hearing how they met. Samantha at twenty years of age was about the same age as Victoria when she first saw John Bartlett. She was in the launderette in Bristol and was so engrossed in her book that she hadn't realised her washing had finished in the dryer. John was so mesmerised by the most beautiful girl he had ever seen, shiny black hair tumbling over her face as she intently read her book, her long legs stretching out in front of her in quite skinny denim cords that he was totally unaware that he was putting his washing in the dryer which still held Victoria's. He put the coins in the slot and just stared at her. He found himself quite unable to take his eyes off her and when she looked up he was visibly shaken by the intensity of the most beautiful palest blue eyes blinking under huge eyelashes. "Oh, oh I am so sorry," she said in the loveliest voice he had ever heard — really from now on everything would be the loveliest, the most beautiful, the most amazing when applied to her —" I think your washing is in the dryer I was using and I think mine is still in there." John looked at the dryer for the first time to see something pink and flimsy whizzing around his dark blue jeans.

"Oh no, I am the one who should be sorry, I just put mine in because I thought it was empty. I am so sorry," and his boyish grin made her heart flip as they laughingly pulled the washing into the basket and sorted it out. He just lumped his into his holdall and she was folding hers very carefully before placing it in the bag. "At least let me buy you a coffee to say sorry for the inconvenience — that is unless you have to be somewhere right now."

"I don't have anything on tonight, I was just catching up on some revision and I would love a coffee thank you." Their cup of coffee lasted two hours and neither noticed. They were so busy learning about each other, both university students, John studying marketing and law and Victoria psychology. They discovered they were one street apart and both marvelled they had never met before, considering they were both in their second year at the same university.

John looked at his watch. "Goodness, time has flown, are you hungry — they do a lasagne here which is wonderful, or maybe you are vegetarian? They do a veggie one too."

She smiled. "I am a meat eater and it sounds a wonderful idea, but only if we go Dutch, we are both in the same boat as students after all." The cafe owner was quite pleased he hadn't made an attempt to clear their cups and sent the order to the kitchen. John was right, it was a delicious meal and they both cleaned their plates.

Needless to say, John would not hear of Victoria contributing anything to the cost of the meal. "Very well then, thank you, but if you are free at the weekend, I would love to cook for you. I can do amazing things with chicken and vegetables if that's OK?"

"Thank you, that would be lovely and Saturday night is just fine. Let me walk you to your flat and I will know where to find you." They walked the short distance to her flat, John carrying her laundry bag with his slung over his shoulder. They said their goodbyes, both equally smitten, and arranged to meet next Saturday at seven p.m.

John was completely over the moon, besotted. This girl was stunning, black hair and blue eyes, a rare commodity in his book and so elegant, so tall and slim and such a wonderful laughing beautiful mouth. He felt she might be attracted to him, she seemed at ease in his company and she had invited him for next Saturday which he guessed would take forever to come. In fact, the week went quite fast for both of them, both having 'hand ins' to be made by the end of the week and Victoria had a particularly in-depth seminar to attend and was still writing it up at midnight on Friday night. She went shopping in the morning and brought all she would need. It was her signature dish, she could do it with her eyes closed and she brought some fresh strawberries for dessert and a bottle of wine. She hoped he liked white wine, and if he wanted beer, she had some lager in her fridge from when her brother, Barry, had come to stay.

There was a wonderful smell of garlic coming from the oven when she opened the front door to John. He was holding a beautiful bouquet of lemon roses and presented her with a chilled bottle of white wine. She managed to find a vase at the back of the cupboard and while he opened the wine, she arranged them and put them on the side table. It was a one-bedroom flat and her grant just about covered the rent. She had shared a house at the start of the year but it had been hassle, one of the girls wanted her friend to move in and Victoria took the opportunity to say she would go and was lucky enough to find the flat. It worked so much better, no quarrels, no one not doing their share.

They learned a lot about each other, John was one of three boys and they lived in Surrey and Victoria was a sister to Juliette and her family lived in Cornwall. They were both enjoying their courses, challenging yet satisfying and each hoped to achieve a first. The summer break was two weeks away and Victoria had lined up her summer job waitressing in the students' pub in Bristol and John was going back to Surrey and planned to work on his father's farm. He had done it for the first summer and earned enough for him to go to New York for five days. He told her he had found it the most amazing place, it had to be the future for him, the buzz and the atmosphere had grabbed him the moment he set foot in Times Square. He was hoping to get an undergraduate placement there, but an awful lot depended on his last year at uni.

Victoria's garlic chicken with new potatoes was superb and the strawberries and cream went down a treat. They finished John's bottle of wine and were halfway down Victorias. They sat on her tiny two-seater sofa and John put his arm around her shoulders. "Victoria, I have had the most wonderful evening, you are a great cook and a wonderful hostess. I have had the best time thank you so much." And it was the most natural thing in the world to kiss her. She kissed him back, a spark fissioned between them and they both felt this was something very special.

John pulled himself away. "Let's do the dishes, I can't leave you with all that in the kitchen."

"No, let's just leave them, we can do them in the morning." So it was, they went to the bedroom as though they had been together forever and there was no awkward fumbling — it was as if this was what they were destined to do from the word go — and neither expected it to be so perfect, so timely and so amazingly complete.

Victoria had really surprised herself. She did not make a habit of going to bed on the first date, and she said this to John in the morning who laughed and said actually it was not the first date, it was the second.

They both finished their exams, both feeling totally exhausted and relieved when they were finally over, now just the waiting for the results and also a parting. They had become inseparable and John was dreading going back to Surrey and Victoria wished with all her might he could find some work in Bristol. Perhaps his father could maybe ask the other boys to work instead of John.

"Victoria, I have been thinking," John said on the last morning as he was due to leave that afternoon. "Would you mind dreadfully if I didn't go to Surrey? I called my dad and he said it wasn't desperate that I work, it was more of a mutual way of me earning money and I enquired at the pizza place and they said I can work there, ten to four and eight to midnight."

Victoria jumped up and whirled around the bed screaming and laughing. "Mind dreadfully? I would mind dreadfully if you went darling. Oh fantastic, I was so worried about us being apart, you might find a jolly farm girl and take her to the hayloft."

It was John's turn to roar with laughter. "I was thinking you are far too gorgeous to be left for a whole summer without me being there to have fun with." They both collapsed and rolled around the bed so very, very, happy. "I love you, Victoria Goldthorpe, I love you I love you I love you."

"I love you, John Bartlett, and I am the happiest girl in the whole wide world."

That summer was an endless whirl of late nights and early mornings and Sundays they had all to themselves and they renewed the tenancy agreement on the flat and were ready for their third and final year of uni. They had both got good results, they were equally thrilled for each other and that set the scene for a year of hard work and a lot of cramming for their final year.

John was invited to spend Christmas in Cornwall and he accepted with pleasure and the Goldthorpes were totally smitten with this handsome young man so very much in love with their daughter. Juliette thought he was drop dead gorgeous, and very sexy and Victoria laughed as Juliette brought all her friends round to 'see' John and they all giggled and totally agreed with Juliette that he was delicious.

They went on the train to Paddington then down to Surrey and Victoria was received by John's family with absolute delight. John's dad thought she was a right cracker and his mum was so pleased he had found a 'normal' girl, not one of those druggy things that wore hardly anything even when it was freezing the end of your nose off.

They both worked really hard, it was such a short term really. They had four days at Easter and just studied, went into the town a couple of nights but otherwise heads down. Victoria thought there was so much to study and the last exam was on everything they had done that year — although it was her favourite part of the course, counselling, she worried she would miss something vital and totally flop. John didn't seem deterred. They were both different in the way they approached their finals, John far more relaxed and he gave Victoria space when she fretted and made sure he pulled his weight on the home front, doing the chores while she studied and stressed.

The exams came and went, there were two weeks of parties where people all got very drunk with the sheer relief of the pressure being off and Victoria and John did their fair share of partying.

They graduated with both sets of parents coming to the ceremony, Juliette was the third guest of Victoria and John asked his brother, Luke, to be his. It was a wonderful day, they had both achieved so much and it was just the beginning. John had secured a placement in a London based marketing company. Victoria was secretly pleased that he hadn't gone for New York. He said he would find his feet in London, make his mark and then decide on what the future might be. Victoria had a placement in the London hospital. She was particularly pleased that she would be using her degree and she was going to work alongside a counsellor and hoped that what she had learned at uni would stand her in good stead. Plus, she was near John and they found a very small flat in Muswell Hill and both parents had helped out with the deposit. They had jobs in the evening in the local pub which would hopefully cover their outgoings.

John was soon making great strides. His farming background had stood him in good stead and he had suggested to his father that they turn part of the farm into a kind of adventure park, catering for the young family market. From this he could see potential for catering and advertising farmland holidays. His enthusiasm for all things new and exciting did not go unnoticed and he was offered a promotion to the pharmaceutical side of the business, something he knew nothing about. However, his knack of discovering new approaches to the promotion and marketing of products would challenge him to achieve amazing results.

A year had passed and Victoria was doing very well at the hospital when she was approached by an independent counselling company to join them as a counsellor for young people with problems at home, be they of bereavement or abuse.

All the time they were making their way Victoria and John were as much in love as when they first met and it was on a wintry day at the end of October that

Victoria Goldthorpe said 'I do' to John Bartlett in the tiny church in Goldstithney in Cornwall where they promised to be husband and wife together, until death did them part.

Juliette was a bridesmaid with her cousin, and John's brother Luke was best man and Juliette thought he was gorgeous, like Mr Darcy and as they walked down the aisle together Juliette's mind went into overdrive — but then she had the most amazing imagination.

John was offered a chance to go to New York by the company. The contract was for a year and the excitement in his voice and the sheer energy bursting from him as he asked Victoria did she think they would be able to go ensured she didn't hesitate in the slightest. She had a good reputation in the world of counselling, many clients would see only her and her company gave her their blessing, wishing her well for an amazing opportunity that would challenge them both.

The island of Manhattan is basically New York city. It is a long, thin island, and is split into three main areas: Downtown, Midtown and Uptown. The company John worked for was based in the financial district near the New York Stock Exchange in Downtown New York, a pleasant part of town with lots of high rises, dominated by the twin towers of the World Trade Centre.

John and Victoria fell in love with New York. They found a small apartment in Greenwich Village, a ten-minute cab ride took John to his office and they both loved the Meat Packing district with its trendy bars, restaurants and shops.

John made many friends through his business associates and Victoria enjoyed the company of their wives and partners who took her under their wing. She was thrilled and amazed to be in the heart of such an exciting, vibrant atmosphere. She was introduced to Japanese food in the famous Nobu restaurant and could not believe the Boom Boom Room at the top of the Standard Hotel.

They found their favourite restaurant in Spring Street in Soho, between Downtown and Midtown. John had taken clients there for lunch and Balthazar was a French bistro-style eatery always packed, with a real buzz frequented by business people to socialites, celebrities as well as families. They got to know Stanton Social, on the east side of Manhattan, with lots of sharing plates and went to their first speakeasy bar which they thought was a very trendy thing to do.

They became quite Americanised, and looked forward to their weekends when they would go to Central Park, meeting their friends for drinks and brunch at the Boat House. They loved Central Park, full of people chilling, running, playing sports, such a busy, buzzing yet relaxing place to be. In the summer they would head out to the beaches on Long Island and on Victoria's birthday John surprised her with a weekend stay at the Hamptons and they loved the colonial style houses and looked in awe at the properties which would set you back twenty million dollars.

A lot of John's business associates ran. It was their habit on a Saturday morning for John and Victoria to get up and go for a run along the Hudson River, come back and shower and enjoy a lazy day, although they often gravitated to Sacks on Fifth Avenue and window shopped in the designer stores there.

John's contract was extended and it was just as well because Paul Bartlett was born in New York General four months into the extension. They had hoped he would be born in England but things didn't quite work out that way and they were the proudest mum and dad, not mom, oh no, mum. Their friends became their family as they all rallied round. Both sets of parents went out to see their new grandson and it was as if love could be seen, felt, tasted, all-encompassing this little family, a cocoon of warmth and genuine endearment, they would feel forever. Victoria often recalled the passage read at their wedding, St Paul's letter to the Corinthians, which she chose although she wasn't religious but just felt that the words were so apt to be spoken in the House of God. She often thought how very true those words were.

"Love bears all things, believes all things, hopes all things, endures all things, faith, hope, love abide. These three, but the greatest of these is love."

They were both sad to leave their friends and they missed New York and the way of life when they returned to England but Paul Bartlett took all of Victoria's time and left little time for her to miss that previous life. John had amassed considerable wealth, being very handsomely paid and investing in the stock market to the extent that he could afford to look for a family house. Paul was two years old and patted his mummy's tummy. "Baby, baby," he would shriek out loud, roaring with laughter and Victoria would cuddle him close and hope with all her heart she could love this little person inside her as much as she loved her little boy.

They found Valley View in a sleepy hamlet in Hertfordshire. It stood on the side of a hill, a long winding drive leading to steps with pillars either side to a wide front door opening on to the longest hall Victoria had ever seen. It was a Georgian house and the old sundial in the garden was dated 1710 and they both fell in love with it in an instant. It was in need of a lot of tender loving care. It had not been maintained in a very long time and Victoria's mother felt it was damp and cold and far too much for them to take on with a toddler and another one on the way. A lot of money was spent and not a lot to show for it, their parents thought. They realised John was 'doing rather well' but the roof had had to be totally retiled and the guttering all replaced. The butler's pantry had a crack in it which seemed to go right through the wall into the back kitchen that lead through a passageway to the tack room. The kitchen was just about usable. A huge Aga was in an alcove and that at least warmed the kitchen which had big wooden cupboards all around it and the lino was curling up around the legs of a wooden table with benches either side which could seat eight. The kitchen sink was so deep a washing up bowl was needed and there was another butler sink in the back kitchen which housed a very antiquated gas stove.

The central heating was the next thing and it took three men six weeks to install the radiators and boilers, new tanks and immersion heaters. The six bedrooms were all very large. No en suites of course and John employed an architect to consolidate the bedrooms down to four using the two spares divided into the en suites for the others. A huge family bathroom was on the main landing and halfway down the back stairs was another landing with a bathroom with a really old-fashioned toilet which you pulled with a chain which periodically worked.

Once the basics had been done Victoria came into her own visiting curtain makers and furniture stores. The kitchen had been tastefully converted and the back kitchen was now the utility room and the tack room had been converted to a study where John could hide himself away from Paul who always wanted his daddy for everything.

Mark Bartlett came into the world a bit unexpectedly when Victoria's waters broke in the park as she was pushing Paul on the swing and her friend popped her son and Paul in the back and drove her to the hospital while she tried to get hold of John. He couldn't get there in time for the birth but the pride on his face when he held his second son in his arms was very moving. Mark was totally the opposite to Paul, an enormous amount of curly white hair sitting on top of a round chubby face with brownish eyes the colour of which fluctuated between hazel and dark brown.

Two months later John announced to Victoria that he was going to purchase a pharmaceutical company. He had been dealing with the owner for some time, it was a family run business and John had created a totally new image. It was doing well but the old man was tired and offered John first refusal to buy it. Thus, John Bartlett Pharmaceuticals was born and everything seemed idyllic.

Victoria was thirty-four when Samantha was born. They called her their precious afterthought, she was a complete surprise as both Victoria and John had thought as nothing was happening on the baby front, that would be that and their family was complete with Paul and Mark. John was bowled over by his daughter. He marvelled at her beautiful hands, so perfect and he said to Victoria he was twice as proud to have two beautiful women in his life.

Victoria never believed she would enjoy motherhood as much as she did. She loved to see her children's development and saw things through their eyes and was as excited as them as they discovered new skills and adventures. John worked hard but they always had their Sundays, and this she realised was a luxury to be able to be together, unless of course John was in New York where he had opened another branch of the company.

When Samantha went to secondary school, she found she really did now have time on her hands. John had insisted she get help with the house and twice a week Mrs Johns came and did upstairs on Mondays and downstairs on Fridays and if they were entertaining, she would often come round on a Saturday morning to help prep the vegetables and organise the dining room. It was a large room with huge windows, still with their original shutters which used to be closed when the families of long ago went away for the summer, and the elegant dining table sat twelve with the sideboards and glass cabinets down either side.

Victoria felt she could now take up her career again and when she mentioned it to John, he was sceptical. "Darling, you really don't need to work. We are fortunate that money is not a problem and the family keep you so busy with all the after-school clubs and the evening tutoring with Paul."

"John, I really need to do something and I could just do two mornings a week and see how I get on. The drawing room would be ideal to see clients, it is private and comfortable. I would become more involved with older clients rather than disturbed youngsters. I am fully qualified and I would love to do it." There was really no contest and Victoria set about establishing herself as a counsellor once more with the added bonus that people could come to her in complete privacy. She contacted the hospital where she began her career and they were only too pleased to refer patients. There was a budget that would cover it and she threw herself into her work, finding that really, she could do with three mornings a week, but settled for the time being with just the two.

Paul didn't want to go to university. It seemed that everyone in the sixth form wanted to go and to be honest he had the grades, but he wanted to get hands on experience and applied to a local law firm to do his articles. Victoria had had many moments in her life as her children achieved their goals but when Paul came down the stairs in his suit, pale blue shirt and tie she saw her John from years ago and tears splashed down. "God, Mum, don't cry, I am only going to work." And she hugged him so tight he wriggled and said, "Love you, Mum, not sure what time I will be back." And off he went on the first day of his new working life.

Mark was not academic and rather thought it would be a jolly good idea to have a gap year before he decided what he would do with his life. John and Victoria were not quite sure what the gap was between, it certainly wouldn't be university, but he had decided he would go with a group of friends 'travelling'. He was a fortunate young man, and although he had worked for John in the post room in the summer holidays, he had a certain comfort cushion which did set him apart from his mates. They applied for their visas to go to Thailand and collected them from the Thai Embassy in London and Victoria drove the three of them to Heathrow and finally stopped crying as she entered her own front door at home.

Paul did well and became a solicitor and said to John it was a good thing he was doing business law because he could always help John out if he had any problems business wise, like sue people, which John found highly amusing.

Samantha had thought she would be a nurse but then wasn't that thrilled at the sight of blood. Her friend Maria was going to be a model — she had been doing odd bits since she was sixteen — but Samantha was not a stick insect and her lovely rounded curves would not be appreciated on the catwalk. She had thought she would go to secretarial college or do a hair and beauty course. She really had no direct ambition, and in the end, it was the fact that she knew she had to do something she enrolled at the Taylor Institute in London to study business administration. None of the children had wanted to go to university which frankly amazed Victoria and John who had so loved their time there, but for what they wanted to do they didn't need a degree. Mrs Johns was all for it always proclaiming she had graduated at the University of Life and had a Master's Degree in common sense.

The John Bartlett Pharmaceutical company was going from strength to strength. John was a hard task master but only expected from his staff what he himself would do and his workforce were hardworking and loyal, he prided himself on that.

It was a telephone call from Peter Carpenter, Mark's friend, that dropped a bombshell into their lives which struck fear into their hearts. They had not heard from the boys for a while but they had told them they were often out of range for contact by phone and when they came across a post office on their travels they would get in touch. Peter was phoning from a post office in Bali. "Mrs Bartlett?" His voice was high pitched and anxious.

"Yes, is that you, Peter, is everything all right?" Maybe it was the concern in her voice, or just the sound of someone 'normal' that caused Peter's voice to choke and he said through his tears that it was Mark, he was in prison in Bali and they were in desperate trouble. She told him to keep calm, to give her a contact number, the number of the post office he was calling from, and she would get hold of John and they would call back in one hour.

Frantic she managed to track John down, he dropped everything and the chauffeur broke the speed limit to get him to Valley View in record time. They clung to each other, so many questions but they had to be calm and they dialled the number of the post office in Bali. Peter answered and seemed to have calmed down, having delivered the initial shock he was able to tell them that they had all been drinking and were in a street market when for absolutely no reason Mark appeared with a piece of salmon, laughing his head off saying wouldn't it be great to have fresh salmon for dinner. He was still laughing when a gun was thrust in his back and a Balanese policeman took the salmon while his partner cuffed Mark's hands behind his back and marched him off. Everyone sobered up within a blink of an eye and followed them to the police jeep and tried to communicate to find out what was going on.

The long and short of it was Mark had stolen the salmon from the fish counter, and the police patrol were there within minutes. It had happened five days earlier and they could get no information as to Mark's fate. John and Victoria listened in horror on the speaker phone. John was immediately in control. "Peter, thank you very much for contacting us and we are grateful that you are all together. You must contact the British Consulate in Bali. I have the details here." Victoria, who never ceased to be amazed by her husband, listened as he gave names and contact numbers. "Peter, I will need your bank details to wire some money straight away. I know Mark will need a lawyer and it will be essential you keep in touch with him. I have heard of the prison in Bali and it is quite dreadful. You have my number and I will give you my mobile number. Use the money to keep in touch, and if possible, to get food to Mark.

"I am making arrangements to come out tonight, or as soon as I can get a flight. Try to keep calm, I will wire the money straight away." Peter was so very glad Mark's dad was so calm, and to be frank, had the money to help out. If it had been his dad, he didn't think the response would have been quite the same. More like you made your bed, you lie on it. One of the reasons he couldn't wait to get out and to be with his best mates was a bonus. None of them knew what on earth had possessed Mark to do such a thing, but they knew it was serious and they would rally to help their friend.

John and Victoria were afraid. Bali they knew was a popular destination for gap year students — using the term loosely in Mark's case — and John had heard it was unbelievably corrupt, from the jailers to the lawyers to the courts and privately he was very worried. John's secretary was on the line with flight details. He could go at six in the morning. Singapore Airlines flew from Heathrow Airport to Singapore which would take about thirteen hours, a wait of about an hour then roughly two and a half hours to Ngurah Rai International Airport in Denpasar in Bali. Ten p.m. GMT and six a.m. local Bali time, as they were eight hours ahead of GMT. They hardly slept for the few hours before John had to leave for the airport.

Both were baffled as to why Mark had acted in the way he had. They had both been so grateful that it appeared the boys had come through with good friends avoiding the heavy drug scene. Victoria once smelled what she thought was herbs, the boys said they were herbal cigarettes, and it was Samantha who informed her, Mum it's weed, grass for goodness sake. Victoria was mortified thinking her boys were on a downward spiral and when she told John he stormed into their rooms and grabbed them by the hair and pulled them into the hall. They were left in no doubt that if that is what they wanted to do they could leave right now and live on the streets. If they wanted to throw their lives away, they could do it on their own time. Maybe it was because it was so very rare to see their father in such a rage they came to their senses. To be honest they had tried it at parties and they both had the same effect of being totally chilled out, but neither particularly enjoyed being out of it and when it wore off the headaches were not worth the chill out.

The only little blip with Samantha was when she decided to get a tattoo. She and her friend were just sixteen at the time and Victoria was mortified when she put her hair up and at the back of her neck were the words 'never look back'. Samantha thought it was quite a daring thing to do and was amazed at Victoria's reaction and John made it very clear he was disgusted and baffled by her actions. She didn't tell them until a year after the event that she and Teresa had had a friendship tattoo. Samantha's was on the left side of her rib cage to balance Teresa's on her right side. Reading from Teresa, 'spread your wings', to Samantha, and 'learn to fly' was they thought the ultimate in cool.

However, the other way of looking at it was standing alone Samantha had 'never look back' and 'learn to fly'! However, the irony was totally lost on her.

John arrived in Bali and took a taxi to where Peter and Simon were waiting. They hugged each other and their pale faces showed the anxiety all of them felt. There was a small shack just down from the Consulate and they sat together to make plans as to how they would be able to visit Mark. The boys introduced John to Es daluman, green grass jelly on ice, which he found quite refreshing and they shared a platter of Nasi Goreng which was welcome and the fried rice was tasty and filling.

John was desperate to see his son, but first had to hire an interpreter and then double the fee for his integrity to give an honest translation. The jail was fifteen minutes by taxi from Denpasar and no one spoke, just so anxious as to what they would find. John was able to bribe the guard at the gate to get them as far as the prison wall. More money exchanged hands and the interpreter asked the head man if it would be possible for Mark to be brought to see his father.

Not possible. Possibly something could be arranged for the afternoon of the next day, but he had committed a serious crime and privileges were not on the agenda.

Disheartened John returned to the boys outside the prison. They made arrangements to stay in a hostel and he managed to call Victoria to say they hoped to be able to see Mark the next day.

Peter and Simon were so grateful for John's presence. He conveyed a feeling of calm, he reassured them that there would be a solution, albeit on the prison authority's timescale. The boys were also very short of money and John was able to make sure they could eat some good food and paid for their clothes to be washed and the bedding to be changed in their room. The next day John had to pay the interpreter the same amount of money and the first guard was paid and the guard at the prison wall demanded even more. He waited and waited and suddenly a man appeared from within the prison walls and said the boy was sick and it would not be possible to see him. "What do you mean sick? Is it malaria? How is he sick? Can I get medicine for him?"

"No, you go away. Two days he may be better."

John was beside himself. "I beg you, please let me see him, please let me at least see how sick he is?"

"Go now, guard, go." John was escorted off the premises, frog-marched by a guard either side to the outside of the prison.

For the first time he felt despair. These people were not normal, not rational. They ruled the roost and judging by the outside of the prison he dreaded to think what terrible conditions Mark must be confined to on the inside.

The boys were very upset and it was for them that John forced every ounce of strength to appear as unruffled as he could. He confided in Victoria he had no idea how you could deal with these people, but his priority was to see Mark. Once he could hold him, talk to him, he could get an idea of what was going on.

Victoria told him the legal department had been able to source a lawyer. Totally corrupt, openly corrupt. He demanded 3,000 US dollars before he would meet John, the amount to be wired to his bank account. Once it was received, he would meet John, in about two days. John noted the details of the lawyer's account and authorised the money to be sent.

They were in limbo, nothing could be done, nothing could be organised and all the time Mark was sick and could be dying for all they knew.

Finally, the lawyer rang John's mobile and agreed to see him, nine days after he had arrived in Bali. The lawyer told him he would need 3,000 US dollars for the judge. There would be no court, no trial, once the money was received Mark would be released. The man that emerged from that dreadful place was not the son John knew. He was wretchedly thin, his face was skeletal and he was covered in sores, which were openly weeping. John ran to him, blinded by tears and lifted him into his arms, he seemed to weigh nothing at all.

John laid Mark across his friend's laps and he sat with the taxi driver as they made their way to the airport. The lawyer had warned John that just because the money had been paid did not mean that Mark was free. He would need to keep a very low profile at the airport, not be seen by security who would rearrest him on sight. This filled the boys with dread and John said they will all go en masse to the toilets in the airport and stay there until the flight was called. Then they would run, as best they could, supporting Mark, to the plane.

The time waiting in the airport toilet, as soon as anyone came in they bundled Mark into a cubicle and stood over him, balancing on the seat, in case it was a policeman, was the worst time John could remember in his entire life.

The flight was announced. They made their way to the gate, the security guards seemed to be everywhere but they had Mark in the middle of them, the passports were handed over and the woman at the desk waved them through. They walked out onto the runway and helped Mark up the steps, into the plane and sat down. They did not look up, they kept their heads down and Mark was just about holding on, and as they secured the cabin, ready for take-off, he fainted into John's arms. Once they were airborne the crew were oblivious of the situation and John ordered hot sweet tea and sugar cakes to try to get some energy into Mark, but he had become unconscious. John asked the steward if there was any medical person on board and in response to the announcement over the tannoy a young Irish girl came to the seat and said he must be laid down in the aisle and put in the recovery position, making sure his airway was clear. She got some blankets and covered him and he was not to be given anything by mouth.

Mark gradually came to, and the nurse got a drip into his arm and the saline solution seemed to bring him round a bit more. He was incredibly dehydrated and so weak from the fever, he looked to John like someone from Belsen POW camp in the last war.

Finally, he slept and luckily it was a short wait at Singapore and they stayed on the plane before it departed again for Heathrow.

John and the boys also slept, completely exhausted, the fear gradually becoming relief. Relief that they were out of the worst kind of hell.

At last, the plane was coming into Heathrow. Peter and Simon had made contact with their parents via John's mobile and it was his money that had brought their tickets, for which they would forever be in his debt, not only from the money angle but for their lives. The parents were waiting in arrivals and many tears and hugs ensued, even Peter Carpenter's dad managed, "You stupid bastard, you stupid bloody bastard, come here." And the tears told the story. They all hugged, Mark was in a wheelchair and the parents thanked John with all their heart. They arranged to meet in a week, would keep in touch by phone, but for now they all needed to get home.

When Victoria opened the door, her mouth dropped open. Her son, her beautiful Mark, was in John's arms, he looked a little boy, not a man of nineteen. His face was gaunt his poor skinny legs flopping over John's arms and his own arms just skin and bone. They carried him onto the sofa, gently laying him down and Victoria rushed for pillows and blankets. The doctor arrived and thought it was malaria and the chauffeur took the blood sample to the hospital laboratory. The doctor examined him and found a tiny piece of coral had embedded itself in his foot and was actually growing. He immediately injected antibiotics. The chauffeur returned with a note from the technician at the tropical diseases department which ruled out malaria. He was running a dangerously high fever from the infection in his foot and it took a week of constant care, changing the mattress and keeping him fully hydrated before the fever subsided. Gradually Mark began to eat, little by little and the process of healing began.

John and Victoria would never forget the harrowing tale he told them of the time he spent in prison which the locals called Hotel K. Twenty in a tiny cell, they were counted in, lined up and lay down, sleeping in forty-degree heat, their limbs entangled with the limbs of strangers. The cells were infested with cockroaches, rats and ants and the toilet in each cell was blocked and many caught dysentery, and were too weak to survive. A favourite form of torture was called the box. Mark was put in the coffin-like structure and was left in the hot sun for one day. The only reason they took him out was that when they opened the box, he appeared to be dead. Mark got taken under the wing of an Australian who was there for life for drug smuggling. He made sure the matting taken by Peter to the jail got to Mark and watched over him at night. He let him help in his garden where he grew lettuces and each day the prisoners were let out from morning till five at night when they were counted into the cell again. Food was crawling with flies and luckily Peter had given the guard enough money to make sure Mark had fresh water. The Australian ruled his little empire and no harm would come to Mark from the other inmates.

John had researched Kerobokan jail. It was built in 1979 for three hundred prisoners and there were now in excess of one thousand four hundred prisoners. Seventy-eight percent were drug sentences and ninety percent were Indonesian. He knew just how very fortunate they had been in managing to get Mark out.

Mark apologised every day for the anxiety and stress he had caused them let alone the huge amount of money they had to pay for his release and he vowed he would get a job and start to pay them back as soon as he was strong. They were just so grateful he was going to recover and Paul and Samantha came whenever they could to support him and show him how much he was loved. Very gradually he recovered and the family were able to settle into normality and the dreadful episode was no longer as raw and vivid as time went on.

28

Victoria heard the car come down the drive and she opened the door and hugged him — she was always so pleased to see him even after just one long day apart. "What news of Sarah?"

"Brilliant. The news is so much better than we first thought. I spoke to Clive and the swelling had considerably reduced to such an extent the surgeon didn't think it necessary to induce a coma. She seems to be fighting hard to get back and please God she continues to make such good progress." Victoria was thrilled to hear this news and asked him about the launch. He told her how pleased he was and particularly praised Andrea for stepping into Sarah's shoes at such short notice. "Do you know Victoria, it astounded me how very well versed she was in the product. I know she had gone over the slides with Sarah beforehand and I think she made several visits to the lab to talk to Kevin about the product and its progress. Her hard work was well rewarded, she was able to answer many questions I didn't think she would have any knowledge about at all."

"That's wonderful darling, I am so proud of you, you had every angle covered anyway, well done you."

She handed him a large scotch and soda and made one for herself as they sank onto the sofa.

"Tomorrow, will be a busy day, always is after a launch, especially such a product as Impactus. There will be lots of feedback and I must congratulate Kevin. Allessandro wasn't there though, that surprised me. He is our keenest competitor in this race and if only for that I am so pleased we got there first." They finished their drinks and although John's head was buzzing, he fell into a deep sleep, a contented, fulfilling sleep, all was well.

Andrea was at her desk bright and early, even after such a full day, fielding calls and typing up the questions and comments she had noted the previous day. "Good morning, Andrea." John positively beamed at her.

"Good morning, John".

"Is Kevin in yet? I would love to see him in my office, he played no small part in the operation and I must reward him. Without his knowledge and persistence to discover that elusive element we would not have Impactus." Kevin was not in the lab. In fact he had left in rather a hurry the previous day. Andrea tried his mobile but she knew there would be no reply. In actual fact it was out of service. John was slightly annoyed. He was on a high and he wanted Kevin to know how much he was appreciated. He did wonder if he had been a little frugal with the bonus, after all although he had provided the lab and the money for the research, the technicians to assist him, Kevin was the catalyst and he had a strong urge to find out where he was. What was going on? HR provided his address and the chauffeur was dispatched to try and get some answers as to his whereabouts.

John went to the lab and all of Kevin's paperwork was on the desk and he found his notes on his age spot research on the computer. Jeff, one of the technicians, asked John where Kevin was. He told him he had been a bit vague over the last couple of days and Jeff wondered if he was OK. John asked him if Kevin had confided in him, any worries, was he in any trouble. Jeff said he was probably the most uncommunicative person he had ever met, no one knew anything about his personal life. He was just one of those guys who seemed to live for his work with seemingly no other outside interests.

John returned to his office. He asked Thomas Clark from the legal department to come and see him. "Tom, I am a little concerned. Kevin Whittaker, our cosmetologist, has not come in today, after leaving in a rush yesterday. Is our patent on Impactus watertight. Is it totally secure?"

"Absolutely John. No problem at all. Right from the beginning we took out patents at every stage, protecting the stem cell production process right through to the branding of the product. It cannot be replicated. The hidden ingredient, Kevin's breakthrough, is as secure as if it were under lock and key."

"I am relieved Tom. I do hope Kevin is all right. He appears to be a bit of a loner, no friends or work colleagues."

"John, there is no way anyone can reproduce Impactus, it's just not possible."

"Thank you, Tom, I knew I could count on you. How is Stephanie by the way?"

"Just fine, thank you. John and the boys are both doing well. We are lucky there really."

"They come from good stock Tom. Now, if you will excuse me, I must deal with my calls."

"Of course, regards to Victoria."

The chauffeur entered the office. "I am sorry, John, it would appear that Kevin Whittaker has completely disappeared. One of the tenants where he rents a room—"

"What do you mean, rents a room? I thought he had a house somewhere near Enfield."

"Well, he has been there for a few months the man said, but anyway he said he came in yesterday afternoon with a man carrying two suitcases and he left thirty minutes later. He got into a black Mercedes and it drove off."

John stared at Jamie. He had been his chauffeur since forever. "What on earth is going on Jamie? He called Andrea on the intercom. She went in and sat down. "Andrea, when you visited Kevin in the lab, did he ever confide in you about his personal life, what he did when he wasn't at work?"

"No John. He didn't have a life outside the lab, although I did notice he always had the racing page open on his desktop. I think he used to study form, so to speak."

"Do you think he was a gambler?"

Inside her head, Andrea was quietly impressed with her acting skills. "I never took much notice, he always seemed pre-occupied but I guessed that was the nature of his work."

"Apparently he left his room with two suitcases accompanied by a man and got into a black Mercedes yesterday afternoon."

Andrea's eyes flew open. "Oh my God John, do you think he was in some sort of trouble, maybe gambling debts or something?"

"It is a distinct possibility. Things are beginning to fit into place. I wonder if I should call the police. He may be in some kind of danger."

Andrea looked totally stunned — maybe she had missed her vocation with this Oscar winning performance, she could have been a film star. "I cannot believe it. He was such an unassuming kind of person, someone you wouldn't notice even if they jumped out at you."

John's mind was in a whirl. So many ifs and buts and what ifs. "The most important thing is to ascertain that he is safe and we cannot do that unless we can find him. I wonder if there is CCTV where he lives. Maybe there would be an image of the man who escorted him, even the number of the car. Jamie, will you be kind enough to go back to his house, or room. See if there are any cameras and maybe the same tenant who spoke to you before could help, if he could concentrate on what he saw." Jamie left and John slumped in his chair. He had been so pleased with everything and was so determined to make sure Kevin enjoyed the success he deserved. What if he was a gambler, and it looked increasingly as if that was the case. What if he got into debt, couldn't pay and was taken off to a dreadful fate?

He had a backlog of calls to answer and Andrea started to dial the numbers and that in some way was pleasing as most of the callers wanted to congratulate and place orders. Several asked about Sarah which touched him and he put a call into the hospital to try and speak to Clive or Adrian. He was so pleased to hear from Clive that she was conscious and trying so hard to speak. That was so amazing and warmed his heart. What a fighter, what a winner. He really missed her and wondered what she would have made of Kevin Whittaker.

Jamie returned. The tenant only remembered that the man was tall and well built. He did not appear to be harassing Kevin, he walked quite willingly to the car.

John called Tom in the legal department and explained what had happened and asked him if he could find a way to get access to the CCTV system. Tom called him back with the news that Dalston was in the London borough of Hackney and there were over two hundred and sixty CCTV cameras operating there. He would need the specific address and a primary request to review data generated by CCTV systems would involve a third party, and he thought in this case it would be the police.

John telephoned the police and a very helpful woman listened to what he had to say. He told her his concern for his employee, namely Kevin Whittaker, who he believed to be a gambler. He explained how he returned to his room in Laburnham Road, Dalston, yesterday afternoon accompanied by a tall heavy-set man. They entered the premises with two cases and left thirty minutes later in a black Mercedes with the cases. It was not in his nature to not turn up for work, in fact he had left early the previous day saying he was unwell. Nothing had been heard of him since that time and he appeared to have totally disappeared. He told her about the CCTV cameras situated in Laburnham Road and there was one above the front door. The point of his call was to ask if the police would consider asking the council to release the data from yesterday afternoon.

She took his number and said she would let him know. She called back to say that a formal request had been made by the police to the London borough of Hackney and an appointment was available at four p.m. that afternoon. John thanked her and Jamie drove him to the offices and in the presence of the police officer the data was put on the screen in the council office. The grey and white film was not very clear, but the road parking camera showed a black Mercedes pulling into the kerb outside a house. Kevin Whittaker was seen getting out of one door as a large man got out of the other. They walked to the door. John asked if it was possible to see inside the windows but they were blacked out but there was part of the number plate visible. The police officer called it in and said he thought it would be comparatively easy to identify such a car. The camera above the door entry showed Kevin and the man quite clearly and the police officer asked for the frames showing the two men to be printed off.

The officer's phone rang and the car was registered to a Mr Alessandro Degen, a Swiss national.

John gripped the desk. His knuckles were white and his face grew pale. Alessandro, his fiercest rival had somehow infiltrated his company to get to his cosmetologist. Kevin Whittaker had been poached away, lured no doubt with offers of large sums of money. He was furious. How could he do this? How could Degan know how far they had got with Impactus? His mind was racing. They must have known about his gambling, it had to be blackmail.

The police officer looked enquiringly at John. "Everything all right sir?"

"No officer, actually it is not. I am grateful for your time and effort on my behalf but I do believe this man is not in danger. I believe he has been persuaded to jump ship. To go with Degen to work for him. I think they call it business piracy or something similar. However, at least I am reassured that Kevin has not been harmed. That in itself is a huge relief. Do I need to sign anything to this effect, what happens now?"

"Well sir, if you are sure there is no harm to the individual, we will complete the paperwork. We know where to contact you if anything develops but it looks as if this is now out of both our hands."

John shook the officer's hand and Jamie drove him back to the office.

He could not comprehend what had happened. There had to be someone inside the corporation who could let Degen know what was going on. They had been scrupulous in their employment of staff. Everyone was vetted. It had to be a technician. A disillusioned person, jealous of Kevin's expertise, knowing he had a problem with gambling and then somehow making contact with Degen. But the technicians would never have known who Degen was. They were not privy to the clients and rivals of the corporation.

His head was pounding and he called Tom to his office, who was mortified to hear what had happened. "But we have Impactus sewn up John, lock stock and barrel. No one can get that formula." Both men looked at each other.

"The only one who can get the formula, is the man who created it. It's all in Kevin's head Tom, that's why they have got him. He can replicate it just like that.

Degen's labs are second to none. I have always envied him that, but I had the chemist and the formula."

The enormity of it was gradually beginning to sink in. Somehow, someone had fed Degen information from the outset. That's why he wasn't at the launch. Why would he need to be? He had the creator in his pocket.

"Tom, I think we need to keep this under our hat right now. Who knew we were going for the CCTV system?"

"Only Jamie and I knew John, unless anyone else was in the office at the time."

"Andrea was here, she left to start sorting the calls, but she is one hundred percent bona fide, Tom."

"It has to be someone with access to the lab and to Degen. The technicians have been with us for so many years, through all our developing products, and they were proud to have worked with Kevin, to see the results and the success."

"John, they don't know Degen from Adam. Do you mind if I run something by you?"

"I am grateful for any input Tom."

"Did you not think it odd, how Andrea would visit the lab? One of the techos told me she would often drop in, just for a chat with Kevin, noting the progress. He said he asked Kevin what she was doing there and Kevin seemed quite flattered that she was interested in what he was doing. John, she knew Degen. I have seen him gravitate towards her and I always thought to myself he had more than a professional interest in her. I don't know of course, but it could be possible. She is the link between Kevin and Degen. She knows them both."

John stared at Tom. "Oh no Tom, not Andrea as well. But why would she, she has a good job. Until Sarah arrived, she was my number one. She was a hard worker and, I thought, loyal."

"Think about it John. You said yourself, until Sarah arrived, she was your number one. Along comes Sarah and usurps her crown. No disrespect to Sarah but maybe Andrea's nose was more than a little put out of joint. Degen is a manipulative bastard. What if he saw how Sarah had replaced her and offered her a deal? He desperately wanted a good cosmetologist. He had the all singing and dancing labs, but no one was a patch on Kevin."

John turned over Tom's words in his mind. He had a point. My God he must have been blind. He didn't see any discord from Andrea, she seemed absolutely fine with Sarah, they worked well together, no animosity on Andrea's part. Yet, he remembered telling Victoria how amazed he was at her knowledge of the product. Would a secretary normally be as well versed in the subject as she obviously was?

"How do we do this Tom? Do we confront her? We have to be very careful. How does it sit legally if we accuse her? Can she take us to court if we are wrong — and although it would appear it could possibly be her, we do not know for sure."

"I think we can start by suggesting that we are at a loss to understand how Degen could be aware of Kevin and his obvious gambling addiction. We could ask the question — was she aware of any communication between the two of them."

"I hate this, Tom. It's industrial espionage at its worst. Yet it's not illegal, is it? No crime has been committed. Kevin has not been harmed. You are right. We will ask Andrea to come in and let her know it was Degen's car and Kevin has gone with him and let's see how she reacts."

He duly buzzed the intercom, but Andrea was not there. He went into her adjoining office and her coat and bag had gone. "That's very unlike her Tom. She would always come in to check if anything else needed to be done before she left for home." The silence between the two men spoke volumes. "It doesn't bode well does it Tom?"

"No, John, I don't think it does."

Andrea had always had an immaculate sense of timing. When to appear and when to disappear. She had planted the seed. The gambling addiction. She had not thought things would have moved so fast and she guessed that if CCTV was available at Kevin's flat it would not be long before the car was identified and the parts of the puzzle would fall into place.

She had always known that when she had to move it would be swift. Her case was permanently packed and ready, and in the taxi to her apartment, she Googled the next flight to Spain. She had planned to go there as a stepping stone to her future. She secured a reservation in the Inter-Continental four-star hotel, in Madrid. It was located in the cultural district yet near the elegant Serrano shopping district. Her passport was always in her handbag together with her driving licence.

She had no regrets. Why would she? She owed John Bartlett nothing. She had given him one hundred and ten percent of her knowledge and hard work and how had he repaid her? Sarah Cook was where she herself should have been in the pecking order.

She had become a hard, determined woman. She knew she was totally on her own. No ties, no past, just a future she had always dreamed of. She collected her case. She would travel with just hand luggage. She had enough money to buy her wardrobe wherever she chose. In the taxi to the airport, she gradually started to relax. She had covered every angle. She got her passport from her bag and smiled at the image smiling back at her. Amanda Barratt, she loved the play on words — Andrea and Bartlett — was on her way, and she knew the business plan she had in her head was solid. She was going to be a big player in the oldest profession in the world. She would be a madam of the highest class of escort girls and she thrilled at the excitement a new project would bring. The fillies in her stable would be the fittest of their breed and she would earn herself a reputation as the top madam in Europe.

John knew it was hopeless but he tried her mobile and her home number. Both calls went to answerphone. "Andrea, when you get this message will you please call me back. It's quite urgent. Thank you."

"Tom, I think our bird has flown the nest. Everything points to the fact that she is the guilty party. No doubt she has covered her tracks and we cannot prove anything. Kevin is now ensconced in Switzerland, and she is on her way to either join Degen or make her own way, her own future and it sure doesn't include this company. Legally we haven't got a leg to stand on, have we? We couldn't have done more than we did to protect Impactus. I guess we just have to wait to see what comes out of Degen's labs."

"John I am so sorry. Degen can dress it up any way he wants but it will certainly be the formula from Kevin that he will launch with a new brand name. However, all is not lost John. Kevin left his notes on his computer and we actually do have the original formula. How do we know that maybe Kevin has some loyalty and the vital ingredient is not in the product he creates for Degen? Degen wouldn't know, he hasn't seen the formula, it's all in Kevin's head."

John was suddenly very tired. He rubbed his eyes and heaved a huge sigh. "Tom, you could be right but we will never know. We have to admit defeat on this one. True we do have the data he was working on and we do know the vital ingredient and how to get it. We must accentuate the positive. Our first and most important move is to find a new cosmetologist. Even if it means headhunting from Europe or America. We need to get on to that right away. The only thing to do with a bad day is to end it, Tom. Tomorrow is another day. We will set the ball rolling and begin afresh. OK, Impactus will earn us a good return. It's the first of its kind on the market and we must vigorously take advantage of that fact and push it far harder than we have ever done with any other product. Our marketing department is second to none. Oh, and I will need a temporary secretary, one already employed here to step into Andrea's shoes. Right Tom, lots to do but that's for tomorrow. Right now, I am going home and suggest you do too. Maybe you can double-check if we have any comeback on what has gone on but I very much doubt it. Lots of lessons have been learned but no amount of careful planning could have foreseen this would happen. Best laid plans of mice and men, and all that." He managed a weak smile, but not from his eyes. He was desperately sad to know that the people who he thought were loyal and true were in fact traitors to the corporation.

Jamie drove him home. Thank God for my wife. Thank God for my family. We didn't come this far to let this defeat us. We have been through far too much and he knew once he was in Victoria's arms things would settle into perspective and he would live to fight another day.

29

Sarah Cook thought of her children. She thought of them with so much love it almost threatened her breathing, it almost overwhelmed her. They were so precious. They meant so much. They consumed her passion, her wanting, her reason to live. They were her everything. The fact that she would not have them had it not been for Clive mattered not, yet it was strange to separate the two.

Once, long ago it seemed, it was all about Clive, with her, starting out on their journey of a lifetime. The children were born, they grew together as a family, and once they were at school she could work and things became easier. She could earn money and she went back to what she was good at. Public relations was her speciality, she knew how to market, how to promote and how to get results. Clive was climbing the ladder. She always supported him and still managed to achieve in her own right. They had a good relationship. They both gave each other space in the marriage. There was time spent apart. Clive was building his career which meant him travelling more and more to America, the head office of the company.

Sarah joined John Bartlett Corporation, a company based in America with an office in London. She was headhunted by the chief executive, John Bartlett, to be his personal assistant, particularly with regard to the promotion of his various cosmetics. Clive knew of the company and encouraged her to accept the position, even though it would mean time spent apart if he was successful in his application for the overseas division of Webbers Franklyn, based in New York.

Sarah thoroughly enjoyed the position of PA to such an easy-going charismatic man. She felt the chemistry between them but they both channelled the electricity into creating a successful enterprise. She knew she was good at what she did. John Bartlett valued her contribution, she was an important component and together they produced the most enigmatic partnership to promote their products.

She was at home when Clive had left in an emergency for the New York office. The call had come at midnight, seven p.m. New York time, saying the president of the company had had a heart attack and Clive needed to be on the next plane out. He had grabbed a few basics and ran, forgetting his mobile in his haste. Sarah had hugged him, kissed him, told him to take care and she loved him. The ringing of the mobile phone startled her awake. Oh no, she thought, he has forgotten his phone. By the time she had put on the light and grabbed the phone it had stopped. The message flashed there was a new voicemail message. "Darling, my poor darling Clive. It is so dreadful, they don't think he will make it through the night, but sweetheart, you will be with me so much sooner than we thought. This must be voicemail, but when you take it, know that I am so waiting for you to show you how much I love you. Be safe honey." Sarah played it back twice, three times. She was trembling. She stared at the phone, willing it to be wrong, not true, a mistake. She knew she was fooling herself. She had had doubts recently, well for months actually. This removed any doubts, any not possibles, maybes. No, this was concrete, absolute proof that he had some woman in New York. She slowly turned around and went to the bathroom where she flushed the phone down the loo.

She never said a word when he called her to say that poor old Jacob Frank was dead when he got there. He would obviously have to stay to sort things out but would keep her in the loop. Actually, he didn't think he would make it back for a couple of weeks. Still, he would let her know. She asked if she should come over for the funeral, although she knew no one in the New York office, but he said thanks anyway, it wouldn't be expected or necessary.

She threw herself into her work. John marvelled at her energy and was thrilled that their trip to Manchester looked set to be a great opportunity when they would unveil their secret product and breathe new life into the cosmetic industry.

She was gradually coming out of a thick black fog. She could see dim lights, hear noise, like a rumbling, a distant murmur. The doctor at her bedside was overwhelmed. "Sarah, Sarah, can you hear me, please squeeze my hand if you can hear me." She could hear a distant sound, it was a voice, it was a man's voice but she couldn't hear what he was saying. She lay there, very afraid of the place she was in, unsure, and she felt a tear roll down her face and she felt a gentle movement, a kiss.

Clive was ecstatic. Somehow his beautiful wife had come through this massive trauma and they had not had to induce a coma, she seemed to be coming round, becoming conscious.

He whispered in her hair kissing her eyes and mouth and saying how much he loved her. She still could not hear, she was only aware of noise and a dim light. "Clive, I must ask you to step away, we need to do a few tests. She is obviously coming back but we don't know what damage has been done. She may not be able to see or talk, but I think she can hear sounds."

Clive stepped back from the bedside and crumbled into a chair. The sheer relief sapped all his energy, he was totally spent. What he had only dared to hope for seemed to be happening. It seemed as if Sarah was regaining the will to live. He prayed so hard, please God, please let her live, let her be OK. His lips moved in his silent prayer and tears rolled down his face.

The surgeon stepped away and the nurses were adjusting the tubes and gently washing her face. "She has made an amazing recovery thus far. Her vital signs are good but we will need to take her for a scan to know if there is any internal damage. I think she is well enough to cope with that now, Clive, so I suggest you go to the canteen, get hold of your son and pass a couple of hours while we sort this out."

Clive grabbed the surgeon's hand. "Your prompt action has probably saved her life, I will never be able to thank you enough." He shook his hand and left to call Adrian.

He dialled the number but no words came out. "Dad, is that you, Christ Dad, what's happened? Please tell me Mum is OK".

"Sorry son, so sorry, yes, Mum seems to be coming round although they don't know what damage may have been done. She is going for a scan. Can you come?"

"I am on my way, Dad, I will be there in thirty minutes. Oh Dad, hang on in there, I will go straight to the canteen on the ground floor."

They both hugged and cried and Clive was surprised how much better he felt after a cup of coffee.

The scan did not show anything untoward and the surgeon was cautiously optimistic. Clive and Adrian sat either side of the bed, desperately hoping Sarah would finally come through her solitary state.

Sarah was becoming aware of a bright light. She tried to close her eyes tighter to stop the glare, but instead they opened, very slowly, like a butterfly's wings, gently fluttering awake and both Clive and Adrian cried out. Sarah! Mum! She looked up and saw both of them, their faces alight with smiles and love. She wasn't sure where she was or what was happening but she was very aware of her darling son. She tried to speak but she couldn't.

The surgeon stepped up and they went to the side of the room as he gently talked to her, reassuring her, telling her she had been in an accident but that she was making the best possible progress and as far as they could tell she should make a full recovery, in time.

Sarah listened to his voice. It was a kind and gentle voice. It was telling her that she was going to be all right. She didn't really feel all right. She felt as though parts of her didn't work properly. She couldn't move anything, she couldn't turn her head and she couldn't speak. Yet this man was telling her it was going to be all right, in the end.

Although nothing seemed to be working, her memory was intact. She remembered how she had felt so betrayed and she remembered the love she had for her children. She remembered the product, the unveiling but she couldn't remember going there. She was not in any pain — the drugs were containing it but she was sad she couldn't speak. She couldn't ask if her daughter was OK, what about her grandchildren, couldn't say to them she loved them.

Clive put his hand on her cheek and gently stroked her hair. "My darling Sarah, we love you so much, we are so glad you are doing so well. The doctor says you will recover completely and you will be able to speak soon, it will just take a little time my darling."

Adrian kissed her and held her hand and told her he loved her, they all did and she was not to stress, just rest and let the healing begin. "You are going to be fine, Mum, we are all here to look after you." He couldn't stop the tears tumbling down his face.

She wished she could tell him how much she loved him, just squeeze his hand to let him know she could hear him, but that would come. Gradually things would return to normal. Normal to her now meant a life without Clive, she knew that. It didn't make her sad, it didn't really seem to matter. The main thing was that she was alive. She had come through a dreadful accident.

She resolved she would get herself well, she would do everything to help herself heal. She sighed, a deep heartfelt sigh as if that sigh could convey how grateful she was that she was going to survive. As she fell into sleep, she remembered what her mother had told her when her father had died, he was so young. "Sarah, no one is indispensable. Put your hand in a bucket of water, pull it out and where is the hole?" From profound loss, seeds of hope are sown and the will to survive takes hold. She knew from that time, this time she would come through and this time, as before, she would flourish.

Plans are made, dreams are fulfilled, if fate allows. The only certainty in life is that we die and we are all guilty of taking so much for granted, but we don't know any other way.

Impactus would prove to be the most amazing cosmetic cream, selling worldwide.

The impact of the worst motorway accident in living memory would continue to ripple in ever widening circles. Life changing, life ending, but also life healing. Precious life to breathe into a new beginning.

Printed in Great Britain
by Amazon

68837445R00182